In the Shadow of Marsfjäll Mountain

FSC
www.fsc.org
MIX
Papper från
ansvarsfulla källor
Paper from
responsible sources
FSC® C105338

BERNHARD NORDH

In the Shadow of Marsfjäll Mountain

Published by the Berhard Nordh Society in 2015.
The cover image and prologue are taken from the edition
printed in 1939 and the rest of the text from the
linguistically edited edition printed in 1967.
The map on the back cover is from
Marsliden's village map of 1903.
A map of the area where the book is set
has been added as an appendix.
This edition has been made possible by the
voluntary efforts of members of the Bernhard Nordh
Society, a literary society founded in 2000 that works to
increase interest in and distribution of Bernhard Nordh's
literary works among readers of all ages and to
stimulate scientific research on his writing.

Original title: I Marsfjällets Skugga
English translation by Emma Davis.

Publisher: BoD · Books on Demand, Östermalmstorg 1, 114 42 Stockholm,
Sweden, bod@bod.se
Printer: Libri Plureos GmbH, Friedensallee 273, 22763 Hamburg, Germany
ISBN: 978-91-8114-746-9

Translator's Notes:

In the original text by Bernhard Nordh, he referred to the indigenous people of Northern Sweden as Lapps, or the Lapp people. The Sami region was formerly known as Lappland and the Sami people have historically been known as Lapps, however this term is regarded as offensive by the Sami, who prefer the area's name in their own language. Since the original text used the term Lapps, it was decided that the translation should reflect this, and the term Lapps was kept. In modern day Swedish the term would be Sami.

The Swedish *Riksdaler* was the name of a Swedish coin first minted in 1604. Between 1777 and 1873, it was the currency of Sweden.

The Sami word *Muorke* means a portage area between two bodies of water.

A Goahti is a Sami hut or tent.

– – –

Emma Davis

When you travel the nearly two-hundred-kilometer route along the Ångermanälven River between Åsele and Kultsjö Lake, you pass through a land that a few hundred years ago was pure, unadulterated wilderness. Here bears roamed the vast forests and marshes. On bitterly cold nights, the hungry cries of wolf packs rose against the sky, shimmering with the Northern Lights. On warm summer evenings, swarms of mosquitoes drifted like clouds above the wetlands of the waterlogged marshes. By streams and forest lakes the beavers built their stick huts and dams, the lynx crept softly among their hiding places in the bushes, and the pine marten wreak havoc among the squirrels chattering in the tree-tops. In narrow rock crevices, the wolverine had its den and ventured out boldly, as it had since days of old, on bloody night hunts, where the reindeer, three times its size, were easy prey. Forest birds abounded – black grouse, wood grouse, hazel grouse… The ptarmigan jumped and flew among the crooked birches of the forest, and at the top of a rugged cliff the golden eagle was perched, brooding like an ancient shadow over this vast land which was scarcely touched by human feet.

It was only the Lapps who passed through here with their reindeer, the Lapps, who with superstition and sorcery coursing in their veins, stole through this wilderness of marsh, forest, and mountain. Here, in some hidden place, strange things might happen – but be quiet about it! no one could see or hear, for woe to those poor wretches, if the men in power should hear anyone whisper that rings had been rattling over the dirty skins of a magic drum! But away in the mountain caves the high and mighty wouldn't hear, and here a Lapp in times of need could retreat in solitude to consult with their ancient gods. Here the magic drum was pulled out from its dark hiding-place into the light. Under the dull beats of the reindeer-horn hammer, the rings performed a fateful dance among the mysterious figures and symbols of the drum. But the younger ones, those who knew that the old gods had long since lost all their power – they sometimes held heated councils around smoky fires, shaking their fists towards the east and brandishing their bear spears…

*

The east is where they came from… tall, grim men, determined to take on the wilderness. One by one they came rowing up the Ångermanälven River, pulled their boat along the shore past the foaming waters of the rapids, and were constantly on the lookout for a suitable place to clear some land. If they saw a simple hut along the riverbank, they had no choice but to keep going. The nearest neighbor had to be at least ten kilometers away, for the well-being of everyone.

The years went by. Smoke from the settlers' primitive chimneys began to rise further and further inland, while the occasional shot from fire-spraying muzzle loaders disturbed the silence of the wilderness. Year after year was carved into the history of the settlement of southwestern Lapland. Råsele was established as a government settlement in 1741, Nästansjö in 1777, Laxbäcken and Strömnäs in 1781, Malgovik in 1788, and so on.

At the beginning of the 19th century, the shores around the wide waters of Lake Malgomaj were overpopulated, for where it was most crowded there was hardly ten kilometers between the small one room cottages.

It was not fishing, and certainly not hunting, that was in dispute. But a person could become so angry if they met a neighbor in the process of mowing a field of marsh grass, which they themselves had had their eye on. You had to have good hayfields if you wanted your cows to still be standing when spring came.

New men came from the east, and the first settlers around Lake Malgomaj began to have children old enough to marry, who, in competition with the newcomers, went westward. New areas, each like a small kingdom were established, and for new land-clearers the only option was to continue up the almost impassable stretch of the Ångermanälven river, which lies between Lake Malgomaj and Kultsjö Lake (the difference in altitude between the lakes is about 200 m), past Dimforsen Falls, and across the Lake Vuollelite and Lake Bielite…

Here was Kultsjö Lake, 540 meters above sea level… a wild, brutal lake, surrounded by mountains. To the north – the wild Marsfjällen Mountains, to the south – Borgafjället Mountain and Burgfjället Mountain with its eternal glacier; in the west – mountains – hardly anything else was to be seen.

But nothing seemed to deter the settlers. Saxnäs was incorporated, and over at the western end of Kultsjö Lake, trees were felled for the first cabins in Lövberg and Klimpfjäll. Other adventurers made their way across the bay to Fatmomakke (an old site used by the Lapps for religious gatherings) and continued up Lake Ransaren, which at 582 meters above sea level spread out its waters in the middle of the inaccessible mountain range, which was connected by Ransarå River to the small spring lakes of the Ångermanälven River, located in Norwegian territory.

Here, at last, further progress seemed impossible. The mountainous area became increasingly difficult to overcome. At least the establishment of a boundary beyond which the cultivation of new land was not allowed, spared the police chief and his assistants from week-long trips to the outermost hiding places in the wilderness. The cultivation boundary was fixed in 1867, and new settlements would not be inspected beyond it. The boundary ran across Ormsjö, Strömnäs, Nästansjö and up towards Lake Storuman, and now a large area, which the settlers had already built on, was beyond the boundary. Klimpfjäll, for example, lay about one hundred kilometers west of the boundary, which the authorities had drawn in the firm conviction that beyond it the conditions were unsuitable for people to make a living.

But the boundary was not drawn with only the settlers in mind. Over the years, there had been enormous encroachments on areas that had belonged to the Lapps since ancient times. The autumn and spring grazing grounds had to be moved higher and higher up the mountains, and in many pastures, previously grazed by the reindeer, the settlers had snatched up all the feed. The authorities also had their views about hunting. For example, a royal regulation of 1749 stated that hunting for furs was the domain of the Lapp people; the settlers were not to engage in "hunting and running about the forests for game" as this distracted them from the cultivation of the land. Henceforth, settlers were only allowed to hunt within five kilometers of their homes.

If the settlers happened to learn that this regulation existed, their harsh reality forced them to ignore it. It was necessary to venture into the great hunting grounds if they were to survive. If their farming gave them a few bushels of potatoes, they had to be grateful.

It was fair to say that not all of these wilderness warriors were Our Lord's best children. And if starvation tore at their stomachs, it might be tempting for someone to shoot a reindeer, which came within firing range. But revenge was lurking, and woe to the poor settlers who had haystacks still standing in the mowing marsh, when the reindeer came down from the mountains towards the woodland! Then the result of weeks of work and sweat could be wiped out in a few minutes, and the settler had to stand there in anger, pulling his hair, not knowing how he was going to feed his cows for the winter.

The seriousness of these disputes can only be partly seen in the court records. Most things were dealt with outside the law, and the rumors about what happened in the shadow of Marsfjället Mountain never traveled the long road back to Åsele...

CHAPTER ONE

One July day in 1852.
The sun was already setting in the west, and the Fjällfjällen Mountain cast long shadows down on to the lower areas of Mount Lill-Gemon and the waterlogged marshes of Stormyran. A sunny haze rested over the high peaks of Marsfjället Mountain, and over in the southwest, the snow on Mount Burgfjället sparkled, greatly vulnerable to the heat that prevailed down in the valleys. Kultsjö Lake glittered, partly framed in black shadows. The lake protruded out from shore ridges and tree lines, and beyond Marsfjället Mountain it spread out eastward into a vast delta, broken up by small lakes.

On this July evening, a young man came walking through the storm-whipped and stunted birch forest west of Östra Fjällfjäll Mountain, along the faint path that led from Klimpfjäll village to Norway. A huge bundle was attached to his wood-framed pack. In front of his chest hung a bag of shot and a powder horn, and at his side dangled a grim, threatening muzzle loader. Sweat ran out from under his squirrel fur cap. However, this did not in any way affect the gentle, plodding gait that was so common to these wilderness folk. They had been thrown into a wilderness where a man without strong legs was doomed to perish pitifully.

It was Abraham, a farmhand from Klimpfjäll, who came wandering along like a plodding pack animal of the mountain ranges. In the morning he had left the Norwegian village of Kroken, waded over gushing streams and rivers, and had climbed up long toiling ascents. With forty kilometers of arduous hiking behind him, he still had more than ten kilometers left to reach Klimpfjäll.

The path here led rather steeply up to the treeless stony wasteland of Dårronskalet Pass, and Abraham paused to rest. He leaned his load against a rock, dug into his pockets and bit off a piece of a juicy brown tobacco braid, straightened the piece with his tongue and then spat out a satisfying spray out over the white bark of the nearest birch.

As Abraham sat tugging at a piece of grass, he wondered if this might be a good spot to have a new settlement inspected, although he should have been aware that attempting to settle up here in the mountain forest would be sheer madness. But it was an old habit. Wherever Abraham went he looked for a suitable place to clear some land of his own. Being a farmhand was not for him. His father was a stately farmer from Hälsingland, and Abraham would not have been sitting here if he had not gone up to Åsele market a few years ago with a bundle of fox skins.

After a fight, which he had only a vague memory of, since it had been fought in the haze of liquor; he had fled west in the company of Jon, the mountain farmer, who had taken part in the bloody fight on Abraham's side.

Ever since then, Abraham had been a farmhand in Klimpfjäll and was unaware that the fur trader who had been stabbed by Abraham's long knife between his shoulder blades, had recovered from his misfortune and was conning people out of their furs, just as cheerfully as before.

There were times when Abraham longed intensely for home, and on light summer evenings he would sometimes sit out on the stone steps with his face turned to the southeast, as if he were trying to catch a glimpse of the flaxen-haired Anna-Stina, who might at this moment be standing on the hill by the mountain pastures, blowing her birch trumpet out over the valleys of her home. But to go back there would mean going to jail and perhaps even having to make the climb up gallows hill, from where no prisoner returned alive.

Abraham considered himself sentenced to life in these harsh mountains, but that sentence was not as bad, and he knew he could endure it. With the exception of these evenings on the stone steps, which, by the way, were becoming more and more rare, the boy from Hälsingland found himself quite comfortable here. He had been wild and hot-tempered before that fateful day in Åsele, but now the mountain world had given him thick skin. If he were to settle here in these parts, the wilderness would find him to be a fierce trespasser who would not give in without a fight.

At Lake Västra Marssjön, just below Mount Marsfjället, Mount Ropen and Mount Såttan, there was a wonderful place where a settler's fire had not yet sent up smoke into the blue sky, but even that place was not available. Four years ago, Jon had applied to the authorities to build a settlement at Lake Marssjön. As of yet, however, no inspectors had set foot in the shadow of Marsfjället Mountain. Jon seemed to be in no hurry to acquire legal claim to the lush surroundings of the lake. But when Abraham had asked a couple of times if he could take over the claim, Jon had been harshly dismissive.

*

Abraham continued his walk and climbed up to the tree line, and just ahead was the huge stone mass that was Dårron Peak. It was a still evening, and all the way up to the edge of the birch forest, the swarms of mosquitoes danced, as if they considered the man a prey to be followed at all costs.

Suddenly, the silence was broken by a piercing cry, which brought Abraham to a standstill. He stood tense for a few moments, but then wriggled out of the pack's carrying straps and, rifle in hand, crept down through the foliage of the dwarf birch trees.

Suddenly he threw himself behind a bush. Across a clearing, fifty meters away, a large man came pulling something. Abraham's eyes narrowed, and his breath hissed through his widening nostrils. The hand holding his rifle trembled noticeably from the intense suspense.

The man who was pulling something had disappeared from the clearing. Abraham hurried after him. In a few minutes he had caught up with the other man, who having suddenly discovered that he was not alone on the mountain, dropped his load to the ground. Abraham drew a deep breath, and the look he fixed on the man before him was full of disgust.

– What is the meaning of this, Jon? he said dully.

Jon shrugged his broad shoulders, and his eyes sharpened.

– The meaning?! Well, Mikael here, fell down a cliff over there.

Jon pointed, and Abraham cast a long glance at the dark mountain walls. It was inconceivable that Jon would have been able to carry the Lapp boy this far in such a short time. Abraham's temper began to rise, but the events in Åsele had taught him to control himself.

– Is he dead?

Jon nodded. He sat down on a rock and told Abraham that he had been walking down the slope and that the Lapp boy had suddenly come tumbling down at his feet. Abraham barely listened to him but just stood staring at Mikael, who lay there limply with his face to the ground. Abraham walked a few steps forward to examine his injuries more closely.

– I guess we'll have to make a stretcher and carry him home with us, he said, when Jon did not seem to have anything else to add.

– What's the point?

Something hot and pressing tightened around Abraham's forehead like an iron band, and his tongue seemed to be stuck at the roof of his mouth.

– The point! he repeated slowly. A Lapp is a person too, and either we have to take him to Fatmomakke or send word to his family to come and get him.

– And get a bear spear between our shoulders, when we turn our backs, eh?

– I can go if you like! said Abraham grimly. I saw reindeer this morning on the other side of the border.

Jon sat chewing on a blade of grass, his thoughts turning heavily behind his broad forehead. He knew better than the inexperienced Hälsingland boy what it meant to bring that kind of message to a Lapp camp. Abraham listened quietly as Jon explained that going to the Lapps was not going to happen.

– Well, then we'll have to carry him home and row him over to Fatmomakke.

Jon gave the farmhand a look as if he had a child in front of him.

– To Fatmomakke? he exclaimed angrily. The Saxnäs farmers will find out, and those fools will scamper off to tell the police chief.

– Well, what of it? No one can be held responsible for an accident! Jon shrugged.

– Well, if you're all for bringing the police chief out here, then I won't stand in your way. He might come right away when he finds out you're up here!

Abraham felt a chill run down his spine, but his face did not move a muscle.

– You may take over my claim at Lake Marssjön, said Jon, but then this will have to stay between us. It is best for all parties involved that Mikael has simply disappeared. He is not the first to do so, and he will not be the last.

An hour later, Abraham and Jon walked through the bleak valley of the Dårronskalet Pass.

Abraham followed silently in Jon's footsteps, and every now and then a groan seemed to force its way out of his chest. He almost expected that the mountain walls would fall down on them, or that something, anything, would come bursting out from some crevice and hurl itself with a hellish screech, down upon its defenseless victims.

After they had left the Pass, Abraham felt more at ease. The Lake Kultsjö area lay before him, and beyond it the last rays of evening light glittered on the peaks of the Marsfjället Mountain. There on the south side of the sunny mountain, was the place he had been promised.

You couldn't tell by Jon's face that he had given away an area which if it had been located further south in Sweden would have been a prime area for farming. Perhaps he didn't even count it as a loss. It was a nice area where someone could settle along Lake Marssjön, but the Lapps traveled through there every spring and autumn. There were whispers about magic and headless dead bodies, which in the autumn darkness traveled secret paths, joining their sounds to the hoarse cries of the buzzards. And after what had just happened on the mountain today, it would be perilous for someone to settle at Lake Marssjön.

Abraham had half-feared that Jon would go back on his promise, once they had left Mikael behind, but as they sat at the table at home in Klimpfjäll in the late evening, sipping their thick fish soup for supper, Jon confirmed his offer.

Jon was somewhat literate, and after their meal he and Abraham went to their neighbor's house, where he and his wife witnessed Jon transferring his claim to the farmhand Abraham Jacobsson. There were no terms of sale recorded in the agreement. Abraham had been given the shore around Lake Marssjön – completely free!

CHAPTER TWO

In Klimpfjäll, the haymaking kept everyone busy for the next few weeks, and Abraham did not have time to apply to the authorities for a settlement permit by Lake Marssjön. There was no hurry either, for it was too late in the summer for the inspectors to make it. Soon, the snow would make the inspection impossible. Abraham was also a little uncertain. He wondered if the police chief in Vilhelmina knew what had happened in Åsele a few years ago.

When the haymaking was over, Abraham borrowed Jon's boat and rowed to northern area around Lake Kultsjön. He was gone for almost a week. He spent the nights on the bare ground under a spruce tree and during the days he explored the area, sometimes going above the tree line. He found quite a lot of fields of native grass, good for haymaking. In the streams coming down from the mountains, there would be places for mills and sawmills. In the pine needle forest between the hills, he sometimes heard grouse. Further up the mountain, Abraham encountered several woodcock birds, and on three occasions in one day he noticed fresh bear droppings.

To get a good view of his surroundings, he climbed up the ravine of a brook up the steep and nearly twelve hundred meters tall Ropen mountain. The Kultsjö Lake area lay exposed and bare below him. At the western side of the lake, he thought he could just glimpse Klimpfjäll's green areas, even though the distance was close to thirty kilometers. But there were neighbors closer than that. There, on the southern part of Lake Kultsjön, was the village of Saxnäs, inhabited by homesteaders. Abraham looked long and thoughtfully in that direction. These three farmers were to be present at the inspection, and they may not be so easy to deal with, when it came to marking the property line between the Saxnäs farms and his new settlement.

Abraham continued further west, where the highest parts of Ropen mountain lay. The mountain heaths, rusty brown this time of year, rose higher and higher, and the young man from Hälsingland thought with some self-trepidation that in just a few weeks the reindeer would have their pastures here.

The future settler left this grand view behind and turned back down across the mountain heaths. He passed the brook ravine and continued towards the part of the mountain that dropped steeply towards Västra Marssjön. And now he stood looking at a glittering mirror of water, which was close to five hundred meters below him. But it was not only Västra Marssjön that sparkled to greet him from above. The whole vast plain to the east was speckled with many ponds and small lakes. Abraham stared intently at one body of water, which was about ten kilometers away. He had heard that one settler had settled nearby ten years ago, and that he would be his nearest neighbor to the east. Would they become friends or foes? Would they accompany each other on long journeys to the trading posts or clash in bloody fist fights over the rights to a meadow?

Abraham was pleased when he finished surveying the area which he was now fully determined to own.

He stayed in Klimpfjäll for the winter, since during this time of year there was not much to be done on a new settlement with no house. He trapped ptarmigans, shot a dozen foxes, and one grueling night he saved his own life by breaking the backbone of three howling wolves.

He sold the ptarmigans and furs in Norway, and at the same time took the opportunity to get tools for the summer. Ax, saw, shovel, scythe, twine for nets and so on. The money he made was also enough to buy a heifer from Jon. He did not intend to have any future connection with Klimpfjäll. He had promised Jon not to tell anyone about the missing Mikael, and he would keep that promise.

In the beginning of March, Abraham discovered something, that six months earlier would have made him abandon all plans for this settlement. One of the farmers in Saxnäs was complaining and cursing over the fact that he had been deceived by a fur trader. From his description, Abraham understood that it was the same swindler he had once pulled a knife on. This now meant that he could, without risk, make the long journey to his home, if he wished to.

Abraham did not consider for a moment to leave the mountains. If he left the area, the pre-emptive right to the new settlement at Lake Marssjön would go back to Jon, and Abraham did not intend to give him any undeserved benefits.

Spring was approaching. Abraham's application had been submitted a long time ago. On the fifteenth of May 1853 a notice was read in Vilhelmina church that the inspection would be held on Monday the eleventh of July. Anyone who considered themselves to have a better claim to the property should appear on that day in Saxnäs village.

*

The evening before the inspection was to take place, Abraham arrived in Saxnäs in his new boat. He brought with him a door, a small lead paned window, an iron pot, and the tools he had purchased in Norway.

At ten o'clock that evening, the inspectors came to the village. It was the police chief P.A. Hellgren from Vilhelmina, the lay judges Salomon Pehrsson from Granliden and Johan Johnsson from Järvsjön.

No one had come to the village to say that they had a better right to the claim at Lake Marssjön. Early the next morning the inspectors were rowed across Lake Kultsjön. The Saxnäs farmers came along to protect their interests during the marking of the property line. It was clear they were sympathetic and wanted to treat the future settler fairly.

When the group arrived at Västra Marssjön, they were met by a man who from the first glance gave Abraham the impression that this was an enemy. The man was Olof Olofsson from Grytsjön,

Abraham's closest neighbor to the east. He was short and stout, and his thick, long arms hung down toward the ground as if pulled by weights. His face was weathered, and his gray eyes had a peculiar expression when he greeted Abraham.

– So, you're the one who is settling here! he said slowly and flatly.

Abraham felt the heat rising to his face. Was this man intending to scare him away?

– That's right, he replied grimly. And you're here to make sure I do not go over your border, I suppose.

Olofsson nodded, and his left eye squinted as if he had his heavy muzzle loader in firing position.

– Yes, although I did not think that anyone would care to have this place inspected. The fact that Jon was here five years ago and looked it over and submitted some kind of application was nothing to worry about, because everyone knew that he would not dare to move here anyway.

– Why is that?

Abraham did not get an answer to that question. The inspectors and the Saxnäs farmers stood off to the side discussing things, and the police chief now called to Abraham that it was time to get started.

The first thing entered in the inspection record was the place where both the house would be built and where the farmed land would be. It was on the sunny side below the wooded, rocky knoll, which rose one hundred and seventy-five meters above Lake Marssjön, overshadowed by Ropen's gray stone ridge. It was entered in the record that the land here consisted "of coarser and finer, less stone-bound rock soil of a better nature".

After this was determined and after they had set the fee for the farmed land (three Swedish riksdaler per 1/3 acre), they set out on the walk through the forest, a sweat-dripping journey, which took several hours. Abraham showed them no less than fourteen different bogs and wet hay meadows, located within an area that stretched from southwest to northeast for nearly ten kilometers. Marking the property line towards the Saxnäs farms did not cause any disputes. The Saxnäs farmers even suggested that the property line markers should be put a good distance out on the muorke, which Abraham had feared he would not get anything of. Nor did Olofsson show any intent he wanted to push Abraham as close to the mountain slopes as possible. He showed his papers and as long as he was allowed to keep his wet hay meadows, it didn't matter to him where the border was drawn. On the north side there was no need to carefully consider the border, since in that direction the desolate mountain range lay like a compact fortress wall against all cultivated land and formed a natural border.

And what would the new settlement be named? Abraham thought Marssjöliden would be appropriate. Erik Eriksson in Saxnäs proposed Mount Marsfjäll, and the police chief wrote Marsliden. Since the new settlement Marsliden was one hundred and ten kilometers from Vilhelmina church, the inspectors decided and put on record that the period of tax exemption should be extended to twenty years, counted from 1854 to 1873.

At six o'clock in the evening the inspection was finished, and the police chief shook Abraham's hand and wished him every success.

– This is a nice place! he said. Strange that no one has settled here before.

Neither the police chief nor Abraham saw the looks the Saxnäs farmers gave each other or the grim look on Olofsson's thin lipped mouth.

The inspectors and the farmers from the other side of Lake Kultsjön left the new settlement and disappeared west down to the muorke. But Olofsson was in no hurry to return home. He was sitting on a rock next to the smoldering remains of the fire they had used to make coffee.

There was obviously something he wanted to say, although it took a long time.

– Well, he said suddenly. I'm wondering why Jon left you this place – you had to pay a good penny, I suppose.

There was something deceptive in Olofsson's gaze that made Abraham think closely before he answered.

– Of course, I had to pay! he said.

– I thought so! Jon's not one to get rid of something just like that, from what I've heard. But this place is not worth many pennies, because you won't be able to live here.

– Not live here! What do you mean?

– Well, the police chief thought it was strange that no one had had this place inspected before. I thought the Saxnäs farmers would say something, but I suppose they would prefer to remain quiet about it. It is not strange at all, that no one has dared to move here, and it is not going to get any better now, since Mikael disappeared last year.

Abraham could feel his blood run cold. Mikael! What did Olofsson know about Mikael?

– Mikael … who … who is that?

Olofsson cast a long glance to the west, and a strange look came over his face.

– A Lapp boy, he said slowly. He disappeared in Fjällfjällen Mountains last summer. The Lapps believe that he did not disappear naturally, and one can understand that they are a little upset.

– Do they think that anyone… anyone did…

– Yes, that is what they're saying. And they got a strange look on their faces when they heard that it was someone from Klimpfjäll who was going to settle here.

A drop of sweat penetrated Abraham's forehead. He had a strong feeling that Olofsson knew how Mikael had disappeared.

– Have you met any of the Lapps?

Olofsson replied that he had last spoken to Niel, Mikael's older brother, a couple of days ago.

– It sounded like he thought that no one would settle by Lake Marssjön, if Mikael had not disappeared.

Abraham's face darkened. Was Olofsson trying to trap him?

– Why would that make a difference?

Olofsson said that he did not know, but there was something in his look that caused Abraham's blood to boil.

– Do you think it was me who ended Mikael?

The other man shrugged.

– I didn't say that! If that's what I thought, the police chief would have brought you with him when he was up here.

Abraham made every effort to appear restrained. He got up and almost instinctively reached for his rifle.

– Since you know the Lapps so well, you can tell them that I do not know anything about Mikael. And then you can tell them that they do not scare me.

Olofsson also got up.

– Well, he said. I have warned you, and this place will not be a blessing to you.

Abraham stood and watched his neighbor as he walked east with long steps. Suddenly he shrugged. He would show both Olofsson and the Lapps that he was not one to mess with.

Abraham took the ax and began to cut some spruce boughs. It looked like it was going to rain, and he had to make a shelter.

It was quite late in the evening before Abraham's spruce bough shelter was ready, and after he had eaten, he crawled in for the night with his loaded rifle close at hand.

CHAPTER THREE

The young settler rose early the next morning. He hadn't heard anything suspicious during the night. However, his mind was still unsettled. If the Lapps thought that he had something to do with Mikael's disappearance, it might not be nice to live in Marsliden.

The more Abraham thought about it, the clearer it became to him that he had to try to talk to his neighbors in the mountains – the sooner, the better.

Abraham felt better once he had made the decision to try to reason with the Lapps, and after a meal he took the ax and saw and began to mark out trees, which were suitable to build his house with. It was his intention to cut and gather logs for the cabin. Building the barn would be out of the question for this year. One of the cabin's two rooms would have to serve as a cowshed for the winter.

After Abraham marked out about twenty mature trees, which grew right next to the spot where the cabin would stand, he cleared away a couple of bushes to be able to cut down the trees. He paused for a few seconds holding the ax with the feeling that this was a significant moment. Here he was, ready to cut down the first tree, and from now on the homestead in Marsliden would be occupied. What no one had dared before, he dared to do now.

Abraham readied himself and swung the ax. The first huge swings bit into the spruce trunk a few inches above the ground. Dull echoes sounded across the mountain hills. But silence followed. There was only a small faint groan to be heard over the nearest bushes.

Abraham stood with one hand propped against the spruce trunk, gasping for breath. He knew exactly how it had happened. In the middle of his swing, the ax glanced off a twig and veered to the side.

His left shoe was almost split in half, and Abraham felt cold sweat begin to seep from his forehead.

He dragged himself back to the shelter. In his birch bark knapsack, he had a clean shirt saved for going to Norway, which he tore into long strips. With his teeth clenched, Abraham exposed his injured foot. A couple of involuntary shivers went up his spine, when he realized that his foot was practically split in half.

Summoning all his willpower, Abraham closed the huge wound and wrapped the shirt strips around it. But they did not help much; they soaked through and stained red in a few seconds. Abraham folded up his coat to use for a bandage. To keep this in place, he had to tear strips of the shirt he was wearing.

Abraham groaned loudly when his foot was wrapped. The whole leg felt heavy and shapeless. The pain was excruciating, and the loss of blood took a heavy toll on his strength. He laid down and touched his hot forehead, which was damp with sweat.

The young settler sat up after a few minutes. It wouldn't do any good to stay here. He must try to get over to Saxnäs as soon as possible. He did not have food for more than one day, because most of the provisions he had brought with him from Klimpfjäll remained in the boat by Lake Kultsjön.

But it was not just about the food. Even if he had had his shelter filled with food, it would have been necessary to try to leave without delay. The foot needed care – and there was also something else. From the moment the ax's sharp edge cut into human flesh, it seemed like an ominous weight was covering Marsliden's new settlement – something gloomy and frightening, which forced Abraham to see the accident for what it was. Marsliden was no longer a good place for a new settlement, but a place where enemy forces had free rein.

Abraham realized that he was now embarking on a journey which might be his last. It was not possible to cross the muorke on one leg without support, so he cut down two young spruces and carved them into a pair of strong poles.

It was already late morning when he finished, and if he was going to make it to Lake Kultsjön before evening, he had to try to leave at once. He packed up his things from the shelter. He held the muzzle loader in his hand for a minute contemplating leaving it behind or bringing it with him. But bringing the gun would be far too cumbersome. The only thing he could bring with him was the reindeer skin he had in the shelter and the food that was left. The skin could be useful down on the muorke. Abraham had an uneasy feeling that it would not be long between rests.

With his reindeer skin rolled up and tied behind his back, Abraham embarked on the arduous journey. He jumped forward on one leg, leaning heavily on the poles. With each hop, his left foot shook, and sharp pain tore through it. Sweat dripped from Abraham's forehead before he was even fifty meters away from the shelter. But he did not think for a moment to turn around.

After four hours of tremendous effort, Abraham had dragged himself to a stream, which just the day before had been marked as Marsliden's boundary line to the west. He lay on the reindeer skin on the bank of the stream as if in a deep sleep. He did not seem aware that blood thirsty swarms of mosquitoes were surrounding him, even though his face was swollen with mosquito bites.

Suddenly he turned over and with a groan rubbed his face on the ground. When he sat up, his cheeks and forehead were striped with red lines from mosquito blood and scrapes. He moved with great difficulty. His left leg felt like a huge lump of lead, and he shook feverishly when he grabbed the poles.

The mountain stream had not yet slowed to the gentle current it had in the muorke. The water rushed over slippery rocks and flowed into a swirling pool below a couple of larger boulders, which rose a few decimeters above the surface. Here is where the inspectors had been able to wade across the stream barely getting their feet wet. Normally the stream would not have stopped Abraham for a second. Now he stood watching the rushing water, barely able to keep himself upright. For the past four hours, his healthy leg had been under terrible strain, which, along with the blood loss drained the settler's strength to the point of despair.

But he had to cross. Following the stream down to the calm waters of the muorke was not appealing. Down there, the water was deeper, the bottom filled with mud and sludge, impossible to cross, even if both legs were usable.

Abraham did not dare to try to jump on to the large boulders. It might have been possible if he had been rested and had taller poles. A few meters above the ford he reached down into the water with the poles. Suddenly his leg slipped into the water, which with a sucking, cold rush came up to his calf.

Abraham stood for a few seconds before attempting another big step. His head ached and pounded, and he had to bite his lip to force back the dizziness creeping up on him, which made him see the water change into red and black.

Abraham put out his poles into the water and nearly fell on his head when one of the poles slipped into a hole. The water rushed around his legs. Big steps were impossible, and Abraham realized that there was only one thing to do.

Half a minute later he crawled, gasping for breath, up the other side of the stream. He had lost his hat and one of the poles. He was dripping wet and shaking from the cold. He took off his vest and shirt and wrung out the icy cold mountain water.

When Abraham was able to continue, he noticed that the reindeer skin had been left on the other side of the stream. There was nothing to be done about that now.

A couple of hours passed. Abraham dragged himself into the muorke, and once out on the muddy ground he was unable to move forward in an upright position. The healthy foot sank down over the ankle, and the pole gave little or no support. Abraham had to crawl. He crawled over swaying tufts of marsh grass, where his hands sometimes lost their grip and sank into the mud that rose above his elbows.

While Abraham struggled mightily, nightmarish thoughts and images entered his exhausted brain. There was Mikael, risen from his undiscovered grave to take revenge. Several times he thought he heard shuffling steps behind him. At one point he gave a small spruce a wide berth, from which glowing eyes seemed to glare at him.

But as the day continued, Abraham became more and more unaware of time and space. He crawled forward almost instinctively, and from time to time he lay for long periods on tufts of grass. He was unable to protect his face from the tormentors of the marshland, which in large swarms sucked until they had had their fill.

The injured settler had been lying under a spruce for a while and was rubbing his face with a piece of damp moss, when he suddenly had an odd feeling that he was not alone. A twig snapped and it seemed as if someone was rubbing against a tree trunk.

Abraham turned cautiously. After his rest, his mind was clear enough to sense danger.

Suddenly, he jerked, and his hands reached for something to hold on to. There – about thirty meters away – stood a bear, rubbing its back against a spruce, shaking the whole tree. Abraham drew his knife, although he was keenly aware that he had no chance of defending himself if the bear attacked him.

The bear had now noticed that someone had invaded his territory. He huffed and sniffed and stroked through the thickets as if to ponder what this would really mean. With swaying, soft steps he moved around Abraham in a tight circle. A curious expression was fixed on his fierce bear face.

Abraham's heart was pounding. He no longer felt his injured foot. His teeth chattered; spit dripped from the corner of his mouth. It was the terrible bear fever. It crept in like an evil spirit to torture his already frayed nerves.

Suddenly a scream split the evening's silence, a gurgling, terrified cry from a man in despair.

Abraham stood upright; his face twisted in horror.

– Mikael! he screamed. Mikael!

The answer was a dull, heavy silence, which came rushing down the slopes of Marsfjället Mountain to throw itself over its defenseless prey.

Suddenly, Abraham rushed recklessly forward, trying to escape the horrors of the wilderness, forgetting that he had a foot that could not carry him. He fell to the ground after a few steps and lay there, his head in a bush.

The bear's circling became tighter and tighter until he stood a couple of meters from Abraham, sniffing suspiciously. But the figure he saw lay motionless, and the forest beast moved forward and snorted the man's legs, stuck its furry head into the bush and let its tongue run down over the man's swollen neck.

Abraham was still lying lifeless, and the bear lay down next to the bush and rubbed his nose against one of his paws as if pondering what to do with this strange creature.

It was close to midnight when Abraham let out a faint groan and regained consciousness. He got up on his elbows and shivered from the cold. From the swamps below a raw, cold mist had come rolling in and wrapped the whole muorke in a gray-white haze. But the fog did not manage to fully darken the bright summer night of the northern land. The nearby bushes and trees appeared almost as clearly as during the day.

Abraham's red-streaked eyes stared in all directions, but there was no sign of the bear.

Almost imperceptibly slipping out of the midnight shadows, the new day began. Abraham crawled towards the west as if guided by some strange instinct…

*

At noon, the farmers in Saxnäs saw a boat drifting in the distance on Lake Kultsjön. There was a light wind from the west, and the boat drifted slowly towards the eastern end of the lake, where it would soon be pulled into the foaming rapids of the Ångermanälven river. The farmers rowed out to recover the boat and found Abraham lying there unconscious in the bottom of it.

It took two months before Abraham had recovered from his adventure as a settler in Marsliden, and he had no desire to return. The things he had left there had been brought back to him by the farmers, and now Abraham was determined to make the long journey to his hometown. The heifer, which was now a cow, had already been sold. Jon had bought it back for the same price that he sold it for last winter. Eric Ericsson was given the boat as compensation for nursing him back to health. After the first snow, which arrived at the end of September, Abraham skied east with the muzzle loader on his back, determined never to return to Marsfjället Mountain again.

In the homes around Lake Kultsjön, they thought Abraham had gotten off lightly. What would have happened to him, if he had been at Lake Marssjön, when the Lapps came around? Now they were more convinced than ever that misfortune and death threatened those who dared to settle on Lake Marssjön. The land had been inspected, but it seemed no settlers would be able to take possession of it.

CHAPTER FOUR

It was a bitterly cold winter evening a couple of years later. The stars shone, and a full moon cast a ghostly, yellowish-white shadow over the snow-covered wilderness.

In a forest clearing near the village of Fjällboberg, about sixty kilometers southeast of Marsfjället Mountain, a bull moose was standing, striking his huge front hooves, making the snow fly. His eyes were weary and blood shot, his breath billowed out in clouds of steam from his nostrils.

In front of the agitated bull moose, two wolves leaped about. Steam stood like clouds around their ragged bodies, and their eyes glowed with a wild desire to kill – to eat – to live. They attacked as one, made lightning-fast jumps and thrusts, but were continually met by the moose's heavy hooves.

The two attackers were not alone. Four pairs of wolf eyes gleamed from the thickets around the clearing. For two hours the wolf pack had been chasing the forest giant, and this was the fourth time he had been forced to stop.

Suddenly the moose turned himself around, trying to run off to escape his enemies but was pushed back by a furious attack from the wolves who had been waiting in the thicket. The next moment a terrible battle began in the moonlit forest clearing.

Snorting and panting, the bull moose danced around on his hind legs, while his front hooves struck at the attackers. Over and over the waves of their attack whirled against the dark giant.

Heavy gasps, interrupted by the metallic sounds of the wolfs' jaws snapping like scissors, mingled with the sweat forming a sacrificial smoke, which settled like a haze over the battlefield.

Suddenly the wolves threw themselves backwards and stood motionless. Their mouths were wide-open, with great drops of drool dripping into the snow. It seemed they wanted to catch their breath for a moment, before putting in the final, decisive blow.

The moose stood still in the center of the ring of wolves. His body quivered with exhaustion, and blood flowed steadily from a huge gash on one of his hind legs. His head sank to the ground as if pushed down by his heavy antlers, and his front legs gave way.

One of the wolves pressed down against the snow and crept forward using its strong front legs. One – two – three meters. The moose remained motionless, seemingly unaware of the approaching danger.

With a lightning-fast leap, the wolf's body lunged forward, but missed. Its dripping jaws snapped barely an inch from the moose's neck. In an instant a terrible blow threw the brute to the ground, howling in pain.

The bull moose roared furiously. His head tossed back and forth. A bloody mist blew out of his nostrils. The wolf under his feet was already trampled to an unrecognizable shape.

Suddenly the wolf pack charged in attack. The moose raised his head, and the next second one of the beasts bit down.

The forest giant got up and threw his head furiously, unable to shake off his enemy. For a moment he stood still with the wolf hanging by his throat and then he collapsed backwards with the whole pack on top of him…

Barely a minute after the giant's fall, there was a flash from the thicket, and a sharp bang was hurled toward the bloody scene in the clearing. One of the wolves collapsed and stayed down, and the other beasts disappeared into the depths of the forest.

Now the clearing was quiet, but after a few seconds a dark shadow came gliding out from the thickets. It was a man on a pair of short, wide skis. His face was almost hidden by his pulled-down leather hat, and some icicles hung glistening from his frosty mustache. He pulled off his mittens and held them in his mouth, while he quickly and routinely reloaded his gun.

The next minute a knife flashed in the moonlight, and after the man had skinned the shot wolf, he began to cut up the moose.

The rest of the wolves now lurked at the edge of the clearing, sniffing the air. They had already gotten a taste and it only increased their voracious hunger which tore at their bellies. Every now and then their fiery eyes gleamed out from between the tree trunks, and a sorrowful howl grew ever more menacingly towards the place where they had made their kill.

But the man paid no attention to them. Hunger gnawed in his belly also. Back home maybe the children were at this moment waking up after a restless slumber, hungrily asking for food. He cut off large chunks of meat, and when he had what a man would be able to carry, he tied it to his load carrier. There was a lot of meat left, but it was not possible to save it from the wolves. As soon as he left, the beasts would come rushing forward. The man picked up the load to test it. It weighed at least forty kilos, and he had not had a bite to eat since early this morning. If he could bring this home, he would be grateful. He was tying the rolled-up wolfskin on top of the load of meat when his hands froze.

From far away in the wilderness, a chorus of distant howling began, which was joined by the wolves nearby.

The man grabbed his gun and fired at a pair of the glowing eyes, shining from the thicket. He didn't take time to reload but momentarily put down the load carrier, turned in the direction where he had aimed the shot, and left the clearing. The snow was covered with wolf tracks, and the man's gray eyes searched about anxiously, but there was nothing in sight. When he realized that the wolf had gotten away, he let out a growl. The last shot had scared the wolves off for a few minutes, but the hunger ruthlessly pulled them back. Half a kilometer away, the new wolf pack came rushing along – a dozen hungry beasts, tumbled forward like a gray ball of yarn with snow swirling around them. They were guided by the instinct that has driven hunting wolf packs to bloody scenes since the beginning of time.

The man briefly reached for his gun, but then he set a course in between the trees and bushes with the tips of his skis facing home. He was far too exhausted to risk a close-up fight with these wild animals.

The skis sank deep into the loose snow, and the man panted under his burden. But Lars Pålsson was used to pushing himself to the limit, and soon his skis came to the trail, which wound along the forest slope down to his home in Fjällboberg. Once on the track, he stopped and listened for a moment. Suddenly he pushed off hard with the poles and skied downhill. The howling pack was after him …!

*

Fjällboberg had three homesteads. In the northernmost one, a thirty-year-old woman sat in front of the open fireplace. Her face was thin, and her brown eyes shone with a peculiar glow, which seemed to increase in strength each time a moan came from the big bed, where the family's six children lay huddled together.

The room was dim, lit only by a pair of glowing logs, and by a narrow streak of moonlight, which shone in through the small, leaded window. Every now and then the woman went to the window, thawed a hole in the frosty glass and peeked out. Each time, her steps became more tired and sluggish.

Suddenly one of the children started crying. It was the youngest, and the woman lifted him up and sat down with the little boy in her lap in front of the fire and laid him to her breast. The little one sucked greedily, and a dull pang cut into the woman's lower back.

Her breast was limp. There was not a drop of milk, and the little boy let go. The little mouth twitched, and the room was again filled with wailing baby cries. The woman rocked and shushed soothingly, but the little one would not be comforted.

It was deceitful to offer the baby her breast. There had been nothing there for a long time, not for at least a month. But he usually fell asleep while he was nursing.

After a few minutes the child fell silent, just lying there, gasping. His brown eyes were dull, and his arms hung limp. His left thumb seemed so strangely narrow and worn out. It was the one he sucked on in his sleep.

The woman stroked the little boy's dark curls. His hair was the only thing that grew – his hair and his stomach. The boy's belly was puffy and bloated, and the woman thought it was because he got to drink too much water. And it was not just little Jonas who looked like this. The other children were equally malformed. Legs and arms like sticks and bloated stomachs.

Last autumn, the potatoes and barley froze. A white fog came rolling in from Lake Kroksjön's wetlands like a flock of evil spirits. When it retreated, the tops of the potato plants lay pressed against the ground, black and slimy and robbed of all life. The hay was also stunted during this year of famine. Since the New Year, there had hardly been anything to feed the cows. They lay as if dormant … two animal skeletons, which may have to be carried out when spring came. One cow had calved and gave a liter of milk a day, but the other's udder did not give a drop.

The woman was thinking about the milk. One liter to divide between the six of them. They had only salted fish to live on, and the children were starting to not tolerate it. They gagged; threw up, groaned, and drank water – lots and lots of water.

When she had put the little boy down, the eldest boy sat up in bed. His face gleamed ghostly white in the moon light.

– Is father back yet?

The mother shook her head and looked away. She dreaded the boy asking her about what she had given little Jonas to eat.

– Is there … is there anything left in … in the bowl?

The boy's voice was thin and trembling, and his eyes shone shyly behind his long eyelashes.

– No! exclaimed the mother with desperate sharpness. Lie down and sleep, Paul, so you do not wake the young ones!

The boy sighed heavily and laid down. His narrow shoulders

were shaking from a muffled sobbing, and he bit down on his fur blanket.

The woman put a couple of logs on the fire and sat down with her chin in her hands. Why hadn't Lars come home? Nothing had happened to him, had it? She shivered at the thought.

Suddenly she startled when she heard a long, drawn-out howl, coming down through the low chimney. Dizziness came over her, and her chest rose in a couple of deep gasps. Right away she grabbed her hat and sheepskin coat and, in her excitement, felt neither hunger nor fatigue. She grabbed the wood ax by the door and hurried out.

The howling wolves sounded like a chorus from up on the forest ridge, and the woman shuddered. Lars had the strength of a giant when there was plenty of food. But now – now he was starving – and what if there were many wolves!

The woman gripped the ax handle more firmly, and the next second, she had on her skis and headed up towards the forest.

Suddenly she stopped, trembling with cold and dread. Over there were the village's two other cabins. Should she go there – go there and knock on the doors – shout: "The wolves are coming!" She trembled and gasped, but then suddenly a steely look came over her face. She stared up at the forest and pushed herself forward.

She would not get any help from the neighboring farms. Bången and Bergelsson were drunk, had screamed and made a row late into the night. They would only yell: "Get out of here, you hag!" There was not any help to be found from them. They would like to see the wolves devour Lars – Lars and all of them. They wanted them gone from Fjällboberg, in order to get their hands on all the hayfields. Last autumn, they stole the best bogland from them. Lars said nothing. He was too kind, letting them do what they wanted …

The howling came closer and closer, and the woman stood breathless at the edge of the forest. Was Lars coming … or was it only the wolves? A scream escaped from her lips.

– Lars!

The chorus of wolves increased in strength and came rolling down in mighty waves from the forest ridge.

– Lars! Lars!

A hoarse, breathless reply came rushing from the depths of the forest, and the woman drew in a sharp breath. Lars was coming! The wolves had not gotten him down – not yet! Sobbing quietly, she moved out into the clearing to wait for the man and the pack of wild animals.

Suddenly a shape came bursting out from the edge of the forest, surrounded in a cloud of steam, and a few seconds later a whirlwind of dark spots danced out into the clearing.

Right in front of his wife, Pålsson turned himself around and let the meat burden fall to the ground. In one breathless moment, he released his poles and grabbed the barrel of his gun, with a dull growl rolling out of his throat.

For a second the wolves stopped at the sight of two people, but they were mad with hunger. Then the pack rushed forward with drool running down their red jowls.

Human shouts and the howls of wolves were mixed into a frenzied chorus, which rose toward the night's twinkling starry sky. Dull crashing, loud cries – wildly moving around in a cloud of sweat. For a bloody second, the woman stared into a pair of glowing wild eyes and then was half-thrown by the impact of a wolf's body, which dropped at her feet with its head split open.

The fierce battle lasted only a few seconds. Leaving three dead wolves behind, the pack scattered and making a howling retreat into the forest.

The man and the woman, bewildered by the heat of battle, raised their weapons, and screamed.

The woman was the first to recover her senses. She stroked her forehead and gasped. The snow changed from red to black before her eyes, and it was with great effort she was able to clear away the dizziness and call out to the man, who about twenty meters away was still pouring out his anger against the howling wild dogs.

The man turned around and trudged through the snow. His blood still boiled in his veins like fire, and his broad chest rose and fell heavily. Hunger and fatigue had been swept away by the excitement, and with the wild strength of an angry bear he threw the bundle of meat up on to his back, grabbed the hind legs of two of the beaten wolves and dragged them with him, one in each hand. The wife struggled with the beast whose head she had split open.

They dragged the wolves home to save the skins from being torn apart by the beasts, which prowled the edge of the forest.

When they arrived at the cabin, and after the man had stacked the wolf bodies on top of each other to prevent them from losing all their heat, he brought the bundle of meat inside. The woman was already standing by the fireplace, lighting a fire under a large kettle.

Pålsson sniffed the air. He smelled the wonderful scent of simmering chunks of meat, and his mouth watered. He had renewed energy, and with a few quick strokes he skinned the wolves. After tossing the skins into the front entry, he stood on the step for a few moments with the delicious smell from the kettle tickling his nose. He glanced at the gleaming points of the Big Dipper, and it was as if some of the grimness on his face was wiped away. Had Our Lord begun to shine His face on them?

CHAPTER FIVE

The widow Bång had been the wife of the soldier Zakris Bång, who would be known to future generations as the controversial inspiration for Runeberg's poem "Sven Dufva". Following the bloody war in Finland, Bång, more dead than alive, managed to cross over to Umeå in a fishing boat. There he was found and taken care of by the local judge's strong willed daughter Greta Baudin, who later became his wife. But Bång's wartime deeds were not over. He took part in a military campaign against Norway in 1814, and there an incident occurred which the grim soldier regretted for the rest of his life.

He was assigned surveillance duty and was patrolling alone in the mountains, when he caught a woman by surprise, who was travelling with eight horses, intended for use by the Norwegians. Bång demanded that she turn over the horses, but the woman spat in his face and said:

– May the devil take you, you Swedish bloodhound, you'll never get my creatures!

Bång stabbed and killed the woman and took the horses. On his deathbed many years later, he said that this act was the only thing he was ashamed of and wished he could undo. He believed he could have taken the horses without shedding blood.

After the war ended, Zakris Bång settled in Lycksele but led such a life that the authorities finally had to expel him. As an outlaw, he went deeper into the wilderness with his wife and in 1827 he put down his stakes near Gaskeliteforsen Rapids on the south side of Ångermanälven River. But he did not find a refuge there either. Four years later, he left Bångnäs Homestead and moved into the forest southeast of the river, becoming the first settler in Fjällboberg.

In 1845, the old warrior closed his eyes for the last time with the words:

"On wide fields I have fought;
In wide fields, I want to rest … "

expressing his wish to be buried in the wilderness. However, he was brought down to the Vilhelmina cemetery. Then, together with their son Reinhold, the widow Bång returned with heavy steps to the cabin in the wilderness. They were seething about the rich relative who had come to the funeral to persuade her to come back with him to Umeå and live on charity.

The second of Pålsson's two neighbors was named Bergelsson. He was from Dalarna, but no one knew why he had wandered through the vast wilderness forests to settle in this remote mountain area. He came here about the same time as Reinhold Bång moved his father's cabin from old to new Fjällboberg, and the two men immediately formed a villainous partnership. Reinhold had inherited both his parents' worst qualities – he lived wildly and out of control, following in the warrior footsteps of Old man Bången, and Bergelsson was not far behind. They were more like forest bandits than settlers, and they had a dangerous reputation for their drinking and wild fights. But back home in Fjällboberg, the widow Bång ruled over these two fighters, and there were times when the old, giant woman completely cleaned house and threw out both the troublemakers and their moonshine distilleries.

That was the only help the men's wives could expect from the widow Bång. She did not even care to help a woman during childbirth. She herself had given birth on a tuft of grass in the forest, while Zakris was fighting an enraged bear close by. Rest – ha! She had not been allowed to lie idly for two or three days as women did nowadays. Just wrap a bearskin around the kid and keep going.

No, the widow Bång was not there to help. She knew nothing about the starving in the Pålsson home, she never set foot in anyone else's cabin. Even if she had known that Pålsson's children were about to succumb to hunger, it would not have made a difference to her. No pity for the weak. If they could not live, then they would die – that's how nature works. This is how she was, hard and ruthless like the wilderness where she had lived most her life. Like a huge female bear, there she sat shabby and gruesome, brooding on memories from the times when she and Zakris had been forced to wander around in the woods like wild animals. Pity? Not from her.

One hardly noticed the men's wives behind the widow's overbearing shadow. But they had one task. They were to give birth to children, do most of the haymaking – and rip Britta Pålsson's hair out, if she swiped even one blade of grass, that they wanted! They sometimes quarreled between themselves over "my children and your kids", but they agreed on one thing. The Pålsson's had to leave. There was one family too many in Fjällboberg. If Britta Pålsson had turned to them for help, it would have been in vain.

*

Pålsson was aware that the neighbors were trying to force them to leave the village. The opportunities to succeed here in Fjällboberg was becoming more and more difficult. Even a good year wouldn't improve things for them. It was too crowded here, not enough space to move around in.

The day after their nighttime adventures with the wolves, she said:

– We must look for a different place to live this spring, Lars.

– Yes, he said slowly. We'll have to think about it. I'll start asking around.

Pålsson had done this before in recent years. But it was not easy to find a suitable place, which hadn't already been inspected and claimed. He hadn't put a real effort into it either. He had hoped that things would improve in Fjällboberg, where they had put in a lot of work, which made it hard to leave. They wouldn't be able to take the cabin and the cleared land with them. They'd have to start over…

– The children are almost big enough to help now, said the woman with a worried glance at the man's brooding face.

They had to move! Did he not understand?

Pålsson nodded and said he would ask around.

Early the next morning, Pålsson went to Strömnäs. He took off heading across Datiksjön Lake, thinking that he would be home again before evening, since it was only five kilometers to the other village. The cold had now subsided. It was overcast, and a bitter wind was blowing from the northwest.

Britta walked around in a daze all day. Would Lars be able to get flour in Strömnäs – flour, so she would get to bake? She resisted, but it was impossible not to take out the baking trough, scrape it clean and lean it up against the bench by the door. It made your mouth water just looking at it.

The children felt better after the robust meals they had had over the last day. But they looked awfully serious and followed their mother's cleaning of the trough with heartbreaking interest.

Paul was tending the fire with a grim look on his young face. He was in charge of the fire and the meat stew! With a seriousness beyond his age, he added water when it got too hot, and with only a look he kept the younger siblings at a proper distance from his important task. Over and over, he stirred the simmering pieces of meat with a wooden stirring stick.

Paul was cooking wolf meat, and it was important that all his movements were done the same way his father had showed him yesterday. When the meat was cooked, it was cut into small pieces and mixed with chopped grass. From what little was left in the hayloft. When you then poured the hot broth over it, it became feed for the cows to eat.

It was getting dark, but there was no sign of Pålsson, and after an hour, his wife got dressed to go and meet him.

Britta followed the trail down towards Datiksjön Lake. After she had skied a couple of kilometers, she saw her husband. He was dragging and pulling a large sled, loaded with a huge load of hay, and Britta shouted with joy. They had hay – hay for the cows.

– You got hay, she said.

– Yes, the man replied breathlessly.

He continued to drag and pull, and the woman threw her skis on top of the hay, grabbed the poles on the back of the sled and pushed with all her might.

– Did you get flour? she gasped after a while.

– Yes, Pålsson panted.

He did not say anything else. It was not possible to speak, when he was pulling as hard as an ox.

The ground sloped up towards the village, and the man and woman struggled hard with the heavy sled, which plowed a deep furrow in the snow. Sweat poured from Britta's face, but she did not feel tired, and her eyes shone. Flour – flour!

Pålsson huffed and puffed as he worked his way up the hillside, where the cabin stood, and they shook from the effort when the sled came to a stop at the outbuildings. Pålsson untied the load of hay and carried armfuls of it into the barn. Britta grabbed some and went into the cows. But she did not take very much hay for them, because you need to carefully steward God's gifts when blessings come.

Inside the cottage, all the children had gone to bed except Paul. He was watching the fire, but when his parents came in, he got up. His looked at the bag his mother placed on the table, and the child inside him slowly crept out of its grim shell.

– Is … is it flour, mother?

His voice sounded strangely distant as if he had guessed something incredible.

Britta could hardly answer. She opened the bag of flour, put her hand in it and savored how the flour felt between her fingers. It was barley flour, mixed with dried and ground bark from live pine trees… a gray, dense pulp, which crumbled between her fingers. Tears welled up in the woman's eyes, and the lines around her mouth seemed to soften. She had to smell, taste with the tip of her tongue – really feel that it was flour.

After Britta had taken out a couple of handfuls of the flour to boil gruel, she put the bag away. It was maybe fifteen kilos, and there was meat in the cupboard. The settler's wife felt so incredibly wealthy that she had a hard time catching her breath.

Now she asked Pålsson to tell her what had happened on his trip.

In Strömnäs they had had a better hay harvest, and after they were offered a good trade, they were accommodating. Tomorrow they would come with a load of hay, and it should last until it was time to let the livestock out for the spring.

The woman forgot to stir the gruel. More hay – that meant milk!

– Did you have to give them both wolf skins for that?

– Yes, but we'll get some more flour too and a bushel of potatoes.

*

A couple of weeks later, Pålsson got ready for a long trip to Åsele. He was to be accompanied by the farmers in Strömnäs, and that was nice, because a journey back and forth from Fjällboberg to Åsele was just over two hundred fifty kilometers.

Pålsson had had an outstanding luck the last week. Two pine martens and a fox had fallen victim to his gun – this seemed remarkable, since it previously during the winter had been impossible to find game. Life felt easier in every way with a bundle of skins on your back. The three skins would be enough for a lot of food and would also put a few coins in his purse.

Before Lars left, Britta urged him not to forget that they needed to figure out a plan for moving in the spring.

Pålsson replied as usual:

– Yes, I will ask around!

The journey took twelve days. The last night, Pålsson rested for a few hours in Strömnäs and then came home to Fjällboberg at noon. From a distance Britta could see that something had happened, and when Pålsson came in, he was so serious that he did not get around to taking off his hat.

– I bring greetings from the ones in Malgovik. They are in good health, and the children are doing well!

Pålsson was sweating and didn't say anything more until he had removed his heavy pack from his shoulders. A secretive look remained on his face. Britta stood there, restless, as if she was barefoot in an anthill. Lars had not looked like this since that day eleven years ago, when he came to find out if she would come with him and start a new settlement.

Pålsson dug into his chest pocket and slowly pulled out a large piece of paper, which he placed on the table. He breathed in deeply.

– What is that?

– A deed for a property, if you can believe it!

Britta gasped and wondered what he meant.

– Well, I met a young man from Hälsingland in Åsele and I bought these papers from him for fifty riksdaler coins.

– Hälsingland?

Britta was completely confused. They could not move to Hälsingland!

– Well, his name was Abraham Jacobsson and he had a new settlement inspected up by Marsfjället Mountain. He had no womenfolk, he said, so it didn't work out for him up there.

Neither Lars nor Britta could read, but Pålsson had had the inspection records read to him at the courthouse in Åsele, when the deal was settled, and these were things that he remembered. He took the papers and "read" to Britta about the farmland "of coarser and finer, less stone-bound rock soil of a better nature" – about the fourteen wet hay meadows; the lake that was close by, about the forest between the mountain slopes – it was all theirs!

Britta was speechless. She couldn't believe it was true. A place called Marsliden – fourteen hay meadows!

The rest of the day, their mother was a mystery to the children. One minute she was laughing and the next crying; she was hugging them and talking a lot about strange things like moving and many loads of hay.

Pålsson was as excited as his wife. After a couple of days, he just had to go. He took his skis, went up Gittsfjället Mountain and on over to Saxnäs, where he was welcomed and spent the night. The next day, Eric Ericsson accompanied him to Marsfjället Mountain, and it exceeded all his expectations. What could not be seen beneath the snow was described by the Saxnäs farmer. You couldn't find a better settlement!

Britta's eyes shone when Pålsson came home and said that Marsliden was even better than what was written in the papers. But this was not the most important thing. It would be so nice to have a place where you could be alone and not have to quarrel with neighbors!

Britta counted the days until spring.

CHAPTER SIX

When spring came and the worst of the snowmelt was over, the Pålsson's got ready to leave Fjällboberg. They didn't have many possessions, but it was important to try to bring what they could – tools, household items, furs and so on. Pålsson took out the cabin's window and took off the door latches and hinges; glass and hardware were too expensive to leave behind. After they had set aside the least necessary items, there were four huge packs, which lay ready to be carried through the wilderness.

Bergelsson paid them a couple of sheep for the cleared field by the cabin. After they and Pålsson's cows had been outside for a few days, getting used to walking around on their own, they were all ready to leave.

The children were still asleep when Lars and Britta headed north, each of them carrying one of the huge packs on their backs. It was impossible to take the same path as Pålsson had skied last winter. You had to try to cross the Ångermanälven River in the village of Stalonnäset and then walk further north and west through Mount Stalon's wild mountain areas, where lynx and wolverines were common.

After Pålsson and his wife had walked three kilometers, they left their packs under a bush and turned back, and about an hour later the whole family stood ready to leave Fjällboberg forever.

Pålsson lifted what was perhaps the most important thing in their entire load onto his shoulders. It was twenty-five kilos of potatoes, which he had bought earlier in the spring in Malgovik. But not a single potato was allowed to end up in the cooking pot – everything would be put in the ground over there in the shadow of Marsfjället Mountain.

They set out, walking in a line. First went Pålsson, leading one of the cows and carrying the potato sack and little Jonas on his back. After him came Paul and his eight-year-old brother Aron, each leading a sheep, and then the rest of the young ones followed in a row. Britta came last with the other cow, hunched forward under her heavy load. Away they went – away from Fjällboberg – away from the place where eleven years of their youth had passed – off into a wilderness where anything could happen.

At the edge of the forest Britta turned around, and with the last glances at their old home, her chest tightened with anxiety. Her eyes watered and stung, and when she turned her gaze forward and saw the two youngest – the last in the row – hand in hand stepping lightly through the forest, she drew in a deep breath. It was as if she wanted to call them back – shouting at Lars in the front to turn around – but then her lips tightened to a straight line, and she hurried to catch up.

*

The moving family walked slowly through the wilderness. Sven and Stina, five and four years old, tried as hard as they could, but last winter's famine had made their legs weak, and after a couple of kilometers of walking over the rough terrain with no paths, the four-year-old began to stumble and fall. Tears rolled down her skinny cheeks, and her legs just gave out. Britta tried to carry her, but it was not possible to have the girl hanging on her arm for long. The weight of her pack was already all she could handle.

– You must try to walk, Stina! she gasped. We are almost there!

The girl's mouth trembled, but she bravely tried to stay on her feet. One of the older siblings led her … dragged and pulled and said – we will be there soon!

Pålsson stopped at a large forest stream, after he had waded across with the cow. He put down his pack and tied the animal to a tree. The current was so deep and fierce that he found it safest to carry the sheep across, the children were transported in the same way. Britta waded and exclaimed "ugh!" when the cold water reached her knees.

Stina stayed where her father had put her down. The little child's body trembled with exhaustion, and Pålsson lifted her up onto the potato sack and put little Jonas on his arm.

– You'll wear yourself out, carrying all that! Britta grumbled.

The man did not answer. He had already started on his way again through the brush and thickets.

That evening, the Pålsson's camped along the Ångermanälven River. Britta was so tired that she was hardly able to hold herself together, and she was barely able to milk the cows. Lars cleared away a small area under some spruce trees, put down some spruce bough and made a bed. After the family had eaten, the children went to bed. The sun was still up, but by morning there might be frost, and Britta looked worried as she wrapped up her little ones. She had gotten them undressed. Their clothes were wet and needed to be dried.

Pålsson had lit a fire. Around the fire, sticks were stuck into the ground, and the wet clothes were hung on them to dry. Britta sat down next to it, put a branch on the fire now and then, and turned over the clothes. In a glade close by, Pålsson cut some grass for the animals. He didn't dare to let them graze freely during the night but wanted them as close to the camp as possible.

Finally, Lars and Britta could also rest after their exhausting day. Since they could only carry two of their packs at a time, they had walked the distance between Fjällboberg and Ångermanälven River three times. They crawled into bed next to their children, after Pålsson had set his loaded rifle within reach. It was the family's first night in the open air. There would be many more to come…

The next morning, Lars and Britta couldn't leave early with half of their packs. Ångermanälven River was in front of them, and it could not be crossed without a boat or raft. Pålsson looked down towards Lake Malgomaj, where the river flowed into the narrow bay of the lake.

– They may not come, Britta said anxiously.

– Yes, they will come!

Pålsson's voice was reassuring, but inside him doubt flickered. Suppose the two men from Strömnäs had been mistaken about which day. Maybe they had been here yesterday – or would come tomorrow.

For an hour Pålsson was tormented with uncertainty, but suddenly Paul yelled – they're coming! Out in the bay, a boat appeared from behind a point, and Pålsson brought his hands to his mouth like a funnel and shouted "ahoy" as loud as he could. An answer came back from the lake. It was the two men that Pålsson had asked to help them across the river.

After two times back and forth, people, animals and packs were now transported across the river. The cows entered the water behind the boat. They swam so hard that Lars did not have much need for the ropes that were tied to their neck halter.

Everyone had made it safely across, and the men from Strömnäs seemed to think that it had gone better than expected, because they offered to go with them for a bit and help them carry their loads. Pålsson thanked them. It would mean a lot to get help for a couple of kilometers. Then the whole family could leave at the same time, and there was something else. Here on this side of the river there were steep climbs – difficult, arduous stretches, that sapped the strength from your legs. Getting help for three kilometers meant half the distance for Lars and Britta.

Step by step, the small caravan pushed forward. Britta breathed heavily in the line and felt that if she had had to go up this incline twice, there would have been no possibility of reaching the village of Dorris before evening. If they had managed to move the camp five kilometers from Ångermanälven River, it would have been impressive.

After an hour's effort, the moving caravan stopped. Sweat dripped from the men's faces, and Britta was out of breath and exhausted, as she let her pack sink to the ground. But there was no rest for her. She prepared food, and after the meal the men from Strömnäs said goodbye and walked back. They would probably have helped them go further, but a twenty-kilometer row awaited them back at Lake Malgomaj, and they had their own chores to do back home.

Britta and Lars continued north. Now they did not dare to walk too far from their camp, two kilometers at the most, since they were up in Mount Stalon's wild mountainous areas. During this stretch, Britta was suddenly startled by a dark shape, that moved out from behind a rock and went into the bushes. It was a lynx, but Pålsson was confident that the giant cat would hesitate to attack the camp in the middle of the day.

When the husband and wife left their children for the second time and set off carrying their packs, their camp was in the middle of a rugged mountain area. Rocks and boulders lay bunched together. The cows did not care for the lichen on the rocks and had just laid down. But the sheep nibbled on the meager food, skillfully climbing among the rocks.

Paul sat curled up on a boulder. His eyes looked like narrow slits, and every now and then he shuddered with a feeling that something was about to happen. Or was it just the wilderness that weighed down on the little boy? Alone with his younger siblings in this lonely place, with a man's responsibility resting on his young shoulders.

Suddenly the sheep started bleating anxiously and moved in close to the camp. The cows rose, snorting and tugging at their tethers, and for a moment it was as if the whole wilderness was holding its breath.

– Something is happening! Aron gasped.

He stood stiff and tense, staring up at his older brother.

Paul did not answer. He stood on the bolder and looked in all directions. His whole body was trembling, and one hand was holding a stick tightly. His mouth was half open, and he breathed in short gasps. Suddenly he yelled and struck at something lurking. It appeared for a second behind a nearby boulder. He yelled and swung. It was a wolverine – a wolverine! A wolverine, coming to take their sheep or the young ones!

It was indeed a wolverine. Its den was in a crevasse nearby. From a safe vantage point, it had witnessed the arrival of the camp and laid motionless until Lars and Britta had disappeared. But now the wolverine was on the prowl, a bear in miniature, but fiercer, wilder – with a long, established thirst for blood, which made him a ruthless killer of the wilderness. When this predator was drawn out by its wild instincts, sheep and goats were defenseless prey.

The wolverine, who the Lapps considered to be as clever as humans, now realized that he was not in danger, but only a matter of rushing forward, clawing, and slashing to get his fill of blood. Paul's scream stopped him just before his intended attack. His green-shifting eyes gleamed, and his claws tore furiously at the ground. With a strange snarl he disappeared behind some rocks to seek a new starting point from which he could attack with the greatest possible speed.

Paul had jumped down from the boulder and stood in front of his siblings with the stick ready to strike. Aron stood just behind him with a rock in his hand, shaking. The sheep bleated. The cows snorted and lowed and shook their heads to tear themselves free. The youngest children cried, and Aron clenched his teeth to choke back a sob.

– The gu--un! he gasped suddenly. The gun!

Paul jerked as if he had been slapped. The gun… it was standing there … should he? But father had forbidden them to touch the gun. He was conflicted for a couple of seconds … But then suddenly, he handed Aron the stick, took a couple of big steps and grabbed the gun. It was heavy. He could barely hold it. The gun was like a small cannon in his hands.

The younger siblings fell silent when Paul grabbed the gun. It was something so bold and inconceivable that they stopped crying in sheer amazement. Aron struck over and over with the stick against the invisible enemy, and meanwhile Paul crawled down beside a rock. His heart was pounding wildly, and sweat was dripping. Now he lay still, and his gray gaze moved sharply and fiercely up to some rocks, where Aron had just said that something was moving.

After a few seconds, the wolverine came rushing down the steep cliff … a rolling, brown mass of flesh and blood, and suddenly the sheep's bleating was interrupted by a shot, which bounced against the mountain and rolled out over the wilderness in a dull echo.

Paul lay gasping on his side. He hadn't held the gun properly against his shoulder, so he got a heavy jolt when the weapon bounced back from the recoil. But he only stayed down for a few seconds. Then he got up.

The moment Pålsson heard the shot, he threw down his pack and ran back. What had happened? Had one of the children disobeyed and touched the gun … or … or …? The man ran, jumped, and flew over rocks and boulders, snorting like a provoked bull moose.

When Pålsson arrived at the camp, everything was as it should be. The sheep grazed, and the children were gathered by the packs.

– Who … who touched the gun? he panted.

– Me! Paul replied trembling.

He felt so small and pitiful just then. He had touched the gun without permission!

– There was a wolverine! Aron said excitedly. Paul shot it!

– A … a wolverine?

– It's up there!

Aron pointed up the mountain, and Pålsson's sharp eyes discovered something below a couple of rocks. Without a word, he climbed up.

The man stood gasping for air for a few moments in front of the felled beast. It was an old, large male, the kind that did not shy away from anything, and Pålsson was well aware of the wolverine's blood thirsty habits. Something terrible could have happened here. He stroked his forehead and suddenly his chest expanded to its breaking point. He had a boy … his son, who had shot a wolverine in the middle of a leap! He glanced down the mountain and then began to skin the animal.

Aron had climbed up to his father, but Paul stayed with his younger siblings. His lower lip trembled, and every so often he looked timidly up the mountain. Was father very angry with him for touching his gun? If father was angry … Paul could hardly hold back the tears.

When Pålsson had skinned the wolverine and come down with the pelt, he nodded to Paul and said that he had done well. The boy lit up. He felt no pain in his shoulder and relief shone from his eyes. Father was not angry!

– Paul fell over when he shot, Aron explained.

Pålsson's eyes widened, and now Paul had to show him how he had held the gun.

– Closer to the shoulder! his father instructed. Like that, real firm!

Paul obeyed. It hurt his shoulder, but it didn't matter. His father grunted with satisfaction and showed the boy how to reload the gun – this much gunpowder …

– But you must not touch the gun unnecessarily – do you promise?

– Yes! Paul gasped and was much too happy to be able to stand still.

He would get to shoot, and father was not angry!

Now Britta appeared, out of breath. When she found out what had happened, she nearly collapsed, but she soon recovered, and there was no time to show any affection. Up with the new packs on their backs. Forward march!

After the adventure with the wolverine, Britta and Lars did not dare to move ahead more than half a kilometer from where they left their children. It took longer with these shorter distances. At each resting place, the animals had to be tethered and the packs tightened.

It was late in the evening, when the husband and wife arrived at Doris with their first packs. A settler had moved to Doris about ten years ago, and when he heard that they were going to Marsliden, a strange look crept into his eyes.

– Marsliden … he said slowly, as if he could not really believe it.

– Yes, I bought the papers from Abraham Jacobsson. He had the place inspected up there a few years ago.

After Pålsson had asked if they could stay overnight, he said that they would go and get the children and the animals from the forest.

– The children?

– Yes.

Pålsson told him how many they were, and the settler gave his wife a strange look.

Lars and Britta left, but when they had gone about twenty meters, the settler finally found his words. He shouted to Britta that he would go instead of her. Britta was grateful. She could barely move her feet.

The settler followed Pålsson with a grim look on his face. If the husband and wife had been alone, he would have strongly advised them not to go to Lake Marssjön. But they had children with them – six of them! and the thought of them made him keep silent. The whole endeavor seemed so incredible to him, that he felt chills run down his spine. What were these two thinking, dragging six small children to Marsfjället Mountain?

The Pålssons were allowed to spend the night in the animals' feed room. Even their animals were given shelter, and Pålsson was able to sleep undisturbed until the morning. But the settler who lived in Doris had a hard time closing his eyes. Should he still tell them that it would be best for them to turn back?

From Doris one could see Marsfjället Mountain in the west, a giant chain of massive hills, wrapped in the morning sun's mist. Before the children woke up, Lars and Britta shouldered their packs and left. Now that the children were in good care, the parents stretched out the first leg a good distance. Returning to Doris they had breakfast and were soon ready to leave.

Unaware of the settler's fears, the Pålsson's worked their way forward in gruesome stages. When evening came, they were seven or eight kilometers away from Doris and set up camp in the woods.

The next evening, the exhausted family arrived at Grytsjö. Olofsson was not at home, and his wife almost didn't let the strangers in. She had Lapp blood in her veins, and Pålsson could hardly understand what she was saying. But her looks and actions spoke clearly, and they were not welcoming. Tired and down-hearted, Pålsson and his wife lay down to rest overnight.

The next morning their mood was better. Today, if luck was with them, they would make it to Marsliden! Britta trembled with excitement as she put on her pack.

Marsfjället Mountain looked so close from here. But there was fog on the mountain tops. The morning was overcast, and the cows smelled rain.

Between Grytsjö and the mountain lay the two Marssjö Lakes, and Pålsson had to head straight north to cross the Marsån River and then follow the shoreline of the lakes. To the right of them, the forest now climbed steeply up towards Mount Såttan's treeless top.

At noon it began to rain, a gray, stubborn drizzle which soaked into their clothes. But Britta didn't feel it. She walked like in a fever, not saying five words an hour – toiled and carried. Her excitement infected the children, and it was as if the whole family worked together in one last, decisive show of strength against the trail-less expanse of wilderness.

The day went by with them working hard, and right before nightfall the children and animals had a rest at Ropenbäcken Creek. They had been walking for a while through areas that belonged to Marsliden.

Lars and Britta continued. It was the last leg of the journey, the last time they had to leave the children and walk ahead with the packs. Britta had a hard time holding back tears of joy. It was unbelievable that they would be there soon!

The ground was overgrown with thick birch forest, which blocked the view of the knoll where the cabin would stand. They came out on a small marsh, and suddenly Pålsson stopped. The big man trembled from head to toe, while his gaze stared at the mountain's black-burnt slope.

– The forest is burnt down! he gasped.

They continued through a grove of small birches and soon the whole devastation was in front of them. Only one large, rough spruce tree remained, rising like a menacing shadow over the bare ground, where the magnificent forest below the mountain had been before.

Pålsson walked towards the spruce tree. Not a word was said, here and there the man kicked the ashes. A week ago, maybe only a few days – the fire was barely burned out.

Britta collapsed after she put down her pack by the spruce tree. She shook as if from a fever, and her teeth chattered against each other between sobs.

– How … will we manage, Lars? she groaned.

Pålsson's chest rose heavily, and his hands were clenched together like huge sledgehammers. He did not answer his wife's question.

– We must go get the children! he said grimly.

And so, they went.

CHAPTER SEVEN

The first thing Pålsson did at Marsliden was to build a home of the most primitive nature. Further up among the hills, the forest was untouched by the fire, and Pålsson cut poles and hauled brush. He drove the poles into the ground on one side under the big spruce tree, attached a pole to the tree and tied other poles together to a sloping roof. Between the poles, spruce branches were woven, making both walls and a roof, and Britta tied together a large birch branch mat and put in a floor. On the other side of the spruce, Pålsson built the "barn". That one was made even simpler. A couple of poles in the ground, cross-bracing the rod in the tree, weaving the branches into the roof – that was it. A few meters from the hut, Pålsson made a fireplace and built up a wind shelter of stone and dirt around it. The whole structure was completed in one day, but then it was also only an improvement on the shelter the spruce tree already provided. The roof would hardly withstand a good rain shower, and there would be no temperature difference to speak of between "outside" and "inside". But despite its shortcomings, the stick hut provided a sense of security. They would not have to sleep under the stars.

However, the fact that the forest was in ashes was a serious matter and would have caused even greater concern if Pålsson had known that it was the Lapps who had set fire to the forest to prevent them from settling here. Either wood had to be hauled from the unburnt places or the cabin had to be built further away. The latter was not an option. The cabin had to stand right here on the sunny hillside facing the lake, protected from all the heavy winds, barely a hundred paces from the lake. And here is where the ground was suitable for planting. Pålsson had already decided where he would break the potato field. There was no other option than to haul logs here, which would be both time-consuming and laborious.

Lots of work awaited the settlers of Marsliden this summer. In addition to building the cabin, there was the hay mowing – cutting, drying, and carrying home the fodder for the winter. Hunting and fishing would take their share of the valuable time, and unforeseen events could cause many disruptions. But first and foremost, it was important to clear some ground, for the potatoes must be planted as soon as possible.

From early morning to late evening, Lars and Britta toiled at the clearing – digging and hoeing, breaking up roots and rocks and sparing no effort. They had no iron rods. The rocks were broken up with the help of a heavy pole, which at the heaviest end was shod with one of the hinges from their house in Fjällboberg. As the ground was broken up, it became littered with rocks, roots, and blackened stumps, and the children dragged away everything they could. After three days' work, the family had cleared about one *kappland* (~1/3 acre), and when the patch was freed from all the rubble, Pålsson took out the precious potato bag.

It was a solemn occasion, when Pålsson put the potatoes in. Lars dug, quietly and reverently, and with every potato Britta put into the young soil of Marsliden, it was as if she were saying a prayer. Her serious face radiated a glow that made her both look older and younger, and her rough hands seemed to caress the ground as she covered the potatoes. The children were infected by the parents' profound seriousness. They stood at the side of the clearing; six small children filled with reverence.

When the potatoes had been set, Pålsson stood and drew a deep breath. Would there be a harvest? Or would the frost come one night in late summer riding in on misty beasts, rising from the muorke's marshes – come and shred the growing greens to black threads?

The day after the potato planting, Pålsson took his axe and went up to the places where the fire had not raged. The forest here was of poorer quality, short, scrubby, and rough at the roots. But there was nothing else to choose from, and in a moment the blows of the axe rang out between the hills. Pålsson lopped off the branches, then he felled the tree, measured the lengths, and trimmed the large ends. There would be many hard days of work here in the forest. The cabin must be built, so that the log walls were at least twelve layers of logs high.

At noon Pålsson went up to the birch forest, and when he came home in the evening, he brought a giant bundle of birch bark, which was to be used for roofing. The birch bark was softened over the fire, so that it could be straightened, and then put into a press so that it would be durable and strong.

During these first days, Pålsson had also tried fishing in Lake Marssjön. He had brought a couple of nets from Fjällboberg, but it was difficult to set them without a boat. He had to push the nets out into the water with a pole, and it was not quite the same. Despite the primitive tools, he was pleased that he got a good catch. There seemed to be plenty of fish in Lake Marssjön.

The days passed. It was not yet hay mowing time, and Lars and Britta worked hard in the woods, while Paul looked after the animals and the little ones. Pålsson had made a log puller, and every mid-day and evening the settlers came back pulling a log. The logs were placed where a few rolled-up stones marked where the cabin would stand.

One day, when Pålsson came home for the mid-day meal, the cows were bellowing and crowding the hut, and one of the sheep was bleating off and on. The children were crying except for Paul, who, pale and trembling, squeezed the heavy muzzle loader. Amid shouts and wild gestures, Aron told them that a bear had taken one of the sheep.

Pålsson took the gun and ran towards Ropenbäcken Creek, and down by the birch grove he came across some bloody remains. But the bear was nowhere to be seen, and after the man had searched in vain for a couple of hours, he returned to the hut with a grim expression on his face.

The loss of the sheep was painful but not the worst of it. They now had a carnivore prowling about Marsliden, a beast that with a single blow could drop a cow to the ground, fling her on its back and disappear. And that the bear would come again was fairly certain. Once such a beast had a taste for meat, it would come back again and again, until there was no more to take.

Pålsson did not go to the woods again that day. But there was plenty to do at home. Lars and Britta leveled the ground, where the cabin was to be built, rolled out rocks and laid the foundation, and before they went to rest that evening, the first level of logs was laid. It was to be a square cabin with one larger and one smaller room.

The boys had been on the lookout all afternoon to warn their father if the bear should be seen down in the lowlands, but the forest beast had not appeared and was apparently content with the prey he had gotten.

From then on, Pålsson could not sleep peacefully. The muzzle loader was always loaded and within reach, and every evening he made a round of the place, before crawling into the hut. And it wasn't just the bear. For a few days now, it was as if the mountain slopes themselves were giving off threatening vapors, some kind of warning of things to come.

Feeling this pressure, Pålsson worked even harder in the forest. He wanted his wife to stay at home by the hut, but Britta refused. She may have been anxious about the children, but she knew that if they were to get the cabin finished before winter, she would have to help in the woods – help now, while she still could work hard. Britta was expecting her seventh child, but Lars didn't know it yet.

The bear roamed around between the hills, constantly threatening the small settlement. Almost every day Pålsson saw fresh bear droppings and huge tracks. Night after night, Lars and Britta took turns keeping watch, and around two o'clock one morning Pålsson saw the furry beast coming out of the birch grove down towards the lake.

Pålsson grabbed his gun and crawled out. The cows lay still without noticing any danger, and under the cover of the hut the man crept to the cabin building site, where he could take up a shooting position unseen. The bear walked cautiously, stopping now and then, sniffing and working its way up the mountainside. It was a great warrior, the biggest bear Pålsson had ever seen, and the man was grimly aware that if he shot and wounded this one, it would be a fight to the death.

The bear now appeared barely a hundred meters of the great spruce tree, and an anxious bleating betrayed that the sheep had warned the enemy. The cows bellowed and Britta came rushing out with an axe at the same moment the shot rang out.

The bear stopped, got up on his hind legs, sniffed and snorted, as if wondering what this could mean – but only for a few seconds. Then he came waddling murderously towards the spruce tree.

Panting with excitement, Pålsson was reloading his weapon. He worked feverishly with his powder horn and ball pouch. Would he make it … make it, before the beast came charging forward …?

It was all a dancing game of seconds, and suddenly a shrill cry cut through the still morning air. Britta rushed forward, swinging her axe wildly. Her eyes flashed, and there was a smoke of rage around her, this rage, which since the infancy of mankind has flamed around mothers who have seen their children's lives threatened.

The bear turned aside as if to evade this unexpected vision, growled menacingly and bared his teeth. Britta rushed forward, shouting and striking, and in a flash the beast quickly took off down the birch grove with the bullet from Pålsson's second shot whistling over his head.

The man looked more than grim as he reloaded his gun. To miss twice in a row had never happened to him before. He took the gun and the axe and ran in the direction where the bear had disappeared.

When Pålsson returned after a couple of hours, his wife had let the animals out to graze, fetched a large bundle of forest moss and spread it on the top level of logs.

They had six or seven logs ready, and although it was only four o'clock in the morning, Lars started with the building, trimming the surfaces of the logs so that they would lie evenly and notching the corner joints. They were now working on the fourth level of logs, which meant that Lars could no longer lay the logs alone. Britta had to help – grabbing the small end of the logs and lifting, feeling like her back would break. The forest moss was pressed together between the logs to fill and seal all the small gaps.

Lars and Britta hesitated to go out into the woods that day. But it was necessary. At any time, they would have to tackle the hay mowing, and how long this would take was impossible to predict. Then, if they got as far as September, a blizzard could come rushing down from the mountain ranges – have mercy, if they had nothing but the hut to crawl into then!

With the muzzle loader in his arms, Paul stood at the post, after his parents had gone off to the woods. The animals had been pushed to the west and to get to them, the bear would have to pass the open space between the mountain and the lake. Standing became tiring after a while, and Paul arranged a comfortable shooting stand for himself next to a rock. And here, hour after hour, lay the defender of Marsliden, a half-naked boy, barefoot and without a hat, pointing the dark gun barrel at the thickets and hide outs of the wilderness.

But either the bear had had enough of the encounter in the morning, or he was equipped with some sort of sixth sense, which told him where he could safely appear. Still, while Paul was looking in vain for the beast, his father had him within good shooting distance up in the woods, and it was little consolation that the beast disappeared when Pålsson went to attack with his axe. This was repeated a couple of times over the next few days, but Pålsson did not dare bring the gun and leave the children without protection. He had to get two things as soon as possible – another gun and a dog.

The bear continued to bother the new settlement, and Lars and Britta almost began to believe that it was not an ordinary bear. Paul had fired one shot at him, and Pålsson had during a day-long hunt sent four bullets towards the rear of the beast. The man became grimmer with each wasted shot. Was it a magic bear that ordinary bullets didn't bite?

*

The hay mowing began. The grass grew tall and lush in the hay meadows, and if you only had time to bring in half of it, there would certainly be no shortage of winter fodder. But it wasn't just mowing. Lars also had to cut down wood for the racks to dry the hay on and carry it to the hay meadows, for the grass would not dry out if it were left to lie. Britta and Aron raked and carried the grass and hung it on the hayrack poles.

One day during the hay mowing, a visitor came to Marsliden. It was Olof Olofsson from Grytsjö, who came for the first time to visit his neighbors. He looked as grim now as he had at the inspection three years ago.

When Pålsson realized that it was his closest neighbor to the east, his face lit up with a kind expression. It would be nice to have good neighbors after all the quarrel in Fjällboberg.

– You weren't home when we stayed overnight at your place, he said.

Olofsson muttered something about having been up in the mountains at that time, and with a nod towards the cabin he said:

– I see you've started building!

– Yes, but there's been a fire here, so it is a long way to haul the timber, replied Pålsson and got caught up in the thought that Olofsson might be willing to help him with the building after the hay mowing.

But it was still too early to say anything about it – let's see after dinner!

Britta was preparing what the "house" had to offer, and the two men went to have a closer look at the log cabin. The children kept their distance and little Jonas thought it safest to hold on to his mother's skirt at all times.

63

– It is the Lapps who have set fire to the forest, Olofsson said softly, so that only Pålsson would hear.

A vein swelled up in Pålsson's face, the fingers of one hand clenched. Set the fire – so that was how it had happened?

– Why did they do it? he asked slowly.

Olofsson pulled Pålsson further away. He told him all about Marsliden, and the more clearly he explained that the place was uninhabitable, the darker Pålsson's face became.

– I haven't done anything to the Lapps, he said in a low voice. Nor do I intend to. Surely, I will leave their reindeers alone.

Olofsson looked searchingly at his neighbor. Didn't this giant man understand what it was all about? "Did not do anything to the Lapps" – and here he was establishing a new settlement on their land! He explained how things were on that matter, but Pålsson was not moved.

– I have papers that say this place is mine! he said grimly. They cost me fifty riksdaler coins.

Olofsson shook his head. The sum seemed inconceivable to him. Fifty riksdaler – surely, there were cheaper ways to die!

– Papers! he exclaimed. Do you think that the reindeer care about some papers when they get to your haystacks!

Pålsson replied that he could put up a fence, but Olofsson shrugged.

– If you think that will help, you will not keep many strands of hay. They would not have to lift more than a few poles before the reindeer are through.

The new settler of Marsliden darkened more and more. If what the neighbor said was true, hard times would come.

– I would have come here sooner, said Olofsson, but I injured myself in the mountains and have had to stay still for a while. It was wrong that I was not home when you came through, so I could have told you at once that you had better turn back. You have a house in Fjällboberg, I have heard.

Pålsson did not answer. His face was like carved in stone, and his eyes were embedded in deep wrinkles.

– I can help you with the move.
– The move …?
Pålsson's voice was strangely sharp.
– Yes, because you cannot stay here. Think of the children!
The men had sat down on the ground, but now Pålsson stood up, and power flowed from his more than six-feet-tall body. His enormous chest heaved deeply.
– It's the children I am thinking of! They almost didn't make it through last winter. Move – no!
Olofsson tried to persuade him, but Pålsson was adamant, and after a while Britta called that the food was ready.
During the meal, consisting mainly of bird meat and broth, the men barely uttered a word. Pålsson suspected that it was pointless to suggest an exchange of work to his neighbor … to try to arrange it so that Olofsson would come to Marsliden after the hay mowing and help with the construction – another year he might need help with his logging. And Pålsson guessed right. He could not expect any help from the neighbor. Olofsson simply would not dare to help build a cabin by Lake Marssjön. It could bring a lot of misfortune to his own house. The children could get sick, the cattle might get lost – anything could happen.
It was Britta who started talking about the bear. Now it had not been seen for a few days, but one was never sure. Had they not noticed it in Grytsjö?
Olofsson replied that it had been several years since they had had any animal taken by bear, and this summer he had not seen any sign of one near Grytsjö.
Pålsson told him about the beast they had roaming here and about the missed shots and wondered if they couldn't join forces and try to bring an end to the rascal before he caused misfortune to either one of them.
Olofsson cast a skittish glance up at the mountain and answered evasively. If Pålsson had not said anything about the bullets not finding their target, the man from Grytsjö would not have hesitated

to bring his dog and gun. He had experienced many strange things in the mountains, and in this case it was clear. The bear was sent by someone who had the power – and could not be shot!

He did not say this so the children heard, but after the meal he nodded to Lars and Britta to walk with him for a bit, and now they got to know his opinion of the bear. Britta trembled. She was a settler's daughter, raised in the wilderness. How many stories had she not heard as a child about magic and strange animals! But when she looked at Lars, she immediately calmed down. They did not believe in magic! And Pålsson explained that, while Olofsson's gaze became more and more strange. Well, they did not believe – they would see! He told about another thing that had happened here on Lake Marssjön, and pleaded to Britta – hadn't they better move?

– We have nowhere to go! Pålsson replied grimly. And if we only can get the cabin ready for the winter, it will be all right.

When Olofsson understood that it was impossible to persuade the settler, he said goodbye and left. At least he had warned him and could sleep with a clear conscience.

CHAPTER EIGHT

Lars and Britta continued with the hay mowing, only getting a few hours of sleep around midnight. Drying rack after drying rack was put up. The weather was beautiful, and the first mowed grass that was cut, was already dry. It had been Pålsson's intention to stack the hay on the spot and then haul it home with the puller when the snow came, but the threat from the Lapps forced him to try to get the feed home before the reindeer arrived to Marsfjället Mountain in early September. Every evening, Lars and Britta came stumbling back from the hayfields carrying large loads of hay, which were put in stacks next to the cabin building area.

As time passed, before the hay mowing was finished it became clear to Pålsson that they had embarked on an endeavor which they had little hope of completing. It was perhaps not primarily the Lapps that would drive them from Marsliden, but a harsh and ruthless winter. The cabin would not be finished in time – too many obstacles all the time – and then this with Britta! It was not possible for her to lift the heavy logs, which for each level had to go higher and higher.

Britta and Lars discussed it, and one evening they decided that Lars should leave to seek help and at the same time buy some food with the few coins they had brought with them when they moved.

Pålsson set off early the next morning, his face bearing the seriousness of the journey. If he couldn't find help, a week would be lost, and with it any prospect of remaining in Marsliden would disappear. He almost turned around at Ropenbäcken Creek. Sweat was beading on his brow, and his chest seemed to be squeezed by a sinking feeling of anxiety. Anything could happen while he was away!

Pålsson forced the thoughts away and continued, almost half-running on the rough ground. On his back he carried a birch bark knapsack, but there was hardly anything in it – a piece of bread, some sun-dried fish, and some bird meat. Tied to the top of the knapsack was an axe, and the man's right hand closed around a strong walking stick. He had not dared to take the gun with him.

As Pålsson approached Grytsjö, Olofsson suddenly came running towards him from a grove next to his settlement. He was extremely upset, and Pålsson could scarcely tell what was going on. One of his cows had been killed. The body was over there, but the head had been dragged away.

Pålsson did not take the time to go and see how the bear had treated its victim. He had many kilometers ahead of him and continued walking. Olofsson looked after him darkly. He was fully and firmly convinced that the bear had killed his cow as a punishment for him visiting Marsliden. Next to the mutilated cow stood Olofsson's wife, wailing, pulling her hair, and spitting westward. Ever since her husband had been to the new settlement at Lake Marssjön, she had known that something would happen… saw it in her dream that night – headless bodies, coming from the mountains. Many generations of people bound by magic had left their mark on her. Oh, my – misfortune was upon them!

Unaware of Sari Olofsson's terrible despair, Pålsson rushed through the wilderness. He ran more than he walked. Distances, which had been day trips during their move were covered in a couple of hours, and before noon he arrived in Doris. Here he rested for half an hour, had a bowl of milk with his fish and bread, and in the meantime talked to the settler there about how to get across Lake Malgomaj by boat, and then continued hurriedly towards Mount Stalon. He pushed and hurried. How were things back at home? After its kill at Grytsjö, would the bear return to Marsliden?

He was so sweaty that steam rose from him. Pålsson arrived at Mount Stalon, which was a few kilometers from the lake. The settler here was out mowing the hay, and Pålsson went out into the fields to find him. The settler had a boat, and if he could borrow it, he would save a day or two. Pålsson met the settler by the brook, and after much discussion he was promised the use of the boat. It was not far to the boat landing from here, and the settler came along to retrieve the hidden oars.

Fifteen minutes later, Pålsson was in the boat out on Lake Malgomaj. Forty kilometers of strenuous travel was behind him, and now a fifty kilometers row awaited him. But Lars was grateful. Without the boat, he would have had to walk along the lakeshore – more arduous, slower and ten kilometers longer.

There was a slight westerly breeze, and it felt even better when the boat passed a point and came out into more open water. Pålsson had so far been so eager to row that he had barely noticed a pole lying in the boat. It was about six feet long. A rope was tied to the top end, and a couple of holes were drilled just over a meter apart. Two sticks were aft, and they seemed to fit in the holes at the top of the pole.

Pålsson wondered if it was a device for a small sail and put up the oars. Just behind the wooden seat was a wooden block with holes in it, nailed to the bottom. The pole fit exactly here, and the rope was just long enough to be tied to a u-shaped nail in the stern. Pålsson put the sticks through the holes in the pole, and now all that was missing was a sail – a sack or a reindeer skin. But neither was in the boat, and Pålsson took off his coat. He put the top stick through the sleeves, and with his shoelaces, he tied the coat corners to the other stick.

The wind blew. The coat was stretched out, and when Pålsson aimed at Strömnäs, he headed for the shore. He might have gone straight to Malgovik and arrived at midnight, but he had a small errand in Strömnäs. One of the farmers there had an old, unusable muzzle loader. Maybe it could be repaired. He sat up for a while and talked, but then crawled into a hay barn, where he fell fast asleep after the day's exertions.

At four o'clock in the morning, Pålsson was out on the lake again. There was almost frost in the air, and he rowed towards Malgovik, his oars creaking. If there was frost here, what would it be like in

Marsliden? In the stern was the old gun, without a stock and with a rusty barrel – not much to have.

Pålsson had many questions to answer at his relatives' house in Malgovik, but when he asked if he could get help with the cabin building, there were suddenly other things to talk about. It had rained so much here in recent weeks. The hay was still hanging on the drying racks – God only knows when it would dry!

Pålsson listened grimly to the complaining. Of course, it was difficult and inconvenient to have hay that didn't dry – but what about him up there then!? Not only did he not have his hay under cover, he didn't even have a cabin for his own family to live in! But he said nothing. In all his days, Pålsson had found it difficult to beg and ask. If they didn't want to help – well then…!

– You should have stayed in Fjällboberg! said his grandmother. There you had a house, and there was food in the forest.

Pålsson did not bother to answer. It was a waste of time to sit here any longer. But there was another matter. The farmers here in Malgovik had horses and usually brought home enough supplies during the winter to sell to the settlers from up the mountain. Pålsson bought as much as he could get for his money and got ready to make the difficult return journey. He stopped at the door. If he told them that Britta was with child, maybe…

He didn't express his thoughts though, and after a solemn farewell, Pålsson left his uncle's cabin.

Pålsson was almost back down to the lake when someone called out to him. From the edge of the forest came a man in his twenties, carrying a loon he had shot. It was Pålsson's cousin Hans Persson. He had been in the village of Laxbäcken for a couple of weeks, helping to build a barn for his future brother-in-law. There was no doubt that Greta in Laxbäcken would be his. But she was young, only seventeen years old, and there was no hurry to marry her. They could always see each other in the meantime anyway.

Hans greeted Pålsson warmly.

– So, you're here! he said. How is it going up there?

Pålsson put down the pack on the ground and began to tell him, and the more he described Marsliden, the more serious Hans' young face became.

– I'll come up with you and build the cabin! he said.

– But do you have time?

Pålsson's voice sounded a little gruff. This sudden offer of help was unexpected.

– Time! Hans laughed, his white teeth gleaming. Oh, you find the time.

Pålsson was almost shaking when he made his way back to his uncle's cabin. Now that he had been promised help, he fully realized what it would have meant to have come home alone.

*

The men arrived at Marsliden the following evening, and Britta had tears in her eyes when she welcomed Hans. But she hardly recognized him. The last time she saw him, he was only a half-grown boy. In honor of the evening, Britta had mysterious activities in the potato field. Her fingers dug gently in the ground, almost as if they were asking for forgiveness for disturbing it. Not a single plant was allowed to be uprooted. Just feel around for the biggest potatoes and then push the soil nicely back in place.

There was a sense of reverence around Britta as she boiled the potatoes, and the children stood there smelling – sniffing, and inhaling a fragrance that made their eyes sparkle. But there were not that many potatoes in the pot. Four each for the men, two each for Britta and the children.

When the potatoes were boiled, the family sat down at a split log table, which Pålsson had set up next to the hut during the first few days. It was getting dark. Dark shadows came creeping down from the mountain slopes. The shores of Lake Marssjön darkened and cast reflections over the lake's shimmering water, which looked more and more like a dark magic eye of the wilderness.

But the people of Marsliden did not look down at the lake. A few logs burned on the hearth, and the glow fluttered against serious faces. There was a sense of reverence at the table that evening. The first potato! The first potato they had eaten in a very long time!

Paul sat next to his father. He ate the bread, the meat, the fish, but it was as if he didn't dare touch his potatoes. They lay on a piece of birch bark in front of him, two oval, yellowish root vegetables. Slowly, almost hesitantly, he picked one up. The potato was no bigger than he could have put it in his mouth at once, but he bit off a piece, which melted in his mouth, while a look of satisfaction spread across his face.

*

The next day, the people of Marsliden received another stern reminder that they were not alone. When Pålsson and Hans came home, pulling two logs, Aron came and showed them a small round, gray ball he had found where the cows were grazing. Pålsson's face froze as soon as he got the ball in his hands. He told Aron to take Paul with him and immediately run to the pasture and see if there were any more balls.

– What is it? Hans wondered.

– A magic ball, I think, Pålsson replied grimly.

– A magic ball?

Pålsson nodded, and without giving any further explanation, he went to the fireplace and lit it. Then he poured some water into a pot and put it over the fire. Britta, meanwhile, came from the forest with a bundle of moss. She hurried to the men and wondered what they were up to.

Pålsson held up the small ball between his thumb and forefinger.

– We'll see how this works! he said grimly and dropped the ball into the water.

All three leaned over the pot, and their faces froze in a tense expression. Only Pålsson had an idea what was going to happen.

The ball moved in the water… a small gray-white shape that neither sank nor floated. A few shiny grease rings began to spread towards the edges of the pot, as the ball slowly melted.

Suddenly, it jumped in the water, and Britta gave a small shout. The ball had disappeared, and feathers, tied together, floated among the water rings the "splash" had stirred up. The water was not yet boiling, and Lars put his hand down and picked up the feathers. His big hand trembled a little when he felt the sharp tips.

Both Hans and Britta understood the terrible significance of the change that had taken place with the "magic ball". Britta was breathing heavily, and her gaze was darting back and forth. She urged them to hurry to the pasture and help the boys look, and no matter how hard it was for Pålsson to leave the urgent work of building, there was no choice but to set off in search of the sinister grease balls.

They were sneaky, these little balls, whose design was as simple as it was refined. Feathers were bent together, so that the tips came close together. Fine thread was wrapped around them, and then the feathers were "baked" in grease, which was rolled into a ball. If an animal or a human swallowed such a ball, their life could not be saved. The grease melted, the feathers stretched out and punctured their intestines, and after a few hours of horrible torment, the "magic" had done its work.

When the men and Britta arrived at the pasture, the cows were lying down, chewing their cud. The boys had found another ball, and all of them started an eager search. Tufts of tall grass were searched especially carefully because the balls they had found were found in those places. The boys said the balls had been put in the grass a few inches from the ground.

An hour passed, and no new death balls were discovered, and the men were about to return to their work, when they were suddenly startled by a horrible scream coming from below. For a second, they stood petrified but then rushed back.

It was the sheep, who, in wild leaps, bleated terrified. It rushed back and forth, leaping, and running as if possessed by an evil spirit.

For a moment it stood still with outstretched legs… a searing, anguished second, that left the men gasping for breath. The next moment the sheep leapt into the air, fell to its knees, got up again and danced around, screaming in pain.

Hans had his gun with him.

– Shoot! Pålsson panted hoarsely, and in a few seconds the animal fell to the ground.

It was unnecessary to look for what had caused the sheep's terrible torments, but Pålsson cut open the body, and one glance at the insides was enough to confirm what was already known. Pålsson's face looked like a thunderstorm as he walked home with the sheep's body over his shoulder.

Britta and the boys followed, driving the cows in front of them. It was perhaps the third and last ball the sheep had ingested, but the incident was too upsetting to dare let the cows stay at the pasture.

Pålsson didn't say much for the rest of the day. He worked as if in dull rage, and it would not have been advisable for the one who had laid out the balls to show himself. It must be the Lapps. But was it entire Lapp families in ruthless collaboration or some lone fool, roaming around?

Hans was even more worked up than Pålsson. He was never more than five steps from his loaded gun, and no matter how hard he worked, the gaze from his steel-blue eyes stared up toward the mountain walls every minute. When evening came, he took his gun and crept to the west.

CHAPTER NINE

Hans had not been able to find anything suspicious on the night he set out with the gun, and the next few weeks passed without any disturbing incidents. There were only a few drying racks on a brook meadow to the west, which had been stacked to dry in place. The reindeer wouldn't come until there was snow up in the mountains, and by then, they hoped that the cabin would be finished, so there would be time to bring home what they had left in the fields.

Pålsson and Hans worked hard – cutting down trees, hauling logs and building. The log hauling took an enormous amount of time, and despite the good help, Pålsson wasn't entirely sure they would have a roof over their heads when the first snowstorm came howling. Britta worked almost even harder than the men. She had the children and animals to look after, but she was also involved with the building work, carrying moss home, tearing, and shaping birch bark, and looking for flat stones to build the chimney.

At noon on one of the first days of September, Britta suddenly spotted a boat out on Lake Marssjön. The men stopped working and stared at the dark spot. The boat was coming from East Lake Marssjön. It could not be anyone other than Olofsson, and they wondered what business he had. But it soon became clear that the rower was not going to Marsliden. The boat slipped behind the small islands near the south shore and was heading straight west.

Pålsson got a suspicious look in his eyes, and when Britta told him that he'd better run over there to see what this might mean, he quickly disappeared down to the lake. One had every reason to be suspicious of anyone who set foot on Marsliden's property.

It was to the west that Pålsson had his haystack, and he reached it before the boat headed for land just north of the stream that flowed from the Merkeskullarna Hills. There were two of them in the boat, Olofsson and his wife.

Pålsson kept out of the way, arranged a few posts around the haystack, and in the meantime heard the neighbors pulling the boat ashore and the rustling in the bushes as the oars were hidden. And now Olofsson came struggling towards the stack with a pack on his back. Olofsson carried a birch bark pack and his wife a Lapp cradle, shaped like a boat. The upper end was open, and a little head stuck up, wearing a lambskin cap.

Olofsson startled as the Marsliden giant stepped out from behind the haystack. Pålsson greeted him and asked politely where they were going.

– To Fatmomakke.

– Oh, Pålsson muttered. What's going on there?

The Olofsson's exchanged a glance as if they had something strange in front of them. Didn't he know what was happening in Fatmomakke now – or was he a heathen who didn't want to understand such things?

Pålsson was told that there was a church service in Fatmomakke the next day and that the people from Grytsjö were on their way there to have their youngest child baptized.

While Olofsson was giving this information, his wife had continued walking, and with an urgent nod he hurried after her into the underbrush. It was as if the settler in Grytsjö feared that accidents would happen on their journey if he did not leave Marsliden as soon as possible.

Britta got worked up when she heard that a pastor was coming to Fatmomakke. Shouldn't they try to go there? She herself could not get away, but Lars and Hans – there should probably be someone representing Marsliden!

The men discussed the matter. They really did not have time.

– We won't have time to finish the cabin, if we start running around in the mountains, Hans said grimly, but it seemed to him that a trip to Fatmomakke was rather tempting.

Pålsson said that they would probably meet some settlers in Fatmomakke and perhaps get to try to reason a little with the Lapps.

– We would lose one day, at the most.

Nevertheless, Pålsson was not very eager to waste a working day, but after strong pressure from Britta, the men finally decided to leave early the next morning for the Lapp chapel.

It was just before dawn when Lars and Hans walked up the mountain. It would have been closer and easier to follow the same path as the Olofsson's, but the service in Fatmomakke meant that the reindeer had now come to Marsfjället Mountain, and the men were very interested in seeing them up close. They would then take the journey home through the forest slope between the mountain and Lake Kultsjön.

They quickly got up above the tree line, where rust-brown mountain heaths brushed up against Mount Kakkankaisse. To the left rose the steeper sides of Mount Ropen, and soon enough they were walking on the bottom of the giant kettle valley, which Abraham had stared down on from the heights of Mount Ropen three years ago. Neither Pålsson nor Hans had been up the mountain before, but Pålsson had heard that there was a pass at the far end of the kettle valley.

It was hard to get up to this opening between the two mountain peaks. They had to crawl more than walk and sweat was dripping off them when they finally reached the top. From here the view to the west was unobstructed, and Pålsson gazed intently at the mountain peaks that rose beyond the Ransardalen valley. This winter he would try use this route to cross over into Norway, if he was able to get some skins to sell. Ericsson had told him last winter that it was much closer to Kroken than to Åsele. Only 80 kilometers from Marsliden.

On this side of the pass there were vast grazing areas, and when the men came down the slope a little way, they saw a herd of reindeer. A little further away, smoke rose from a *goahti*. Hans wondered if they should go there, but Pålsson said that they should probably hurry and go straight to Fatmomakke. They made a wide turn so as not to disturb the grazing herd of reindeer but did not avoid getting barked at thoroughly by a couple of dogs, who followed them halfway down to the tree line, ready at any moment to sink their teeth into the men's calves.

Fatmomakke lay on the south side of the narrow bay which cut from Lake Kultsjön towards the mouth of the Ransarån river. The place was uninhabited and completely deserted except on those occasions when the Lapps gathered for religious meetings, which happened only twice a year. The first was held at midsummer, when the reindeer were still on the nearby mountains, and the second church weekend was celebrated in early September on their return from the summer work in the Norwegian border mountains. If the small chapel in the wilderness was dead and quiet for long periods, it was all the more lively on these weekends. In addition to sermons, there was a bizarre variety of weddings, funerals, and infant baptisms. And there was time for other things as well. On the hillside between the chapel and the bay, goahtis were erected, and it could be quite lively during those days, when the liquor began to go to the heads of thirsty Lapps and settlers.

Already at a distance Pålsson and Hans could hear that it was a happy day in Fatmomakke. There were dogs barking, laughter, and shouting. They came down to the bay just before the start of the service and called for a boat.

As Pålsson expected, a lot of settlers had gathered in Fatmomakke. The Saxnäs farmers were there, settlers from Lövberg and Klimp-fjäll and a few more. Jon in Klimpfjäll had his daughter Inga with him, and there was a look of interest in her eyes when she saw Hans' young face.

The men from Marsliden attracted attention. It was as if an icy wind had come rushing down from the mountains. The noise outside the goahtis was cut down to whispers, and from the smoky interiors of the goahtis a head or two came sticking out with set faces. At the far goahti an old Lapp rose and shaded his eyes with his hand to see better, while his thin lips moved as if to ward off this sight with a spell. Next to him stood Niel, hard and grim, with one hand unconsciously resting on the handle of his knife. The old man asked something, and this was answered with a short nod.

The settlers, too, seemed a little surprised, but that did not prevent the Saxnäs farmers from greeting their neighbor to the north cordially, and before Hans could really understand how it had happened, he was sitting on the ground with a cup of steaming hot coffee in his hand. It was Jon's daughter who had quickly and firmly taken care of the young man from Marsliden.

After the service, which included a sermon in Lapp and Swedish, there were two funerals. The coffins had been buried earlier. The graves had been filled back in except for a space which was kept open with a wooden tube, and through the tube the three scoops of dirt were sent down to the coffins. When Pålsson saw the Lapps mourning, he had a hard time believing that they had evil intentions towards him. They were like children in their humble pain.

The Saxnäs farmers and Jon were gathered and invited Pålsson and Hans to eat with them. Today was a feast. They had bread and cheese, meat, new potatoes, and plenty of alcohol. Pålsson was careful with his drinking. He took a couple of shots to be polite, but then he had enough. Meanwhile, he cautiously brought the conversation to the relationship with the Lapps – that Olofsson had said this and that.

The farmers from Saxnäs laughed. Olofsson – you shouldn't listen to him! He just wants you out of Marsliden, that's all. You don't have to worry about the Lapps either. They are just cowards who don't dare to do anything. Jon agreed, and they drank to that.

The Lapps – ha!

Pålsson listened intently. He wondered what they would say if he took the "magic ball" out of his pocket and showed them and told them how the sheep had fared. But Pålsson left the ball where it was. He suspected that the men would be too upset if they understood what had happened, and he did not want there to be trouble in a place like this. He didn't even ask if they knew that the forest in Marsliden had been burned down.

Down among the goahtis, the mood was high this afternoon. A young couple had just been married. Pålsson went down there, determined to try to talk with one of the Lapps. Surely it would not be impossible to reach a peaceful agreement. If there was a dispute, he was the one who had been wronged. The burned down forest, the sinister grease balls – what would they have to say about them? But he would not go that far but would listen calmly and quietly inquire whether they considered his settlement an encroachment on their grazing lands. If the answer was yes, then perhaps a solution could be found. Pålsson went alone. Inga had preoccupied Hans, who seemed to have forgotten that there was someone called Greta.

There was celebration and joy everywhere by the goahtis, but when Pålsson approached, the mood shifted. Laughter died down, and happy faces stiffened in dull hostility. Pålsson noticed this change but pretended not to. He stopped here and there and said a few kind words. The answer was silence or some sentence in Lapp, which he did not understand.

Olofsson's wife was sitting by one of the goahtis. She pretended not to recognize him, and a shadow passed over Pålsson's face. Between a couple of goahtis he almost bumped into a young Lapp girl, who ran around like a whirlwind. He nodded kindly, but the girl recoiled as if she had encountered the evil one. She drew back, gasping for air, and disappeared.

Pålsson darkened. What did this really mean? Did the Lapps have to behave like this because he had moved to Marsliden? Or was there something else underneath all this – something he didn't know about? He continued down to the lake shore, deep in thought.

Pålsson went back the way he came. No Lapp was visible outside the goahtis, not even Niel. The settler stopped at the largest one.

– I would like to talk to someone in here! he said loud and clear.

A murmur was heard in reply, then silence, no one came out.

Pålsson left. The position of the Lapps was clear enough. They did not want anything to do with him.

It was getting towards evening. Pålsson was in a bad mood, and when he finally caught up with Hans, he thought they should go home. He asked Jon if he would be willing to row them across the bay. Inga asked her father if it was time for them to go home as well. Jon thought for a moment and then said it would be good if they all left together.

Five minutes later they left Fatmomakke, but Pålsson would never have climbed into Jon's boat, if he had known what conclusions the Lapps would draw from this.

The rowing would save the men from Marsliden about seven kilometers of walking, and while they were rowing the boat south, Pålsson and Jon had much to talk about. The two men had previously met at the market in Åsele, and now Pålsson was interested in hearing how business was done in Norway. Jon had good things to say about it. There were good people in Kroken, decent people to do business with – twenty *öre* for grouse and seven or eight *kronor* for fox-skin. They could go there together sometime this winter. It was not too far out of the way to take the road over Klimpfjäll mountain.

Pålsson's face brightened. How easy it was to talk to someone like Jon – different than Olofsson's gloomy predictions!

But it wasn't only future trips to Norway that needed to be discussed. Jon showed great interest in Marsliden, and Pålsson told him how they were getting on. He told him about the forest nearest the homestead being burnt down but said nothing about the dangerous balls. This was something he still wanted to keep secret. But the fact that the place was nice did not need to be kept secret. Good hay crop, and no frost had yet been felt. The potatoes thrived and were ready to be harvested any day.

Hans and Inga sat huddled together on the seat in the stern and spoke of their own things. It was mostly whispers and glances, stolen hand squeezing and the occasional little laugh. Pålsson hardly noticed them, but Jon nodded now and then and seemed pleased.

It had clouded over, and a sharp wind came in from the opening between the two Nassjo Mountains, which bordered the lake on the west side. Here in Nassjoviken Bay was a dangerous place for a boat. If the wind blew just right, the air was pushed together between two parts of the mountain creating huge waves down in the bay. Jon said that a few years ago a boat and its load had perished here. But today there was no risk. The wind wasn't coming from that direction.

When they got close to Stornäs, Jon headed for the north shore to put Pålsson and Hans ashore. The wind had picked up, and beyond Stornäs the waves were high. Here there were no mountains to block the wind, so the wind had free rein along the valley of Lake Kultsjön to the west. Jon looked grimly at the white, foamy crests. It would soon be dark and rowing the more than twenty kilometers to Klimpfjäll in a strong headwind was not appealing. Inga thought they should all go to Marsliden for the night. Pålsson said that they were welcome to do so. It would be a bit crowded, and hard to find a spot for everyone to lie down, but if there was not too much of a storm, it could be arranged. There was hay outside to sleep in.

When it had been decided that Jon and his daughter would spend the night in Marsliden, they continued along the lake again, and keeping a few hundred meters from the northern shore, the boat was pushed along with the wind sweeping from stern to bow.

After five kilometers, the boat was hauled ashore, and then the four of them hurried across the muorke to get to the new settlement before it got dark. But if Jon and his daughter were only wanting a place to spend the night, Marsliden was not the most convenient place to stop on their way home. They could have spent the night in Stornäs, which was right next to the channel up to Klimpfjäll.

There was no storm that night, and the next morning the weather was calm and still. Jon seemed to be in no hurry to get home. He was looking around in Marsliden. He went up to the woods for a while and helped Pålsson haul home a huge load of logs and did not save his strength. But there was something inside that nagged him. This place would have been his, if not... if not... He had been stupid to have handed over the claim to Abraham. But he tried to remember – did Pålsson have any papers proving that he had a legal right to the new settlement? Jon asked a few cautious questions and Pålsson showed the papers he had bought from Abraham.

Jon was superior to Pålsson in one respect, and that was that he could read. He looked carefully through the papers. It said that he (Jon) transferred his claim to Abraham, but there was not a word to indicate that Abraham had transferred the new settlement to Pålsson. It was Abraham who still had the legal claim to the place, but that right would be forfeited in two years.

This applied to Abraham. When the time had expired, the place was available for a new inspection. The fact that Pålsson had settled here did not matter, as far as Jon could understand. The papers Pålsson had bought were useless to anyone but Abraham. But were there any other documents – court records that Abraham had transferred the right to Pålsson?

Jon was careful not to ask about that. He could find out in Åsele what the situation was.

– These are some nice papers! he said. Was it fifty riksdaler coins you paid for them?

Pålsson nodded.

– Yes, fifty riksdaler coins!

Inga hardly left Hans' side all morning. But she was not in the way. She was healthy and strong, used to doing the toughest of chores, and she helped with the work, until sweat dripped off her tanned face.

After dinner, Jon said a few words to his daughter in private. She nodded cheerfully, and although it was now really time for the visitors from Klimpfjäll to leave, if they were to get home before evening, she went with Hans to the woods to fetch a couple of logs.

Jon helped with the building of the cabin for a while but then said that he had to think about returning home.

– Inga could stay and help you for a week or so. We don't have much to do at home, since we are done with the hay mowing.

Pålsson found it difficult to find an answer. Sure, he was grateful for help, but…

– Well, you don't have to think about any payment, said Jon, who thought that was the sticking point. And she'll earn her keep.

There wasn't much for Pålsson to say. He was reluctant to upset Jon. When Hans and Inga came back from the forest, the farmer from Klimpfjäll had left.

Hans was a little apprehensive when he learned that Inga would be staying in Marsliden. He couldn't shake the feeling that there was a snare tightening around him.

CHAPTER TEN

A couple of weeks after the visit to Fatmomakke, Pålsson woke up one night to the sound of cows bellowing. There was a storm raging outside. The huge spruce shook, so that the roof of the lean-to was close to being torn apart. Pålsson crawled out and gasped for breath when he was hit by a huge gust of wind. It was a blizzard, the first howling storm of autumn.

The cows stomped around in the snow seeking protection for their heads as close to the spruce trunk as possible. Earlier in the autumn, Pålsson had tied up branch walls around the animals' night camp, but now the storm had ripped one of them apart, and at any moment the roof could collapse.

Pålsson did not bother to try to fix the wall. He groped his way in the dark towards the cabin. The doorway was to the south ... a gaping hole in the solid log building. Pålsson went in, felt his way to the fireplace, built just the day before, and managed to light a fire after a lot of trouble. The man forgot for a moment the animals out there. Would there be a good draft out through the primitive chimney, or would the smoke make its way into the room? The fire fizzled on the unused hearth of stone and dirt. The smoke stung his eyes as it bounced against the stones of the flue. Pålsson took a few steps back, and in a moment he nodded. There was a good draft! And it would be even better after the stones warmed up.

The fire flared up and cast a flickering light over the room, giving the gray, shaggy walls a magnificent look. Long strands of moss hung from the gaps between the logs. The moss moved in the draft from a window opening, a slit where the blizzard came cascading in. There was no floor. The floor beams were in place, but in between them, only dark dirt was visible, cold, and gloomy. The split wood of the roof shone brightly, where the flames were reflected in the splinters and slivers. There hadn't been time to carve the inner layer of the roof smoothly, nor was it necessary. They did not need to touch the inside of the roof.

Pålsson went out to get a bundle of hay and used it to close up the window opening. While he was getting the cabin's other room ready for the cows, Britta came in, panting. She heard rustling but couldn't see anything in the dark.

– Are you here, Lars?

– Yes, we have to bring in the cows.

Britta went to the fireplace where some long pieces of kindling lay to one side. She took one and lit it over the fire and a few seconds later she stood in the opening to the other room with a smoking torch. There was no floor here either, and Lars was spreading moss between two floor beams.

The cows were led in. They snorted and resisted, and there was a great risk that they would break their legs stepping over the threshold, which lay about half a meter above the dirt floor. But they got in, and after Pålsson gave them some hay, they seemed fully satisfied with their new surroundings. This is where they would stay until spring. Pålsson had always intended that one of the cabin's rooms would be used as a barn for the first winter.

The animals were protected from the storm, but they were not any warmer. The window opening in this room had also been stuffed with hay, but there was no door, and Pålsson went to the damaged lean-to to get material for a cover. Meanwhile, Hans crawled out of the lean-to and carefully closed the opening with a door, braided from birch branches.

The two men now helped each other to cover the opening which led from the entry into the rooms with the cows. It was difficult in the dark. The light from the fireplace in the big room did little good out here. They had to feel around in the dark while putting up support rods and braid branches together. When there was daylight, they could make a real door.

While the men were busy with this, Britta crawled into the lean-to to see if the children were awake and cold. But the snow was covering it like a blanket, and it was quite warm inside. The children slept, and Britta laid her and Lars' fur blanket over them. Someone was moving by one of the walls.

– Are you awake? whispered Britta.

– Yes, are you up?

– It's snowing.

Oh, Inga gasped, and sat up. She couldn't see anything in the pitch-black darkness, but she heard the storm pulling at the spruce branches.

– Are the men outside?

– Yes, we have brought the cows into the cabin.

Inga felt around to find her shoes. She was otherwise fully clothed, and it did not take many seconds for her to get them on. She crawled out into the storm, followed by Britta.

The two women made their way to the fireplace outside the lean-to and started looking in the snow for pots and other kitchenware. When they entered the cabin with their hands full, the men had finished their work and sat on one of the floor beams in front of the fire, discussing what to do from here. Pålsson›s face was grim but not hopeless. Had the storm held off for a few more days, the outside of the cabin would have at least been finished.

There was more to carry in, and Pålsson and Hans helped the women. The storm roared and howled with undiminished force, and it was difficult to find all the things in the devastating snowstorm. But everything eventually made it inside, and Britta went to the fireplace to prepare something hot to drink.

They didn't know what time it was. Pålsson used to have a watch, but it was destroyed during their move from Fjällboberg. It might only be midnight, but no one felt like crawling into the lean-to to wait for dawn. More firewood was brought in, and in the light from the fire Pålsson began to carve windowsills, Hans went out and dug around in the snow and dragged in some rough poles, which he cut off to door lengths. It was necessary to get a proper door ready and put it up as soon as possible.

In the dark night the blows of the ax were heard inside the cabin, accompanied by the howling of the storm in the low chimney. Despite the fire, there was no heat in the room.

The walls were damp and cold, and from the doorway a stream of cold air swept along the dirt floor.

Britta sat next to the fire with worry showing on her face. The snow had come several weeks earlier than expected, and if they had not had Hans' help, they would not have had a roof on the cabin, maybe the walls would not have even been completed. Britta shuddered when she thought of what this would have meant for them. But how were the children doing out there in the lean-to? Britta was tormented. If only they could have brought them in here! They were probably freezing to death out there under the spruce branches.

– Maybe we should bring in the children, Lars.

Pålsson stopped working, and a thoughtful wrinkle was seen between his eyebrows.

– They are probably better where they are, he said slowly.

– But what if they are awake and cold?

Pålsson replied that he did not think so, but Britta was worried. She went out, found her way to the lean-to and crawled in. Once there, she immediately calmed down. The children were breathing calmly and quietly under the furs, unaware of the howling storm that was raging outside the walls. Britta lay down next to them and soon felt that it was much warmer and more comfortable here than in the cabin. She laid still, thinking, and after a while her thoughts faded, and the settler wife slept …

But the cabin was bustling with work. Hans was building a door and went about it in the same way as when you put together a picture frame. The rods were carved square, holes drilled, pins driven in, moss between the rods, and these were driven together. The result was a sturdy door, at least four inches thick, and no one would be able to put it on their back and run off with it. Hans did not say many words to Inga, who was sitting on one of the beams, carving thick plugs for the door's mortise and narrow ones to be used as nails. But it was the girl from Klimpfjäll he was thinking of. What did she really mean? She was after him every day and wanted him to ask Pålsson to share the new homestead. Oh, he understood where this was heading.

There were times when Hans was close to giving in. In many ways there was no better place to settle. Here the potatoes survived the frost better than in Malgovik. It was as if the mountain walls radiated warmth, and this pushed away the chilly mists that crept in from the shore. And there was fodder on the vast meadows of Marsliden – not just hay for two, four or six cows but for thirty or forty. And Pålsson was probably not averse to the idea. He had heard him say so several times. He knew that if he settled in Marsliden, it would be in the company of Inga. He was captivated by this strong, agile woman, who could make his blood run up like fire through his veins. And she was sure of herself. She said they could stay in Klimpfjäll for the winter.

But tonight, Hans felt like she was trying to ensnare him. With each blow of the axe, he vowed to himself that this would have to end! And perhaps it would be best if he could get Jon's daughter out of his mind. She was pretty, but there was something voracious and predatory in her eyes, and those full lips could never conjure up the sun-warm smile that used to meet Hans from Greta in Laxbäcken.

*

The storm subsided towards morning, and by the time daylight came, the wind had shifted to the southwest. The wet snow was dripping from the roof of the cabin. It seemed like the early snow was going away again. But it would not disappear today. In some places large drifts had formed, and the lean-to looked like a snow cave.

Today it was impossible to haul anything back from the forest, but there was work to be done anyway. The roof was not finished on one side, and there were windows and doors to be fitted in place. Britta found it hard to hold back her tears as the small window in the kitchen was put in. A window to look out of, that was a long time ago! The doors were just as remarkable. Not having to crawl in and out, just turn the wooden handle – open and close.

As evening approached, the sun peeked through the clouds, and it was decided to move into the cabin, even though it had no floor. It might get cold that night after the snowstorm. If it had been earlier in the autumn and no danger of severe cold, Britta might not have relented. Walls and a roof and fireplace, it felt like paradise since they had been sleeping under a spruce tree all summer. Hay was brought in to sleep on, since the dirt floor was cold and damp, even though there had been a fire in the hearth since last night.

The children were delighted. They climbed on the floor beams and tumbled in the hay, but when daylight stopped seeping in through the window, they stayed reverently still. They sat in the hay and stared at the fire. There was something so unfamiliar about having light where you were supposed to be sleeping.

When the people of Marsliden had gone to sleep that night, there was a glow of happiness on Britta's face. They had somewhere to live, a roof over their heads like other people. It was almost too won-derful to be true. Her eyes shimmered as she looked at the mossy walls, which radiated comfort and warmth. She didn't think about lying on a pair of beams on a dirt floor. The children and Lars were asleep, and from Hans came a heavy snore. But Inga was awake. Britta heard her moving in the hay, and amidst all the feelings of happiness a wonder intruded. Would anything develop between Hans and Inga, she wondered?

There was no frost that night, and the next morning the ground was practically clear of snow. The birches that were sheltered from the wind glowed fiery yellow. It was still autumn, even though it had been winter weather the night before.

Hans was unusually quiet this morning, and after breakfast he said he had to think about going home before it became too difficult to travel across the ground. Soon the streams would be too risky to cross, and they might worry at home if he stayed until winter when the streams were completely frozen over. It was evident from Hans that he'd prefer not to leave Marsliden before the cabin was fully finished, but Pålsson reassured him they would be fine now that they had come this far. There was no hurry about the floor. They could pull in one log at a time. Despite his stoic ways, Pålsson was observant. It wasn't the journey Hans feared. There was something else underneath that wasn't wise to meddle with. Otherwise, he would probably have asked Hans if he wanted to stay in Marsliden. Two men could manage better than one, and there was plenty of room here for several families.

Britta prepared some food for Hans, and Pålsson said that he would pay for his work when he had some skins to sell. Hans dismissed any talk of a wage. They didn't have to worry about paying him! This is how Hans was. He was quick to help but didn't understand that his work was worth something. So, Hans' father was actually right when he said that his second oldest boy would never amount to anything. If you wanted to be something and get your own place, you couldn't act in this way.

But Hans had no fears about his future when he was ready to leave Marsliden. The worries of the past few days had been erased from his mind. His eyes were bright, and he laughed as carefree as he had before.

– You'll come up sometime and visit, right? said Britta.

Hans nodded. Yes, he would. He would have promised anything at that moment.

After a heartfelt farewell, Hans walked east, accompanied by Inga. She would walk with him the first part of the way and then come back.

– I wonder what they will figure out, Britta said, when the two young people had disappeared towards Ropenbäcken Creek.

– Figure out?

– If there will be anything between them.

Pålsson did not answer. He knew more than Britta – that there was someone else, named Greta – but he did not discuss other people's love affairs, not even with his wife.

– Didn't Hans say anything to you?

– No.

– Inga has been after him a little too much, I think.

Lars did not answer this either. If he had any particular opinion about Jon's daughter, he kept it to himself.

Whatever Pålsson and his wife thought of Inga, she was earning her keep in Marsliden. Thanks to her, Britta had had time to pick berries. Fish, both dried and salted, was available for their needs this winter, and it was Inga who had shown Britta how to cook "juombo". The plant "Jierja" (Mulgedium alpinum) grew in the mountain valleys. The long stalk would be boiled, chopped up and put into a small barrel to ferment. When the plant was eaten, it would be mixed with sour milk. Inga was knowledgeable about many things that were part of life in these remote mountain areas, and it was at her instructions that the men had built a small storehouse on four poles. Here the food could be stored without being spoiled by the cabin heat or dragged away by wild animals.

Paul was most delighted that she was staying with them. It was thanks to Inga that he now had a working gun, the old musket Pålsson had received in Strömnäs. She had scrubbed the barrel clean of rust with fine sand and greased the steel with sheep tallow. She had carved a new stock and fitted it in, and the boy was beyond proud of the bear Jon's handy daughter had carved into one side of the stock. Sometimes Inga's actions and knowledge seemed to come from an unnatural source, but she had the stuff that was needed to make the mightiest settler's wife to ever wield a clearing axe in the Lappland wilderness.

It was a couple of hours before Inga returned, by which time she seemed to have lost all desire for work. After a while she climbed up to the top of the hill, which lay just behind the cabin, and looked to the west. Would her father come for her? He hadn't said anything about that – just "You can stay here."

If Jon did not come for his daughter, she would have to make an arduous hike if she did not want to wait until the lakes were frozen. A fifty-kilometer journey through a wilderness many times more rugged than the one Hans had to cross to reach Malgovik, along the mountains beyond and past Fatmomakke to Lake Gikasjön. Here there was a settler who could help her cross the roaring Ransarån River, then a hike across the Gemon Mountains at a time of year when some mountain lands were impassable and the days so short that she'd have to spend the night in a rock cleft or a thicket.

Inga was fully aware of what the journey required. At least she would not set out this day, maybe not the next either, but could she bear to be in Marsliden much longer? She didn't think so. Inga still stood looking towards Klimpfjäll Mountain, and for a moment something anxious gleamed in her gray-brown eyes. What would her father say when she came home and told him that nothing had come of it? Father was the only man Inga feared. Sometimes he became wild and just yelled and hit. He had been like that for a couple, three years.

With a deep sigh, Inga turned to the vast delta to the east. To the right, snow glistened at the top of the north slope of Mount Gittsfjället, but the girl could hardly see it. Her eyes sort of searched the woodland beyond Grytsjö. He was somewhere over there. Despair and desire flamed in Inga's face. Wasn't she good enough? Wasn't she as good as anyone else? Her breathing was heavy. Her cheeks turned red and hot, and her bosom swelled so that the dress was close to bursting.

When Inga came down to the cabin again, she was perfectly calm, almost lethargic, and for the rest of the day she sat by the fireplace in the cabin without saying a word. Britta didn't ask her anything, and neither did Lars.

The next day Jon came, and there was not the slightest shadow on his face when he found that Hans had disappeared. He said that he had come to fetch his daughter before the lake became impassable, stayed in Marsliden for only an hour, and then the Pålsson's were again alone at Lake Marssjön.

Inga had expected to hear harsh words when she was left alone with her father, but Jon was in a great mood. During these two weeks he made a trip to Vilhelmina and talked to the police chief. It was, as Jon had thought, Abraham, who still owned the claim, Pålsson's possession was illegal. But he was welcome to stay in Marsliden for now and clear the land. Jon was sure that this winter he would be able to meet Abraham in Åsele, and then he had to get Abraham to hand over the deed to him and immediately have the land transfer registered. The fact that Pålsson had the papers meant nothing. Abraham could say that they had been stolen. And if Abraham did not agree to the deal, it was only a matter of pretending like nothing happened. After two years, Abraham's deed would expire, and then...

Jon's face shone. Marsliden was almost as good as his.

CHAPTER ELEVEN

The weeks passed, and suddenly the winter arrived in earnest. The peaks of Marsfjället Mountain had long since turned white, and the meadows on the mountain heaths were covered with snow half a meter deep. But it seemed that this year the reindeer did not want to leave the mountains. With their broad hooves they dug holes down to the lichen and sometimes made breakneck climbs up the steep stone walls, where the moss shone green on wind-cleared ledges.

Niel came skiing along the foot of the great peak. His face was hard and cold, and every movement expressed grim determination. Tonight, it would happen – tonight, when the settler at Lake Marssjön lay asleep, judgment would come upon him!

There had been many heated deliberations by the fires in recent weeks. The more sensible Lapps said that there was nothing to be done about it, but that it was best to be careful lest misfortune should befall them. Remember what happened to Nutti! He was hanged – hanged! It was better to settle for letting the reindeer destroy the haystacks – no one could help that – no one at all! And maybe next year lightning struck the part of the forest that was left – surely lightning would strike!

But Niel and Ante were not satisfied to allow the settler to get off so easily. Ante was old and could talk about the time when there was not a single settler west of Lake Malgomaj. In those days, no reindeer meat was cooked in foreign pots. The settlers were like the wolf. They prowled the outskirts of the herds and pounced on reindeer that were not being watched. And were they satisfied with the reindeer? When Ante was young, during the migrations between the forest land and the mountains, you could come across beavers –

fine meat and skins that were worth a lot to trade. But where were the beavers now? Ask the settlers – the ones who did nothing but run around with their guns! Did they shoot the wolves? No! They fed the beasts with reindeer meat, which they couldn't bring home. Those wolves knew that they would get food – just keep on the trail, and they'd get to the bloody remains. And what would it be like this year? They could tell that the reindeer didn't dare to leave the mountains! This year another settler had come … one worse than all the others. Almost settling in the mountains. Could he make a living from it? No! He intended to stuff his belly with reindeer.

And had they forgotten Mikael? Was anyone hanged because Mikael "disappeared"? No! Had they not all seen that the settler at Lake Marssjön had left Fatmomakke in Jon's boat? That meant something. Or did they not remember that Ante had pointed to the Fjällfjällen and Klimpfjäll Mountains the night after Mikael disappeared – Ante, who could see "visions"? Pointed and held up one, two fingers in the air. Two that had made Mikael disappear – the second one. And now that second one had built a cabin to stay by Lake Marssjön. How much misfortune would he bring upon them! The reindeer cows would calve prematurely, the dogs would become mangy and go mad – should they allow this to happen? Did they think the reindeer would destroy his haystacks? He hadn't left a single straw out in the fields – knew that revenge was coming – hauled it home – a large stack – sat on top of it with the gun – the reindeer, no way! He needed to go away, away…!

Niel was so full of thoughts and plans of revenge, that he flinched when the angry sounds of dogs suddenly came echoing from the pass. He pushed his staff against the ground and threw himself forward with all his might.

Below the mountain slope, which rose just before the passage to the kettle valley, a pair of other Lapps stood beside a gray bundle and stared upward. On a ledge fifty meters above them two dogs were barking and jumping furiously in wild attempts to get higher up. But their blunt claws scratched in vain at the hard rock, and when suddenly one of the Lapps called them, they tumbled downward like gray balls with the snow flying around them. Their tongues hung from their red jaws, their nostrils were wide, and their eyes were sparkling. Coming down to the men, they first made a few circles around the bundle on the snow and then sat down with their noses pointed up, spouting their angry barks at the impertinence above them.

Seven reindeer, agile like mountain goats, had for some hours been seeking their way higher and higher up the mountain side, attracted by these little green clusters, which stuck out from crevasses and ledges. From ledge to ledge, they had worked their way upwards and were now one hundred and fifty meters above the mountain heath, with deep slopes on their side.

The Lapps knew that there was nothing to do but stand and wait for the meat. The reindeer would not be able to get down, and it was only to speed up the slaughter that the dogs had been allowed to make their attack. One had fallen. That was the gray bundle lying in the snow.

Unaware of the danger, the six doomed reindeer continued to nibble at the thin moss that was barely a centimeter high. The reindeer on top had licked its narrow ledge clean and was staring longingly at a small tuft on the rock wall above. It rose on its hind legs to reach it. It ate it all at once, and its big eyes looked greedily for more clusters of green. But now it was impossible for even a reindeer to climb any further. Not even a snowflake had stuck to this wall. The reindeer moved backwards a few inches, sort of felt its way with outstretched hooves, pressed its short tail against the mountain wall, pressed its feet close together and turned its head – the next second the reindeer flipped around in the air, hit a ledge thirty meters below and kept bouncing down…

Although the Lapps had long ago since realized the inevitable, they were upset as one reindeer after another came tumbling down the mountain. The last three came at once, almost colliding in the air and ending up with legs outstretched and broken backs in front of the men, like a quivering mass.

The butchering knives were brought out, but it didn't feel like it usually did when the reindeer had to give up their lives. Something hollow and menacing lay lurking over the bloody scene – an oppressive, icy cold atmosphere, occasionally shattered by the dogs' yelping for morsels. Niel cut into the reindeer carcasses with an expression on his face as if he wished he had something else under his knife. He was so filled with hatred for the settlers that he was fully convinced that they were responsible of the reindeer falling.

It was quick work to take care of the dead reindeer, and the incident was like a signal that it was now time to leave the mountain. The dogs ran around panting and herding the reindeer together, and like a gray stream the large herd ran down into the kettle valley. At dusk, there was not a single reindeer west of the pass.

*

The night grew grey and dark. There was no wind, only a couple of degrees below freezing.

Through the spruce forest in the opening between Mount Ropen and Mount Suttan, Niel came sneaking like a wolf. His eyes glowed, and his chest heaved in deep, half-stifled gasps. In his hands he held his strong, spiky ski pole, and on his back hung a roll of dry birch bark.

Arriving at Marsliden, Niel made a circle around the new homestead, sucking in the air through his nostrils as if he was sniffing. But it was quiet, no smoke stung his nose. The lonely cabin lay like a dead, gray lump below the hillside. Niel had been down here before and knew there was no dog. He glided silently forward on his skis, stood for a few seconds at the corner of the cabin and listened, and then floated like a shadow to the haystack. There was a fence around it, and Niel drew his knife, cut off the thin birch branch ties and carefully lifted the fence posts away.

Armload after armload, Niel carried bundles of hay from the haystack, putting them behind the cabin. Sweat dripped from his brow, and his eyes gleamed as if with ecstasy. He put some hay bundles outside the door and pushed up a bundle just below the eaves, while a dull squeak came from his clenched teeth. No one would be able to get out. Away they would go – away, away…!

Niel pulled hay from the stack to get more fuel when a shadow suddenly appeared just next to him. Niel grabbed his ski pole and crouched down, a hoarse growl twisting up from his throat.

– Hey, Niel!

The whisper was that of a woman, and the Lapp youth straightened up when he saw who it was. He stepped forward and grasped the girl tightly by the arm pulling her behind the stack.

– Get lost, he hissed and pushed her away, so that she almost fell.

– What are you… what are you going to do, Niel?

The girl's face was barely discernible in the darkness, but the ragged gasp revealed her excitement.

– Go, Vanni go, I say!

– You're going to burn them!

Niel drew a snorting breath, and at that moment he remembered that Vanni was the one who had listened most eagerly to Ante and him. He nodded, and the girl stifled a little scream.

– But the children? she gasped.

– The children?

– The six children!

Now Niel was standing so close to Vanni that he could see that her face was twisted in horror. Her whole body trembled, and suddenly she grabbed Niel's arm.

– Don't burn them! she moaned. The six children!

Niel spat out a grunt and tore himself free. Would the whole thing be ruined because…?

– Go! he hissed between clenched teeth, and when the girl didn't move, he pushed her away, meter after meter.

– I'll scream and wake them up!

Niel threw herself upon her. They tumbled around in the snow, and the man pushed snow into the girl's face, as he pressed his hand over her mouth.

Vanni lay still. She had no way to defend herself against the strong Niel. She groaned for air and suddenly became aware of what Niel intended to do to her – tie her up – put something in her mouth… The grip over her mouth relaxed a bit, and Vanni got out a few words and said she would not scream.

Niel paused with the rope and suddenly it was as if a thought that he was behaving rudely towards Vanni cut through his overheated brain – Vanni, whom he was to marry next spring! Maybe she understood now… understood, that something must be done tonight, so that the place would be free from bad luck.

Niel released the girl, and they stood swaying opposite each other. Not a word was uttered during those long seconds, but then Niel said – that now she should leave!

Vanni didn't answer. She had lost her skis in the commotion, and she searched for them, fitting the peaked Lapp shoes into the bindings. For a few seconds she stood motionless on her skis, caught her breath and then she left.

Niel was taking the first step back towards the haystack, when a powerful blow from Vanni's ski pole knocked him over. He rolled once but quickly got to his feet and saw Vanni hurrying towards the cabin. Catching up with her was impossible, and exasperated, Niel raised his ski pole over his head intending to prevent her from warning the settler with a whistling throw. But then Niel lowered his terrible weapon and crept like a gray shadow to get behind the cabin unseen.

Vanni rushed towards the door of the cabin as if chased by evil spirits. With a single motion, she brushed away the hay, bumped into and banged on the door. Not a sound came from her lips, only a hollow, heavy gasp.

Suddenly the door was jerked open from within, and the glow of a fatwood torch blazed against the girl's face. She stood motionless with her hands pressed to her chest – as if mesmerized by the towering man in the doorway. Pålsson, too, stood still for a few breathless, silent seconds, when it became clear to him that this was the same girl who had recoiled from him back in Fatmomakke. Only now did he seem to notice the hay strewn all over.

– What is the meaning of this? he exclaimed grimly taking a few steps towards the girl.

The torch was still in his hand, but it was going out.

Vanni did not move, she was trembling, and her legs could hardly support her. She wanted to escape – disappear – to run away, but her limbs refused to obey, and the next second it was too late.

Pålsson threw away the smoking torch and grabbed the girl tightly by the shoulders, it felt like being grabbed by the paws of a bear, and in her mind, she imagined "grab her – carry her in – boil her in a pot …!"

– What is the meaning of this? Pålsson growled. Can't you speak? Come inside!

When no answer came, Pålsson lifted the Lapp girl as if she was a small child. At the same moment, Vanni heard a faint crackling sound.

– Look … behind you! she whimpered.

A light at the cabin gable caught Pålsson's eye, and he dropped the girl and rushed around the corner, where he came upon a lit fire. With a wild roar, Pålsson rushed forward and kicked a fiery bundle of birch bark, so that it flew like a fireball far away into the snow. He jumped and stomped, and after a few seconds what had been the beginnings of a giant, deadly fire was smothered. It was only the birch bark bundle, which fifteen or twenty meters away continued to burn, casting a blazing glow over the scene.

Pålsson breathed heavily when the fire in the hay was put out. Another ten seconds or so and all the hay next to the cabin wall would have been on fire. The thought of what that might have meant made the new settler's face stiffen.

The fire was out, but to be sure, Pålsson brushed all the hay away from the cabin, and only when that was done, did he remember the Lapp girl. He hurried around the corner, but there was nothing to be seen.

Vanni had disappeared.

Pålsson got no more sleep that night. He stayed inside for a while and comforted Britta, not saying a word that they had been in danger of fire. His wife was in such an advanced stage of her pregnancy that any intense emotions could be disastrous. The settler spent the rest of the night outdoors, carrying the hay back to the stack, repairing the fence and checked up in the woods. At a distance, he heard the occasional dog bark, but he could not detect a reindeer, much less the glimpse of a human being.

As Pålsson walked and looked around, he wrestled with the question of what to do. It would cost the Lapps dearly if this matter was reported. He had seen a shadow fleeing away in the darkness when he had rushed forward to kick away the crackling birch bark firebomb. But which one of the Lapps had done it? If he knew, there would be no need to report it! There was one who did know – the Lapp girl, whom he had held in his arms for a few seconds, and he would recognize her from among a hundred. Maybe she was involved in the attempted arson. No, not her – not this mild-mannered girl, who looked as if she could do no one any harm. But who would she have accompanied – one, two or more Lapps – he had to find out!

Pålsson decided not to report the horrible murder attempt for the time being. Even if the right person was punished, the innocent might suffer. Pålsson didn't realize this yet, but when he thought of the innocent, it was the Lapp girl who he had in mind. One thing was certain: if Vanni had fled as Pålsson yanked open the door, the settler would have regarded all the Lapps as criminals, for whom no punishment would have been severe enough.

No new attack seemed to be directed toward the homestead that night, and in the morning Pålsson went into the cabin and found the children asleep safely. Britta was awake, but not many words were spoken.

*

They now had a floor in their cabin. Planed logs lay pressed together, and the settler had put a lot of work into making them so smooth that no bare children's feet would be scratched by any splinters. At one side stood a primitive bed, made of round logs, and built in two levels. It was not movable. The inner two poles reached up to the ceiling and were attached to a beam. The table by the small window was made of peeled logs, and the benches next to it consisted of three, carved poles, held together by a crossbar. A pair of new skis leaned against the other wall. They were tied in tension to give them their proper bend. In the ceiling lay wood to dry on poles for several more skis. Up there between the beams was also wood for storage vessels, knotty burls, intended for bowls and wooden ladles, and stripped birch branches – there was plenty of work here for his woodworking knife during long winter evenings.

The next few days were full of excitement for the people of Marsliden. The reindeer were now roaming the forest, and Lars and Britta took turns watching over the precious haystack at night. But no reindeer came near the cabin. It was as if the Lapps had drawn a sharp line, which the reindeer were not allowed to cross. If a reindeer tried to make its way down to the homestead, its hind legs were immediately in danger from the sharp fangs of the guard dogs.

Pålsson had thought that the reindeer would make on pass through Marsliden and continue eastward, but here in the strip of forest on the southern edge of the mountain there had not been much snowfall. The reindeer had good access to grazing and were in no hurry. The controlling of the herd was exemplary. Only on a couple of occasions could a few reindeer be seen from the settlement's yard.

Several times Pålsson attempted to speak with his neighbors in the mountains, but all his efforts fell short because of the Lapps' incredible ability to keep out of sight. He did manage to get close to two of the mountain men, but he didn't have any success to speak of. They answered him in Lappish and were so preoccupied with urgent matters that they could not pause for even a minute. Pålsson began to give up hope. Did they not understand Swedish – or did they not want to?

On the fifth day that the reindeer were on Marsliden's land, suddenly a couple of shots rang out from down by the muorke. Pålsson wondered if a wolf had come. He took his rifle and skis and headed west.

Down on the muorke, Pålsson saw several tracks from reindeer. He immediately discovered a bloody scene, which made his eyes narrow. Bloody parts of reindeer lay strewn on the snow, and it was immediately apparent that it hadn't been a wolf. It had been slaughtered with a knife, the best pieces cut away and the rest had been left to the wild animals.

Pålsson followed the ski track that led from the place, and after ten minutes he had found three new bloody areas.

Lars was upset. If he hadn't understood before why the Lapps objected to anyone settling by Lake Marssjön, he understood why now. This was a bloody theft – no wonder the Lapps were angry! Pålsson remained at the last kill, while a dull anger boiled up inside him. It was so rude to behave like this! If you wanted reindeer meat, it probably wouldn't be that expensive to buy an animal from the Lapps.

Pålsson was ready to follow the ski tracks to see in which direction they were heading, when someone appeared between the spruce trees, and suddenly Niel came rushing forward. He stopped twenty meters away, and his eyes flashed.

– You take reindeer!

– No!

– You take reindeer! repeated the young Lapp, panting.

– No!

Niel took such a threatening position that Pålsson almost feared that he would come charging forward with the ski pole like a lance in front of him.

– You take reindeer!

– No, I said! Lars exclaimed furiously. You can come with me home and look for meat, but you'll find them easier, if you follow these tracks!

Pålsson pointed south, but Niel did not take his eyes off him. Tracks meant nothing at that moment. He had a bloody area and a man in front of him – that was enough!

The settler soon realized the futility of trying to convince the angry Lapp that the culprit was somewhere else. Niels' attitude became more and more threatening, while he stubbornly clung to his accusation. Pålsson looked grimly at him, and suddenly he said:

– Maybe you were involved in trying to burn down my place the other night!

Niel did not answer. His chest worked heavily, and his hand gripped the ski pole tighter.

– You could go to jail for that, you know!

The word "jail" struck Niel like a whip, and a sound came from his throat. Jail! He had heard of it – a dark hole – walk around, around – never getting out.

– You were there!

Niel didn't hear him. He could see red flames before his eyes. Jail – he'd rather...!

With a swiftness that no one could have believed Pålsson capable of, he swerved aside, and in the same second flung out his right hand and caught Niels' terrible throwing weapon in mid-air.

The settler let out a roar after he had caught it. Between the trees he caught a glimpse of Niel, who had set off on his skis and fled. For a moment it looked as if Pålsson was going to follow, but he stopped after the first glide and stroked his forehead in frustration.

The settler inspected the weapon that could easily have become the death of him. It was more like a spear than a pole, and the sharpened point was as sharp as a needle. Pålsson lifted one knee as if to break the pole into pieces but then pushed the dangerous weapon into the ground and went straight home.

Niel had not gone far when he noticed that he was not being pursued and snuck back. Ten minutes after Pålsson had left the muorke,

Niel was back at the scene of his failed throw. He flinched when he saw his pole standing upright in the snow.

His body trembled when he pulled up the pole and found it completely unharmed. It was astonishing that the settler had caught the weapon in mid-air, but that was nothing compared to this – returning it … like a harmless stick! The expression on Niels' face looked like an illustration from a cruel nightmare.

The young Lapp crept away like a moving shadow. The fact that roaming reindeer had fallen victim to murderous knives was erased from his mind. Generations of magic-whipped wilderness blood threw forth its explanation. The settler was "anointed" for fire and steel! If the settler lived – a dark hole – walk around, around – never getting out…

To this son of the mountain, jail was more terrifying than a noose.

Nothing happened during the final two days the reindeer stayed in the Marsliden area. After the incident down on the muorke, Pålsson did not try to communicate with the Lapps, and it was with great joy that he saw the last gray dots disappearing to the east. Now he could work in peace again.

CHAPTER TWELVE

Lake Marssjön was frozen over, and Pålsson had long ago hung up his primitive fishing gear. He did not have a large supply of fish but hoped that the hunting would be more bountiful than in Fjällboberg.

It was mainly grouse and fox that the settler was interested in, and after the reindeer had left Marsliden, it didn't take many days before Pålsson had a number of grouse snares put out among the birch trees and willow thickets. It required more time to make and set out the fox traps. From medium-sized logs he sawed stakes about seven feet long. He made the lower ends pointed, so that the stakes could be driven into the ground and stand firm, and the upper ends he made flat. This is where the traps themselves would be cut out. He sawed a long, narrow fork with sharp edges. One point was made slightly longer than the other and sharpened. The bait was then placed on this point – now let the fox come!

Despite their simple construction, these traps were extremely effective. To reach the bait, the fox had to jump, and in nine cases out of ten its foot sought support in the fork of the trap. When the sly fox lowered his body, his foot was firmly trapped, and as the animal could not reach the ground with his hind feet, he had no chance of freeing himself and was left hanging, until the trap was checked.

The very first week the settler had four foxes in his cunning wooden traps. The grouse haul was good too, although Pålsson grumbled that some snares were emptied by four-legged hunters. He was even more exasperated when he found a half-eaten fox in one of the traps one morning. It was not difficult to see who had been there. The clumsy tracks clearly revealed the mountain's furry marauder.

Pålsson let the fox sit, and in a thicket fifteen meters away he prepared a blind; cut off some obscuring twigs and sealed off the sides of the thicket. Pålsson was almost certain that the wolverine would return. That scoundrel would certainly not let any food go to waste.

When evening came, the settler snuck into his hiding place, bringing a small bundle of hay with him to have something warm to sit on. There could be many hours to wait, and the starlit evening was chilly and clear.

The settler sat as still as a statue in his hideout, his gray wilderness eyes peering out at the moonlit clearing before him. Trees and bushes cast sharp shadows, not a movement could be sensed, not a creak. In the middle of the clearing stood the fox trap.

Suddenly a faint sound came from one of the nearest bushes, and in a flash a hare leapt out into the clearing. It stopped by a small spruce and began to eat its shoots, its long, black-pointed ears moving in every direction.

Pålsson did not move a finger to try to shoot this unexpected prize for the stew pot, although it was only a few meters from the muzzle of his gun. Instead, he made a rustling sound with his foot, and that was all it took for the hare to take off in long strides. The settler gave off a silent grunt. There! Now the place was free again. A hare could cause a lot of trouble if the wolverine came running.

Suddenly the hidden hunter perked up his ears, and his eyes peered sharply toward the streaks of moonlight beyond the clearing. The muzzle of his gun silently moved forward, and he pulled off his right mitten with his teeth.

Following its old track, the wolverine came along with clumsy leaps, its disproportionately powerful hind body seemed to bounce forward by itself. When it reached the trap, it turned its head in every direction to convince itself that it would be able to eat in peace. It wasn't exactly afraid of anyone in the wild. It was three times heavier and stronger than the fox and would have eaten all the foxes a long time ago, if they hadn't had such long legs to run with. Nor was it afraid of a fight with a lone wolf, nor did it have any undue respect for old man bear, who was content to eat ants, and who, by the way, was asleep this time of year.

After the wolverine had made sure that there were no uninvited spectators nearby, it climbed up the pole and placed one paw on the shortest point of the fork – one second, and the wolverine tumbled down into the snow again, as the echo of a shot rolled between the mountain sides. A few minutes later, Pålsson was on his way home with the furry thief on his back.

A couple days after he had taken care of the wolverine, Pålsson went over to Saxnäs and let the farmers there hear his opinion regarding the reindeer slaughtering out on the muorke. This deed had been troubling him for several weeks, but he had not had the time to go there – and it would have been just as well if he had not done so now either.

At first the farmers at Saxnäs listened and laughed it off. The reindeer! So, he had seen the tracks. You had to get something for the stew pot – how many reindeer had he gotten himself? Couldn't he just stand in his doorway and lure them in!

When Pålsson then grimly explained that he was no reindeer thief and that the bloody business must end, the farmers' jovial attitude changed. Oh, is that the way it was going to be? If he thought it was all right to come here and tell them what or what not to do, he would have another thing coming!

– I am not telling you what to do, but it is despicable to steal reindeer and slaughter them. It must be possible to ask the Lapps about buying reindeer.

– You try that! And starve to death if you want to – it makes no difference to us! You'll sing a different tune when the reindeer break your hayracks one of these autumns!

– The hayracks would probably be left alone if no reindeer were stolen! said Pålsson grimly. Both we and the Lapps would benefit if this could be arranged.

The exchange of words continued until eventually things took such a turn that the Saxnäs farmers would have thrown themselves at the settler from Marsliden, if they had thought themselves able to beat the giant.

Pålsson's face was dark when he left Saxnäs. He had done himself more harm than good on this journey. But he did not regret that he had spoken out. He felt somehow cleaner inside.

Pålsson had better luck, when a few days later he went to Klimpfjäll Mountain to ask Jon if they could go to Norway together before Christmas. The two men agreed to make a trading trip in the first half of December, Pålsson would just come over to Klimpfjäll Mountain, when he had enough furs.

*

As the early winter approached Christmas, Pålsson grew more and more satisfied with the hunting. He now had fourteen fox skins stretched out to dry inside the cabin, and despite the good ventilation through the chimney, the air in the room was permeated with a sharp, pungent odor. It was everywhere and even made the milk taste like fox as soon as it came inside the door. However, they soon became accustomed to this nuisance, and they didn't mind it since they knew that the skins would give them good things in return. Since the fox hunt has been so successful, Pålsson decided not to bring any grouse this time. It didn't pay more for a sack of grouse than for a skin, and it would be difficult to transport them such a long way. The hundred or so grouses he had caught lay frozen out in the storage shed and could stay that way until spring without becoming spoiled.

The day before leaving for Norway, the settler picked up all the snares he had set in the grouse forest. He might be gone for a whole week and thought it unnecessary for any trapped animal to sit in snares for so long. If Britta hadn't been in the condition she was, she could have checked the snares, but now it was far too hard for her to work her way up to the tree line. Even though he knew that some settlers would have a refreshing laugh if they found out, he made the fox traps unusable. Turning the traps into harmless stumps was easy – just remove the bait from the longest point of the fork – and that evening the unusual thing happened that Pålsson came home from the woods with fish he had used to bait the traps. Only the three closest traps were still set with bait. They were no further away than the boys could keep an eye on them and get Britta to help if some fox made the worst mistake of his life. Paul had admittedly claimed that he and Aron could watch over all the traps, but Pålsson was not inclined to let the boys go too far from the cabin. Because of the wolves it was not safe.

Early in the morning, long before the gray dawn of the short winter day, Pålsson set off with the bundle of skins on his back. It had snowed since he had last come by here, and the skiing was quite hard. The settler arrived at Klimpfjäll Mountain shortly past noon. Jon was not home, but Pålsson was welcomed by Inga, who said that her father had only gone out to check his snares.

– Look how many skins you have! she exclaimed, impressed, and stroked her hand gently over the wolverine's fuzzy fur.

– Oh, there aren't that many.

– Aren't there any grouse over there?

– Yes, but I couldn't bring them with me this time.

Pålsson had brought food with him, but Jon's wife said he didn't need to sit there and eat a cold lunch. She invited him to sit at the table and set out what the house had to offer. Jon's wife seemed to have great respect for the man from Marsliden, and there was a hidden fear in her eyes. That he could live over there in that magic hole! He had fine skins, but misfortune would certainly come upon him one day!

Inga asked about Hans, and Pålsson replied that he had not heard anything from him since he had left Marsliden.

– Will he come up and help you build the barn next summer?

– There was no talk of that.

– Maybe he got married?

Inga's voice sounded strained, and Pålsson gave her a long look.

– Don't think so, he said.

While Pålsson was talking to Inga, he was thinking that Hans was a bit of a fool. It wouldn't be easy to find a more capable girl than this one. Maybe he should ask Hans to come up for a while next summer.

Jon came home shortly after dark with a bundle of grouse. Pålsson's skin bundle astonished him, although he had probably known that the hunting grounds over there around the Marsfjället Mountain were better than here. Fourteen foxes and a wolverine! He had only gotten six. Jon knew about furs, and one glance was enough to see that Pålsson was not too far behind him. In both Åsele and Kroken Jon had sometimes seen furs that were shrunken and matted, but these had been stretched well, and the fur was combed out, so that the hairs shone.

– You ought to get nine riksdaler coins each for these! he said.

Long before daybreak Jon and Pålsson were on their way to Kroken. The Saxnäs farmers had taken a load a couple of days earlier, and Jon's horse was willingly walking along the well-trodden track with a sled behind it. In the sled was a large bundle of hay, and two bags of grouse were hidden under Pålsson's bundle of skins. Jon's six fox skins didn't take up much space. They were pressed against four snowshoes that the horse would use if there was deep snow. A pair of reindeer skins and a food box were in their proper place in the sled, and along one edge the butt of Jon's gun was just visible. Pålsson was unarmed. He expected such a large load on the return journey that the gun would be too much trouble to bring. And this was not a hunting trip but a trading trip.

The men walked behind the sled as they climbed up the steep slopes towards the stony, treeless, snow covered Dårronskalet pass. It was still completely dark in the narrow pass, but Pålsson didn't need to see much of his surroundings to know that it wouldn't be worth the risk to try to come through here during a roaring blizzard. Jon walked silently ahead of him on the track. These days he did not like to go through the Dårronskal pass alone.

On the other side of the pass, it was downhill, and here the men could ride now and then. Jon said that there was a rest cabin between the Ransarån River and Tjåkkolafjället Mountain, but the conditions today were so good that they could probably get to Kroken without spending the night on the road.

The daylight came eventually – a grayish pale light, which had difficulty outlining the contours of the mountains. But the lines became more and more sharp. The sky was clear, and in the south a flaming redness appeared. The sun suddenly broke out and cast glittering rays on the peaks of Lasterfjället Mountain. But the rays lasted only a few minutes. The globe of light sank again behind the horizon, leaving behind it the same blood-red hue of color that had just announced it. The colors faded, and after a while the wilderness was enveloped in a strange gray-white glow, which seemed to come more from the snow than from any light source in the sky. But even that light faded, and it was not long into the afternoon when the long winter night of the northern lands came once more with a curtain of darkness.

Through mountain valleys and storm-whipped birch forests, over rivers and streams, where rushing water lurked under false ice and snow bridges, the route entered Norwegian territory. It had been dark for several hours, but it was still a good distance to Kroken, for there were close to sixty long wilderness kilometers between Klimpfjäll and the Norwegian village.

Jon's horse strained and pulled uphill, making its breath rise like a mist over its head. There had been a couple of breaks, but now the horse seemed to understand that there would be no more rest until it reached the stable in Kroken.

Jon and Pålsson walked close to the sled. The minutes and hours went by without a word being said. Only the light scraping of the sled against the snow broke the silence of the wilderness – the sound of the sled and the faint thumping of the horse's hooves, occasionally interrupted by the gloomy howls from some lone arctic fox.

*

A day and a half later, Jon and Pålsson came back across the border again. Pålsson was more than satisfied with their business dealings in Kroken and was determined to continue to make his sales and purchases with the Norwegians. He now carried more goods than he had ever traded for before. There were two big bundles in Jon's sled, and on his back, he carried a heavy pack, because it weighed the sled down when they went downhill. Pålsson was almost taken by surprise by how accommodating Jon had been. He had limited his own purchases in order to be able to transport more for the settler. Pålsson offered to compensate him, but Jon immediately waved it away.

– Don't mention it! he said. I have a horse and can go back whenever it suits me.

But the reason for the Klimpfjäll farmer's helpfulness went deeper than that. It was in his interest that the settler would be able to bring goods home more easily from Norway than from Åsele, making him less tempted to make trips to the east. However, Jon himself intended to go down to the large skin market in Åsele after the New Year and try to reach an agreement with Abraham. And if he was not willing – well, all the more reason to keep the settlers of Marsliden away from the courthouse. Who knows – Pålsson might happen to show his papers to someone who could read and then have the claim to the new settlement legally transferred to him – this must be prevented!

The weather was still ideal, but the travelers decided to rest for a few hours in the cabin next to Tjåkkolafjället Mountain. The cabin was of the most primitive kind, without windows and with a door that could hardly be closed, but there was a fireplace, and on a wide bench were two sheepskins. The men made coffee, and here in front of the fire Pålsson talked about the reindeer thefts. Jon was eager to talk about it. He had heard from the Saxnäs farmers that Pålsson had been over to their place and was fully aware of the settler's position – even though it seemed absurd to him.

– The police chief should be sent after them! Pålsson said. Even better, the pastor could sort it out.

Jon's jaw dropped. The very idea of the pastor interfering in their external affairs was ludicrous. The pastor! As if he didn't have enough to do with baptizing kids, preaching, performing weddings and funerals when he came twice a year to Fatmomakke!

– The pastor could talk to the Lapps and us and say that it is not Christian to do anything bad to each other.

Jon had recovered from his surprise and nodded seriously. Yes, the pastor could say that.

Not much more was said, and after a while the men covered up with the furs. Despite the difficult day's walk, Jon found it hard to fall asleep. He was starting to suspect that things were not right in Pålsson's head. Bringing up the pastor because some reindeer had gotten lost and disappeared!

At dusk the next day, the men arrived at Klimpfjäll. Pålsson still had just over 30 km to go before he reached home and thought it safest to stay in the village for the night.

While Jon had been in Norway, one of his cows had calved, and Pålsson followed him to the barn to look at the new arrival. It was a bull calf, and the settler made a suggestion, which Jon found un-expectedly sensible. To exchange calves, so that there would be no inbreeding – he agreed!

– So, you've got a calf, too, this late in the year!

Pålsson nodded. He didn't mention the fact that his calf was a few weeks older.

It was overcast and almost mild weather the next morning, and Pålsson had reason to be even more pleased with his first trip to Norway. Jon thought that since the weather was so suitable, they might as well exchange calves right away. That suggestion meant more to Pålsson than the switching of the calves. This meant he could bring his whole load with him at once.

It was also with great gratitude that the settler said goodbye to Jon, when he was ready to leave Marsliden with Pålsson's calf in the sled. Jon paused with the reins in hand.

– Are you going down to the market in Åsele? he wondered.

– Don't know if there's a point. I was well paid in Norway, you know.

– I don't care about going there, either. Poor prices down there this year and a long way away. They have better goods in Kroken too.

As Jon drove home, he was as pleased as Pålsson with the trip they had made together. What did it matter if he had wasted time transporting goods to Marsliden? The settler wasn't planning to go to Åsele – that was worth much more!

CHAPTER THIRTEEN

Britta now had more flour than she had ever dared to dream of, and it was pure, fine flour, where not a single dark grain of bark could be detected. She felt almost anxious with this wealth in front of her. How could she bake with such fine flour! But there was no choice, for they had not had time to get any bark during the summer. Anyway, there were just no green pines near Marsliden, and it was this bark they needed for flour. The trees were peeled in the springtime when the sap started to run. The green on the bark was cleaned off, and the now white bark sections were hung up to dry, and then they were ground into fine powder in special bark mills.

But now Britta had to get by without bark, and it was almost as if she had forgotten what to do with pure flour. Even the children looked puzzled, and their mother had trouble keeping their fingers away when she finally got around to making dough.

Pålsson did not have the same worry. If things continued as well as it had started in Marsliden, they would no longer have to eat bark bread. He was now busy making a baking oven for Britta. Before the snow came, he had found four even-sized stones, suitable for a base. He placed the stones on the hearth and on top of them a smooth and even stone slab. The oven was ready! It was only a matter of having a gentle fire burning under the slab, and when it got hot, Britta could bake her thin loaves easily.

These were busy days leading up to Christmas. Pålsson had more than just his traps and snares to see to. In the forest there were many treetops left over after the logs were cut, and the settler brought these home and chopped them into firewood. When time permitted, he also cut down a tree or two and hauled the logs to the place where he intended to build a barn next summer. The evenings were strictly occupied with wood carving, and after the children had gone to bed, Lars and Britta sometimes sat in front of the fire and talked. There was no getting away from the fact that they had been lucky to acquire Marsliden.

Christmas was celebrated. In a flash it was a new year, and Britta's difficult moment approached with frightening speed for Pålsson. How would things work out? When the other children had come into the world, one of the neighboring women in Fjällboberg had been at hand, but now he was all alone. He was hesitant to ask for help from Saxnäs or Grytsjö. He felt that they wouldn't have any time to spare for them at Marsliden. He thought of Inga sometimes. Maybe he should ask her to come and be here, until the difficult part was over? But Inga was young – did she know how to deliver a child and how the mother should be cared for? In any case, he asked Britta if it wouldn't be best that he went over to Klimpfjäll and picked up Jon's daughter. Britta did not agree to this. Who knew how long it would take? Inga could have to stay here for weeks before anything happened!

That was the terrible thing for Pålsson – not knowing the day and the hour when it would happen! At night, maybe – and to rush to the neighboring village and grab a woman for help, while Britta… Pålsson sweated at the thought. And what if it happened during the day… when he wasn't home! It happened so fast sometimes. Maybe she felt nothing in the morning – but then – when he was up in the grouse forest – a contraction – and Britta was alone with the children! No one, who could be help her with any of it… Maybe the children started to cry – thought their mother was acting strange. Would try to handle things herself… Britta would not be able to… collapse… not know what to do… and then… then… there would be no Britta!

Pålsson's concerns were far too clear for Britta not to notice.

– It will be all right! she said reassuringly. I usually have an easy time of it.

And that was true for the first five children, but when Jonas was born, there had been such difficult moments, that the women in

Fjällboberg had been almost helpless. Pålsson knew nothing about that struggle.

The days passed, while the expected event lay like a terrible shadow over Marsliden. Pålsson clung to Britta's: "It will be all right!" but the comfort soon left. When he went out to check on his snares, it would sometimes occur to him that it was happening right now! Like a frenzied animal he would rush home, dripping with sweat, to find that Britta was on her feet and that nothing had happened!

A storm came, which made it impossible to go outside for three days, and Pålsson both hoped and feared that the snowstorm would force the event to start. But it turned out to be several days of only anxious waiting. Every morning, before Pålsson left for his hunting grounds, he looked questioningly at his wife. Britta shook her head. No, nothing!

*

One morning in early February, Britta said:

– Best you stay home today, Lars!

Pålsson turned pale and began to tremble all over. In those first, stinging seconds, he felt the same urge that millions of men before and after him felt in the face of events like this – to run, to flee anywhere – to attack a taunted bear with his bare hands rather than to be a part of what was happening.

Without a word, Pålsson threw on his coat and grabbed his hat.

– Where are you going?

– To Saxnäs to get help!

His voice was so mumbled that the words could hardly be made out.

– Never mind that, you!

– Never… never mind… yes!

– No, it will be all right anyway, and it may be a while before someone comes from Saxnäs.

119

Pålsson went outside anyway because the cabin seemed far too small to breathe in. The day began to dawn. It was clear and at least twenty-five degrees below freezing, but the cold just melted against the settler's hot face. There was a red glow in the southeast… like bloody streaks on the horizon – something gloomy and ominous, which forced a groan out of Pålsson.

He went over to his felled logs, moved a couple of them and stroked his forehead. How foolish to get worked up like this! He knew as well as any woman from Saxnäs what was to be done. It would probably be all right – it had to be! After a while he had calmed down enough that he could go back into the cabin. He took off his coat, sat down by the window and began carving a bowl.

Britta walked around as usual, tidying up the cabin, but sometimes she stopped and grabbed hold of something. Pålsson hardly dared to look at her. He carved the birch burl with such zeal and determination that the whole piece of wood was in danger of being turned into shavings.

The children seemed to understand that all was not as it should be this morning. They kept unusually still, and Paul's thin lips were sometimes pursed into a narrow line. If any of the littlest ones showed any signs of playfulness, he gave them a sharp look – don't do that! The whole cabin seemed wrapped in a tense atmosphere, and at last Pålsson couldn't stand it anymore.

– I'll go out and chop some wood," he said. You can call me if you need anything.

He disappeared hurriedly through the door, and Britta gave his back a strange look. He was usually so calm and confident, not afraid of anything – but now…!

The sun was up, and over the southern edges of Marsfjället Mountain there was a sparkling, white light that cut and burned the eyes. Pålsson stood still and blinked. Such bright sunshine in early February! Or was it his eyes that couldn't handle it? He took the few steps to the pile of treetops and grabbed the axe. He chopped like mad for a couple of minutes but then stopped and wiped the sweat from his brow. His hands trembled, and an aching pain pressed in his stomach, almost making him feel dizzy. How easy it would be to cut his leg on a day like this!

Pålsson continued more carefully with the wood-chopping and for long moments stood still, sometime staring at the fuzzy, wooden walls of the cabin, and sometimes out over the vast wilderness that stretched beyond Lake Marssjön. Once he looked up at the mountain… at the cold snowy heights, where merciless death seemed to have taken up residence.

What if Britta were to die!

The thought tore at him, and nearly drove the strong man to despair. Then he would be only half a man – and what would become of the children? It was Paul, who would take the mother's place until Stina had grown up. She was five years old now. It would be another four or five years before she could take care of herself, the cabin, the animals …

Pålsson was so preoccupied with his thoughts that he jumped when he suddenly saw Paul beside him. The boy's face was unnaturally calm and firm. It was only his gaze that seemed to shy away from something.

– Father should come inside! he said.

Pålsson drew a deep breath and dropped the axe without knowing it.

– Did… did Mother tell you to get me?

The man's voice was heavy and breathless, and the boy's voice trembled when he replied:

– Yes, mother is down on her knees!

Pålsson stumbled into the cabin with the uncomfortable feeling of walking around in empty air without legs. The sunrays gleamed against a patch of cloud above Mount Såttan's soft lines – a white, woolly cloud, which appeared to Pålsson as a smoky haze with blood-red splashes.

When the settler entered the cabin, he found his wife kneeling on a sack of moss. She was in the darkest corner of the room, her face turned to the wall. On the hearth stood a pot of steaming hot water. Lars knew that the moment had come. It was on their knees that the women fought. Only when everything was ready, was it time for her to go to the bed.

In those moments, when it was make or break time, a great calm came over Pålsson.

– Take the children with you, Paul, and go to the cows! he said firmly.

Paul instantly obeyed and herded his siblings in front of him like a flock of sheep. He closed the door, and for a few seconds the group of children stood huddled in the darkness of the entryway. Jonas whined and wanted to go to back to his mother but calmed down when Aron opened the door to the cows.

It was dim in this part, which was used as a barn. The small window on the gable was greyish white, covered with rosy ice flowers.

There was no wooden floor, and the youngest children began to climb on the floor beams in the narrow passage behind the cows. A couple of hay bundles were just right for jumping in, and Jonas was soon completely preoccupied with the thrilling feat of jumping; jumping so that the calf from Klimpfjäll bounced inside its pen.

– Calm down, Jonas!

Paul's voice was stern and firm, and the three-year-old was silent at once. He crawled over to the calf and quietly tried to get it to lick his fingers.

A few minutes passed, and suddenly a shrill cry was heard. The little ones looked at Paul with frightened looks.

– What was that?

Paul did not answer, and now Stina sprang up towards the door. Paul grabbed her.

– You may not go in!

– Yes, go to Mother!

– No, Father will be angry!

That helped. The girl crawled back into the hay, but her lower lip trembled, and her eyes glistened with a wet gleam. She moved closer to Sven and leaned her head on his shoulder as if to listen. But now there was no sound from the room next door, and it was as if all the living things in the cabin held their breath for a few moments.

Outside the sun was still shining, but soon the gleaming fireball would roll down behind Borgafjällen Mountain's easternmost point. The land around Lake Kultsjön was already in the shadows, and the dark line crept silently up towards the cabin below Marsfjället Mountain's slopes – this cabin, where big events were happening, and where six children sat in the semi-darkness of the barn in trepidation of the unknown.

A last glistening ray of sunlight brushed against the low chimney when the door suddenly opened and Pålsson appeared. He was bareheaded and took a few stumbling steps out into the yard, his breath rising like smoke from his mouth. With a grunt, he grabbed a shovel and began shoveling snow, only to throw the shovel down a few seconds later and make a few sharp turns. He paced back and forth as if he didn't know how to behave. Suddenly he stood still, and at last there was something sensible in his eyes. The children! He had to tell them. They were probably freezing to death with the cows!

After a few minutes, the settler came out again, and now he had a hat on his head. He walked with giant strides to his pile of logs. He poked and prodded at the logs, but suddenly it was as if he had realized it was pointless to keep moving the logs around. He stood looking at the cabin, and a brightness came over his rough face. It had gone well for Britta! From the cabin he looked up at the sky. There would be moonlight tonight. And he would go out to check the traps, after he had milked the cows…

Inside the cabin, the children stood amazed by the bed, looking at a small bundle lying at their mother's breast.

CHAPTER FOURTEEN

After a couple of days of rest, Britta was back on her feet, and Pålsson eagerly took care of his outdoor chores. He continued to be very successful with his hunting and made two trips to Norway during early spring.

March and April did not offer any major events, but the second week of May brought a surprise. Pålsson came back home late that night, and when he put his birch bark pack down on the floor, a strange sound came from the thin birch bark. Pålsson opened the lid and lifted out a small gray bundle.

– A dog! Aron exclaimed delighted, bending down to pet it.

His father pushed him away.

– Don't touch it! he said grimly. It's a wolf cub!

Aron pulled back, and the other children also moved away. Jonas and Stina took cover behind their mother. A wolf – yikes! They became somewhat more confident when they discovered that the wolf cub could barely stand on its legs. Its eyes were not open yet, which meant that it was no more than ten days old.

– What are you doing bringing that thing home? Britta asked.

She was almost as stunned as the children.

– We don't have a dog.

– That rascal won't turn into a dog.

– We'll see, Lars replied. Do you have some warm milk to give him?

Britta warmed some milk and poured it into a wooden bowl, but it did not occur to her to approach the wolf cub. If Lars wanted the beast to live, he would have to feed it himself.

Pålsson put out the bowl, but the wolf cub knew of no other way to eat than to seek out the warm body of its mother. His nose bumped against the edge of the bowl. His awkward head seemed way too heavy for the cub to hold up. Pålsson took it by the scruff of the neck and dipped its nose in the milk. The wolf cub spread his legs and snorted, but he didn't get any milk.

After the unsuccessful attempt to teach the wolf cub to drink, Pålsson lifted it on his lap, dipped a finger in the milk and then stuck it in the mouth of the little helpless beast. The wolf cub sucked bravely, and Pålsson asked for a spoon. The three oldest boys almost ran each other over to get him what he wanted.

Pålsson opened the mouth on the little rascal and began to pour milk into him. Most of the first spoonfuls spilled out again, but then the wolf cub began to sip and suck. The children barely knew what to do with themselves and stood as close as they could. Watching their father feed a wolf cub was for them a most interesting and exciting event.

When the bowl was empty, Pålsson laid his charge down on a sheepskin. A sheepskin which constantly reminded the settler of the attack with the "magic balls" last summer. The wolf curled up like a ball, and Lars slid the warm skin around its back.

– What's his name? asked Stina, who couldn't imagine an animal indoors without a name.

– Sappo.

After the wolf cub had been cared for, the settler sat down at the table, and only now could Britta see that he was both tired and hungry. He had traveled far and wide that day, and it was on the far side of Mount Såttan that he had found the wolf's den under an uprooted tree. It had been rather difficult to get the four pups out of the hole, and it was only the little chap on the floor that had escaped with his life. The settler certainly would not have saved this one either if it had not seemed so unusually strong in comparison to his siblings. Pålsson was not very convinced that it would be possible to tame the beast into a dog. But it was worth a try.

The wolf den was not Pålsson's only find today. Over by Garsbäcken Creek he had seen clear tracks of huge bear feet, and the settler suspected that it was the same beast that had been prowling around Marsliden last summer. It hadn't bothered their homestead since the attack in Grytsjö, but what would happen when the cows were let out to graze?

*

The reindeer did not cause Pålsson any trouble when they came up from the forest this spring. They climbed up the mountain in a hurry, and the people of Marsliden hardly saw a glimpse of any Lapps. Pålsson looked grimly up at the clearing between the mountain hills. What kind of "magic" mischief would come from up there this summer? He could not hope that the Lapps would completely leave the homestead alone.

Over the remaining crusty snow, Pålsson hauled home the rest of the timber needed for the summer's construction and it became a considerable pile laying there waiting to be built.

Suddenly, the snow was gone on the southern slope of Marsfjället Mountain. Lake Marssjön broke out of its icy shackles to the accompanying roar of the strong rapids of Ropenbäcken Creek. The birch trees were leafed out, and then came the long-awaited day when the cows could finally be let out to graze in the meadow.

It was a big job for Britta to clean the part of the cabin that had been used as a barn. The window was taken out. The top layers of soaked dirt were removed with the manure out through the window opening, and roof and walls were scrubbed with a stiff birch broom and hot water. When this was done, she filled the window opening with hay, carried in a bundle of juniper branches, and laid it in the middle of the floor and lit it. Then she closed the door and fetched a bucket of water. All day long the room remained closed and filled up with billowing juniper smoke. When Britta opened the door late in the evening, there was not a trace of the smell of cattle inside. She removed the hay from the window opening, and after a few minutes the cross wind had cleared the air of smoke. Now it was ready for Lars to build the floor.

126

Pålsson, however, was busy with a building project that was more important to him at the time than putting in a floor. The wolf cub was beginning to show his wild instincts and could no longer be kept indoors. It was not a good idea to let him roam freely yet. Aron had been bitten by his sharp, beastly teeth, and Stina persistently refused to leave her bed under the eaves, when the "woff" was down on the floor, even if her father held it by the scruff of the neck. The easiest thing would have been for Sappo to join his siblings in that place of blissful sleep, but Pålsson had not yet lost hope. Surely it should be possible to teach this rascal some good manners.

Pålsson drove down stakes and fenced off a small place about twenty meters from the cabin. He dug a hole in the slope and put in some moss. After he had put a thin roof of poles over it, Sappo's home was completed.

The settler, however, had not brought the wolf cub home to keep it in captivity, and it was not many days before Pålsson just happened to forget to close the little hatch that was placed on the front of the enclosure. He then casually dropped a wiggling trout on the grass and continued unconcernedly to the field, where he was expanding the clearing by a few fathoms. (1 fathom = ~0.5 meter) The children sat with their noses pressed against the cabin window. The wolf cub was left to his own fate.

It did not take many seconds before Sappo discovered the bright gap in the fence, and suddenly he took a leap into the open to explore the world beyond the fence. But it was a world full of dangers even for a wolf cub, and Sappo shrank back in a startled bounce when the trout suddenly wiggled in front of his nose. It wouldn't have taken much for Sappo to rush back to his safe den. A strange, rasping sound came from his throat, and his bristles stood up like a brush on his back. He made a couple of leaps on stiff front legs, but when the trout seemed unwilling to engage in battle, he took a leap forward, put his paws over the wiggly nuisance and resolutely bit the fish's head off.

When Sappo had eaten his catch, he ran around, sniffing, as if expecting to meet more of those pleasant fellows.

It was actually exciting few minutes for Pålsson, when the wolf cub had disappeared among the tufts of grass. He had agreed with Britta that if the wolf cub did not return to its den on its own, it would get to run free. Now he almost regretted saying that. Maybe he shouldn't have let the rascal out so soon.

Pålsson's concern was unnecessary. Frightened by something, Sappo suddenly came running – a gray ball, which rolled up against the enclosure and disappeared into the den. A grim smile crossed the settler's face. The first round was won.

The process of opening the hatch was repeated day after day, but one day there wasn't any fish in the grass. The wolf sniffed and smelled, but couldn't detect anything, and after that disappointment he didn't react much to Paul approaching with one hand behind his back. When the boy was four steps away, he threw a fish, and it landed in the grass between them. In a flash, Sappo rushed forward, put one paw over the fish and growled angrily. Paul stayed, despite all the clear warnings to leave, and at last the wolf cub took his prey and retreated backwards. His eyes flashed, and it would not have been a good idea for Paul to try to take back the fish.

This exercise continued for a week or so, and finally it seemed as if the wolf cub had learned that if he got something to eat from a human, he did not have to show his teeth to keep it.

The hatch to the enclosure was now open all day, and Sappo made interesting excursions in the immediate vicinity and did not mind any of the boys joining him, as long as they didn't get too close to him when there were nice holes to explore.

The youngest children were still so intimidated by the wolf cub that they did not dare approach it by themselves. There was a great commotion one meal, when a loud scream made Lars and Britta rush up from the table.

A few feet from the steps Jonas had been knocked over, and around the screaming and kicking boy, the wolf pup was leaping around him in a wild war dance, making fierce lunges and his teeth were gleaming under his drawn upper lip.

Pålsson didn't take what had happened too seriously, for it was soon clear to him that Sappo's rage was mostly him playing. If nothing had happened out there by Mount Såttan, these days the wolf pup would have been tumbling around with his siblings in wild games outside their den.

– It's the puppy in him, he said, as Britta waved her arms wildly, scaring Sappo away and then lifted Jonas up.

– A puppy! Britta gasped.

A wolf was a wolf, in her opinion. That Lars would think it was possible to make a dog out of that ugly thing! It would probably bite one of the children to death one day.

Jonas soon calmed down, and Pålsson asked him how it had happened.

– I jumped like this, the boy answered and made a few jumps, and then the wolf came and pushed me and was trying to bite me.

– He just wanted to play, their father said calmly, although he was fully aware that Sappo's play could turn into a tragic incident.

But that was precisely why it was necessary to impress upon the children that the wolf cub was not dangerous. If they didn't run away from Sappo, he would have no desire to sink his teeth into their legs.

The children were strictly forbidden to try to pet this wilderness dog and Pålsson was prepared for anything to happen when he himself stroked Sappo's back. Growling and with raised bristles the wolf cub accepted this and made no attempt to bite.

The wolf cub developed quickly. The body became more and more proportionate to his large head, and his clumsy "puppy movements" began to resemble the agility of a predator. If things turned out as Pålsson hoped, in a few months' time Marsliden would have the most dangerous guard who had ever bared its teeth in front of a homestead.

*

In the weeks before midsummer, Pålsson laid the barn's first level of logs, and the settler family could celebrate the anniversary of their arrival at Marsliden with the confidence that they had accomplished a great deal in the past year. This summer, they didn't have to live under a spruce tree and would be able to get their tasks done without breaking their backs.

However, mixed in with his sense of security, Pålsson worried that the Lapps would bring unpleasant surprises, and the guarding that Sappo provided would perhaps make no difference, if the killer bear came prowling.

When midsummer came, Lars and Britta set out to visit Fatmomakke. The baby needed to be baptized and Pålsson wondered if it wouldn't be a good idea to hint to the pastor that there was something else to be said beyond the sermon itself. It seemed unsafe to leave the children alone at the homestead, but Pålsson thought it even less advisable to let Britta go to Fatmomakke alone. After all, Paul was eleven years old now and had learned how to milk a long time ago. The younger siblings mostly took care of themselves, and if the settlement was not disturbed by something from the outside, the risk was not that great. And during this time, the Lapps would be gathered in Fatmomakke.

In Fatmomakke, there were even more people gathered than during the church days last autumn. The nights were bright. You didn't need to have a goahti or church cottage, but people could sleep in the open air. Down among the goahtis, Lars spotted Vanni, but the Lapp girl disappeared, even before the settler had time to show that he had recognized her. Pålsson felt an uncomfortable knot in his stomach when he could not spot Niel anywhere. Was the young Lapp on his way to the homestead perhaps? Had he figured out that the children were alone? Pålsson tried to reassure himself that the Lapp was staying away and would appear when the church services began.

Pålsson sought out the pastor to tell him that they had a child who needed to be baptized, and even though he was a very busy man

at the moment, he listened for a few minutes to what the settler
had to say. Pålsson mentioned the reindeer thefts in careful terms,
mentioning no names or places, and was just as careful in pointing
out that the Lapps were not always in the right either.

The pastor's facial expression did not change once. There was
only a small impatient frown, which came creeping across one
side of his mouth. He had certainly heard that there were a few
things going on in these wild mountains, but it was not his responsibility to sort them out. He was a soul-saver. If anyone felt
he was suffering a worldly wrong, there were other authorities
to turn to. Where would it end if he started to deal with reindeer
thefts and haystacks?

Pålsson nodded seriously. Of course, the pastor was right. He had
come here to care for souls, baptize children and bury the dead. Your
earthly body was your responsibility to take care of, as best you
could. If you were in a bloody fight and survived, you could always
go talk to the police chief.

When the service began, Pålsson sat in the very back by the door
in the small chapel. He scrutinized every face that came in but could
not see the Lapp that had thrown the spear at him out on the muorke. How were things at home? Had the hostile Lapp gone there?
Pålsson brushed a few drops of sweat from his forehead and wished
that Sappo was fully grown.

With this worry on his mind, Pålsson found it difficult to hear the
pastor's sermon. There was a God, and if you believed in him, you
would go to heaven. But if you did not believe in the living God, you
would be thrown into the lake of fire on judgment day.

At the mention of eternal damnation, a chorus of sighs and groans
rose from the Lapps, and Pålsson felt a hard lump form in his chest.
They were fearful of being punished but not convicted about doing
good works. Think how different it would be if the sermon could
also convict them of the blessing of doing good works in their daily
life – to treat each other like brothers, helping them instead of beat-
ing them down.

Pålsson's thoughts strayed and pondered this as he listened to the Lapps' lament in the face of eternal punishment. Now their souls were soft and tender, but when the smoke from hell's stinking sulfur wells no longer moved them, life would return to normal. Eternal punishment was only for the afterlife and had nothing to do with events on earth.

Britta listened with a completely different devotion. Just sitting in a room with many other people made a deep impression on her, being confined for long periods of time to a particular place in the wilderness without the possibility of seeing anyone but her own family. She listened with an open mind to what the pastor had to say. The words flowed in and filled her, there were no dark thoughts standing in the way. Her brown eyes shimmered with emotion. To share in eternal life – to go to heaven, where there were no worries.

After the sermon there was communion. Pålsson held the little one, while Britta went forward. There was a big crowd. The chapel was filled with trepidation from their trembling human hearts; would they get up there fast enough?

When Britta came back, her face shone as with an inner, holy fire. She took the child, and when Lars did not show a sign of getting up, she pushed him. He had to go up there, too!

A few drops of sweat appeared on Pålsson›s forehead, and he drew a deep breath. But then he stood up. For Britta's sake, so that it would not be spread all over the mountains, that he was a heathen above all heathens. Everyone took communion. There would be some bad gossip if he did not.

Slowly and heavily the settler of Marsliden walked up to the altar and knelt down. Next to him was Jon, two of the brothers from Saxnäs and some Lapps. Pålsson was tormented. There seemed to be a smoky haze before his eyes, and the sighing around him felt like whips. One believed, received the sacrament, and went to heaven; it meant nothing how you acted on earth! The wafer grew in his mouth. It wanted to suffocate him… a punishment from the Lord for not receiving the sacrament with a humble mind.

Dripping with sweat, Pålsson returned to his place by the door. His eyes had a grim expression, but perhaps that was because he had had an anxious feeling at the altar, that things were not right at home – that something was happening over by Lake Marssjön, while the sacraments were being distributed in the Lord's house.

A few hours later, Pålsson left Fatmomakke in a depressed mood, as if the noise from a marketplace was pounding in his ears. Now the time for devotion was over. It had ended as soon as they had stepped outside the chapel doors. How many skulking glances he had received from both settlers and Lapps alike!

The noise gradually died away, as if erased by the winds from Marsfjället Mountain's snow-capped peaks. With long, determined strides, Lars and Britta walked home, and on Britta's back the baby rode in her carrier. She had been baptized and her name was Erika.

CHAPTER FIFTEEN

It had been decided that Niel and Vanni would marry this mid-summer, but the Lapp girl seemed to have lost all desire for that after the night when Marsliden had nearly burned down. All winter she had stayed away from Niel and had said outright that she did not want to marry him.

Niel interpreted Vanni's reluctance in dark musings. It was the settler at Lake Marssjön who was to blame. Maybe he had put a spell on Vanni. Or why else did Vanni sometimes have such a strange expression in her eyes – as if she was seeing visions far, far away?

But Niel considered the terrible threat of imprisonment to be even worse. It had loomed over him like a nightmare all winter, and many a night he had woken up in an anxious sweat and needed to rush outside into the open air to be able to tell that he was not in a dungeon. No one had been more eager than Niel to up into the mountains this spring – no one had tried so hard to make the journey easier for old Ante. Ante had not been doing very well during the winter. He had sat coughing for hours on end, gasping for breath.

Ante got better when they got up to Marsfjället Mountain, and Niel did not have to worry about the old man dying before he could help Niel discover what should be done. Steel and fire did not work, the Sami drum would have to provide a solution to what had to be done. Once the settler was gone, everything would be fine – no thoughts of imprisonment would creep up to smother him, and Vanni would turn her gaze back to his face.

*

When the other Lapps headed for Fatmomakke, Niel stayed in the mountains. Ante also wanted to go down to the church gathering, for it would maybe be his last time, but Niel half-forced him to stay. Had he forgotten what he had promised last winter, when Niel skied himself half to death to get medicine for his chest? Seventy kilometers in a snowstorm – and didn't his chest get better?

The old man trembled in every limb when it became clear to him what Niel demanded.

– There's nothing else for me to do? he complained.

– The drum! said Niel bitterly. You can ask the drum!

– No drum – do not have a drum!

Niel darkened.

– You have a drum. Should I show the pastor where you keep it?

Ante slumped with a groan, and over his dirt-yellow, wrinkled face a flaming red color drew, as the air seemed to get caught in his throat.

– Me…me…di-ci-ne!

The whisper was so faint that Niel more sensed it than heard it. He hurriedly looked for the old man's medicine bottle, poured some into an antler spoon and poured it into Ante's toothless mouth. There was wheezing from his throat, and a groan went through his whole shrunken body. But then the breath came, first irregular and then more and more evenly. The attack was over.

Niel was more careful after this episode. Scaring the old man could be fatal. He did not say another word about the drum but turned the conversation to old wrongdoings. He knew that it would not take much for Ante's mind to turn in the direction that events demanded. Some Lapps said that there was something wrong in Ante's head … that he was lost – sometimes not quite knowing what he was doing. Niel didn't believe it. Ante, "lost" – Ante, who knew more than anyone else and who could see and hear what others couldn't even sense!

Ante and Niel sat inside the goahti, which had been put up at the border of the birch forest. It was semi-dark inside, and in the fireplace a burning fire sent up a faint smoke towards the opening in the roof. Ante sat on a reindeer skin with his body rocking and his head shaking. His old, gnarled fingers twitched and his eyes glowed.

– You take reindeer calf, he suddenly croaked and gave Niel a look, which made him shudder.

But only for a second. Then Niel's face became drawn together into a stiff, grim mask. Now the time had come for him to find out the solution!

Ante took a wooden bowl from the goahti wall, fastened it to his belt and crawled out. He blinked in the bright sunlight and brought up one hand to shield from the brightness. Peering, he turned in all directions.

To the east, the view was shorter with close by mountain heaths curving up towards the snowy ridges of Marsfjället Mountain. In the south, his gaze was drawn to the Borgafjällen Mountains, where the sun haze lay like a sacrificial smoke over its mighty lines, and to the west the horizon was broken by the peaked mountains near the border.

Leaning on his walking stick, Ante stood motionless facing north when Niel came out. But there wasn't much to see there, just a hilly ridge, with a few shadows of clouds, swirling like dark spirits. Ante did not see them. His gaze seemed to go right through them to a distant point where neither sun nor moon shone.

– Shall we go now?

Niels' voice hissed with excitement. He had attached a leather bag to his belt. In the bag was meat and reindeer cheese. Niel knew it would be a long walk.

The old man nodded, felt to see if his broad slaughtering knife was in place, and began to work his way up the mountain.

Today it was only the dogs and a couple of boys who were watching the reindeer. In a valley to the west, a smaller group had separated from the herd, and usually the boys would have had a harsh rebuke from Niel. Now, instead, there was a pleased twinkle in his eyes. Now he could take a calf without anyone knowing.

While Ante continued straight ahead, Niel crept towards the unsuspecting herd, and already at a hundred meters away he had picked out the calf that would join them. Niel came closer and closer with his eyes fixed to his victim, and in an instant, he threw his rope – a few jumps, a jerk, and the calf lay sprawled on the ground, while the other animals rushed away.

The calf lay panting, when Niel with a few long leaps threw himself over him. Its shiny, moist eyes were full of fright, and its tongue hung outside its trembling mouth.

Out of habit, Niel quickly fastened a rope around the calf's neck. Another jerk, and the reindeer calf stood upright again on long, wobbly legs. He was not much more than a month old, still reddish brown and scrawny.

Ante had disappeared, and Niel set off in haste with the calf up to the low ridge, which obscured his view. Arriving at the crest, he saw the old man a few hundred meters ahead of him, a small, bent figure, who with unsteady steps was making his way straight north.

*

The sun stood like a fiery red globe beyond the spines of the western mountains, when after many hours of arduous hiking, Ante and Niel finally arrived. It was a desolate place they had come to, downright frightening in the dim glow of the night. Surrounded on all sides by high mountain walls, was a small mountain lake with water shimmering in green and black. No rays of light penetrated it except in the middle of the day. There was a ring of birch trees, that wrapped around the lake like lashes around an eye, their leaves had dark shadows in their tender greenery. Or was it the strange lighting, which gave the impression of black leaves on green birches, a light that came only from above and merged with the darkness that seemed to radiate from the damp mountain walls? Seen from above, the place was like the bottom of a huge well, where the ring of birch trees around the shimmering depths of the water evoked the strange feeling that a forest was growing underground.

Niel had tied the reindeer calf to a birch trunk, and the exhausted animal lay on the ground, nibbling at the succulent grass that grew between the tree trunks. A few meters away, Ante silently made his humble preparations. He had pulled off his hat and stands of his hair hung down over his furrowed brow. His breathing was short and wheezy, his lips moved in inaudible mutterings. Between the old man's swollen edges of his red streaked eyes, a senseless look gleamed. No fatigue could be sensed in his quiet movements. Every fiber of his shrunken body seemed permeated by a secret power. That power had not been present during their walk over the mountains, when his legs had sometimes been like withered blades of grass, and when for long stretches he had hung like a helpless bundle on Niels' back.

A little closer to the mountain side, a strangely shaped stone rose above the ground. Now it was green with moss, but there had been a time when it was shiny from animal fat. On this spot, in ancient pagan times, the mountain people had gathered to offer their sacrifice to the mighty ones. They came creeping like dark shadows through the narrow gorge of the pass – first the *noaidi*, the Sami shaman, with a heavy iron pot. He was followed by an entourage of humble people, approaching the place of the gods with trepidation, dragging a sacrificial animal.

Like a spirit from days gone by, the withered figure of Ante moved around the pagan sacrificial site. But he was more subdued than his forefathers, and there was no sign that he intended to approach the stone with shouts and wailing and smear the *sieidi*, the stone, with blood and fat. For Ante, the stone was only a stone.

It was to the "little ones" under the earth that the Lapp turned to, to the little invisible ones who in the darkness controlled the beginnings of new life. It was "the little ones" who made the grass sprout from the ground and the forest to grow, and if you were not in their good graces, the cows would not give birth to calves and the women would only be able to long for children. The "little ones" were the masters of life itself, more powerful than anything else.

It was almost midnight. For a brief moment the sun had sunk below the horizon, leaving behind it a red wall, from which violet streaks shot up towards the floating clouds in the air. The sky was otherwise clear, and in the cool glow of midnight the contours of the mountains became almost sharper than during the day.

Compared to the light above, the area near the small lake was where dark shadows dwelled. A gloomy semi-darkness lay brooding over the reflective, shiny, black water. Not a movement could be detected in the birch leaves, and only a few heavy rustles disturbed the eerie silence.

Ante knelt between two birches and cut out a piece of sod with his knife, which he placed next to the hole. For a few seconds he stared down into the dark dirt, then crawled backwards towards the reindeer calf, where Niel stood ready with an axe and a wooden bowl.

Now it was done, and while the calf's body was still trembling with life, Ante crawled back to the hole with the wooden bowl filled with blood, emptied the bowl into the pit and placed the piece of sod back over it.

Sweat dripped from his brow, and with a wail he began to crawl around the bloody spot.

Niel stood trembling by the slaughtered sacrificial animal. The desolate place, the act of the bloodletting, Antes' wailing, and the pressure of his own misfortunes pressed together into something terrible, forcing him to his knees. His eyes were wide open with horror, and for a few seconds the terror nearly made him run away. Then he let go of all reason. He was pulled in, as if hypnotized. Drooling, Niel began to creep forward, while a couple of stray thoughts fluttered like raven wings through his overheated brain. The solution – he must find the solution! Closer and closer he was drawn to the scene of the sacrifice, and with horrible groans the two bewildered Lapps crawled like worms around the piece of sod, its underside wet with blood.

Finally, reason seemed to return. Ante and Niel got up and staggered toward the nearest mountain wall. Beside a stunted birch they disappeared into an opening, which seemed to go straight into the mountain.

Soon a faint smoke drifted out of the cave, and the glow of a fire cast a flickering light out into the semi-darkness.

Inside the opening, Ante and Niel sat with the firelight reflecting on their faces. Ante's body stayed as close to the heat as possible, but his soul seemed to be wandering. His eyes were strangely rigid, and his breathing was so weak that his spark of life seemed to be fluttering above his head.

Niel had regained control of himself and sat hard and grim, staring into the fire he had previously gathered fuel for. Now he was about to hear what the drum had to tell Ante – find out the solution that would destroy the settler at Lake Marssjön.

The Sami drum was already in the old man's lap. A white-tanned, reindeer calfskin was stretched on an oval frame that was about one meter long and half as wide. It was dirty gray with age, and on the drumskin were painted the strangest symbols and signs. Deities and people; mountains, lakes, and rivers; reindeer, dogs, wolves, and other animals. Here were roads leading to Fatmomakke, here and there crossed by the unseen spirit paths of the headless dead, who sought their way down to the dark abysses of the underworld. Birru (the devil) had his symbol. Bieggagales, the god of the storm, and Horagales, who thundered among the clouds…

Ante was still motionless. It was as if he did not dare let the rings begin their rattling dance across the skin. He held them tightly in one hand, and his lips were pressed together in a bloodless line. He seemed oblivious to Niel and to time and space. He sat like a shadow from the past with death reflected in his eyes.

Niel was still too, and not a single look on his rigid face betrayed the impatience that lay within him. The old man must not be disturbed – not now, when he was to see future events swirling between the symbols on the drum. Now and again Niel took a stick from the pile of brushwood and threw it on the fire, its blazing light sought in vain to reach the darkest corners of the cave.

Suddenly a jolt went through Ante's body, and with a violent movement he flung the bundle of rings down on the drum skin. Now his stiffness was gone. His breath came out in wheezing pulses through the narrow opening of his lips, and his eyes glowed with a fanatical shimmer as the first dull blows from a small reindeer horn hammer began to set the rings in motion.

Niel sat spellbound, while his eyes stared at the rings dancing around on the skin. His mouth was open wide, and a sweaty wad of hair moved across his forehead. His thoughts stood still. The present was swept away.

The drumbeats got wilder and wilder, and as the dull rattle of the rings penetrated every crevice and recess of the cave, two incredible shadows were seen on the damp cave wall – a smaller shadow, swinging to and fro with violent movements, and a larger one, rocking slowly back and forth. Deep groans began to mix with the rattle and beat of the drum, and the fire crackled on some wet twigs and sent a fiery, blue-black smoke out towards the opening of the cave.

The light blazed against Ante's face. The old man had lost all sense of reason. Seized by a hysterical madness, he hammered furiously on the drumskin. His eyes glowed and sweat poured from his brow.

– Bad times! he suddenly wheezed. The wolf will not find food.

Niel leaned forward, and every line of his heated face expressed intense tension. Now the solution would be revealed!

But Niel listened in vain. Not a word could be discerned in the stream of blurred whispers that poured over the old man's bloodless lips.

– The solution! groaned Niel. The solution, Ante!

The old man dropped the reindeer horn hammer. An ashen gaze shot out from his eyes and landed on Niels' face, while the rings rested after their magic dance. For a few seconds Ante was motionless but then began to tremble and suddenly cried out loudly.

– Jesus Christ! Father God in heaven!

It was like the cry of a soul in distress, and before Niel could understand what was going on, the old man had risen to his feet and with a single blow smashed the drum against the stone wall and thrown the pieces on the fire. He took a few staggering steps, came out into the open air, and then stood motionless with his hands raised to the sky, until he suddenly sank to the ground.

CHAPTER SIXTEEN

It was a terrible drought that summer. During the month of July, not a drop of rain fell on Marsliden. The potatoes were stunted, wilting away in the heat of the sun below the steep mountainside. Even the grass suffered, the tops yellowed and seemed to grow more downwards than upwards. However, the situation was better in the marsh hayfields, and Pålsson did not have to worry about a lack of winter feed, although it could be quite strenuous to cut among the bushes and thorns.

Pålsson had almost finished the barn when it came time to start mowing in earnest. No bad encounters with either the Lapps or the bear had disrupted their work. As for the Lapps, they were far away on the Norwegian border in the summer, and Pålsson began to think that he had little more to fear from them.

One day in early August, Ericsson from Saxnäs came walking across the muorke. He really had no important business but was just out to satisfy his curiosity. When he came close to the homestead, he was suddenly attacked by a gray wild animal, charging with lightning speed and with a horrible howl, nearly knocking him over. Ericsson could barely protect himself from its shiny teeth and wiped the sweat from his brow as Pålsson came running and pushed the furious Sappo away.

The angry young wolf only half obeyed, and raspy growls came from his throat. The man from Saxnäs did not take his eyes off him.

– That's a feisty rascal of a dog you've gotten, he exclaimed, gasping.

Pålsson smiled in his usual stern way.

– Not a dog exactly, he said slowly. I took him from a wolf's den last spring!

After that announcement, Ericsson did not spend many minutes in Marsliden. He suddenly was in a desperate hurry – very busy with the mowing now – just came for a quick visit since he was nearby.

Ericsson's visit to Marsliden brought with it much curious gossip in the cabins in the Lake Kultsjö area, and there were even voices whispering of a pact with the evil one. One person thought he had heard from Ericsson that flames of fire had erupted out of the jaws of the beast, and another thought that the wolf didn't have ordinary paws but hooves like a goat. When Ericsson was asked about the hooves, he could not give a definite answer – but it sure was a terrible beast!

Over and over the wolf story was being told and added to. Now people began to understand why the settler at Lake Marssjön had been able to manage as well as he had in a place that no one else had dared to settle at. It didn't make sense. Some recalled old events and added them to the context. Had they noticed how the settler had behaved at Fatmomakke when he had taken communion? He had not dared to come forward… and how the sweat had run off him when he knelt at the altar! Hardly able to breathe when the pastor had put the holy sacrament in his mouth. Didn't they understand… that it had been the evil one who had been in the settler, tormenting him? And who knows – maybe this drought was God's punishment for the devil being inside the house of the Lord.

In mid-August, the rain came. A fierce thunderstorm broke out, moving across the wilderness with a thunderous roar and nearly rocking the huge mountains. A torrential downpour – a flood unparalleled in human memory – filled the dried-up furrows of the mountain streams in a few hours. The marshes were flooded. The downpour eventually turned into a drizzle that seemed never-ending. Day after day – the same chilling gray weather continued, which did not even let the mountain peaks appear for a minute.

For the settler in Marsliden, the flooding was far more terrifying than the summer's drought. He had almost all his mowing done in the lower meadows. Some of the hay had already dried and been gathered into small stacks when the flood came. These stacks now swam around without Pålsson having any chance to save them. Most of the hay was still in hay drying racks, the two bottom layers of them were submerged in these muddy swamp lakes.

It looked almost hopeless, and one day Pålsson put the scythe on his shoulder and walked up the mountain. He had previously noticed that there were good hayfields on the mountain heaths above the forest line, and surely there couldn't be flooding up there. He had to make sure to get some of these fields officially inspected and registered. Admittedly, they were more than five kilometers from Lake Marssjön, but with the help of sledges it would be quite easy to get the hay down.

On the plateau between Mount Såttan and Mount Kakkankaisse, Pålsson found what he was looking for. The grass was not very long, but thick and lush after the rain, and here the settler began the second mowing of the summer. It had finally started to clear, and if autumn gave them good weather, all hope was not lost. But no forest grew near here, and every morning Pålsson went there weighed down under huge loads of wood. One drying rack after another began to appear on the bare mountainside.

Pålsson worked alone on the mountain. The water had now receded, and Britta and the boys had a good deal of work to do to save what they could of the hay on the marshfields. The bottom parts of the haystacks that had been under water were hopelessly lost — half-rotten and soaked with sludge — and the rest of the hay was not in great condition either. But something had to be used, and if it was laid out in the sun and then hung up again, it was at least better than the black lumps they had had to feed the animals their last winter in Fjällboberg.

Some days Sappo was up in the mountains, and there was plenty to keep the energetic young wolf busy. His contact with humans had taught him that they were not dangerous, and his clash with Ericsson had given him a voracious appetite for similar events. Anything unfamiliar immediately put him on high alert.

In the mountains, Sappo was most interested in the lemmings and quickly mastered the art of catching these colorful mountain rats. A single slight rustling could make him stop and be completely still, a stillness that instantly turned into a lightning-fast leap that no lemming could escape.

Usually not a sound was heard from Sappo while he hunted. It was for this reason that Pålsson froze with his scythe in mid-swing when one day, towards evening, he suddenly heard a howl coming from the west.

Pålsson threw down the scythe, stood for a second as if sniffing the air, and then the echo of his huge thunderous voice rolled between the mountain ridges.

– Sappo! Sappo!

The answer was another howl, now mixed with a scream, which gave the settler goose bumps. He set off at a wild run in that direction. Sappo couldn't have… He could rip a man's throat in a single bite.

Arriving at a creek, he had his bad suspicions confirmed. At the very edge of the creek lay a motionless human figure with the head pushed against the ground. With a couple of long leaps, Pålsson arrived, pushed Sappo away with a grim roar and grabbed the shoulders of the person.

A cry made the settler release his grip, and the next second a face turned up to him, distorted in fear and horror. Pålsson barely saw the face. Sappo had not spilled blood! Pålsson stood panting and stroking his forehead, trembling with relief.

It was Vanni, who lay terrified on the ground, staring up at the giant man, who was bent over her. Her body shook, and her brown eyes begged for mercy.

– What are you doing here?

Pålsson had now fully recovered from the shock, and his voice had a strong note of suspicion. There were no reindeer around. What reason did she have for sneaking over here?

The girl gave only a whimper in reply, and suddenly Pålsson saw that her left leg was in an oddly twisted position.

– Have you hurt yourself?

Again, the settler did not get a proper answer, but the matter was clear. The Lapp girl had somehow been injured. All grimness was wiped from Pålsson's face. Whatever the reason she had for coming – here was a fellow human being, who needed help.

There were two options to choose from, either carry the Lapp girl along the kettle valley up through the pass, to find some goahti which should be on the other side, or to take her home to Marsliden. Pålsson quickly decided on the latter.

But first he had to get something to support the girl's leg. It would probably be painful enough without having her leg dangling here and there during the uneven hike down the mountain. He said that he would be right back and hurried down toward the birch forest. He took Sappo with him.

After the settler had put a splint on the girl's leg, he started wondering whether it wasn't better to carry the girl to where she belonged. He could not help but notice the horror with which she looked at him. But there were good reasons to put an end to that thought. It would take all night to bring Vanni west – what would Britta think if he did not come home by nightfall? And was it humane to drag and haul the victim further than necessary? No, she was going to Marsliden!

When the leg was in a splint, Pålsson lifted Vanni up, so that she was hanging with her head over one of his shoulders and began to walk east with long strides. Vanni noticed which way they were going, but she protested only with a faint whimper. She was helpless, entirely at the mercy of this large, powerful man.

CHAPTER SEVENTEEN

Vanni lay staring up at the ceiling in Marsliden's front room. It was her second week at Marsliden. The pain in her leg had been purely excruciating during the first days, now it was not felt anymore. The leg was only stiff and awkward and could not be moved, and the settler had said that it would be at least two months before she could move around as before.

But that was not what the Lapp girl was thinking about. Everything was so strange. How kind Britta was to her! And Lars…! It wasn't true, the way they talked in the goahtis. She would tell them that when her leg was well – say that the settler at Lake Marssjön meant them no harm.

During the long hours in solitude, many thoughts stirred within Vanni, and it was with trepidation that she anticipated the day when Niel would show up. Maybe he would come one night, like last fall, to burn the cabin with them all inside. Niel was so strange now after that day, when he had come back, carrying with him the dead body of Ante from the northern mountains. What had Ante and Niel been up to? Oh, Nikku and her father had whispered about it one night, when they thought no one was listening, something terrible about a reindeer calf getting lost and that there was something over there in the mountains that would bring them much harm if the pastor or the police chief found out. That Niel had dared to! And what had he been brooding about all summer? Just staring at the ground and muttering to himself.

When her thoughts wandered in this direction, it could take hours before Vanni could think of anything else.

Henni had whispered to her one afternoon that Niel had been at Finn-Märi's – she lived far down in a valley on the Norwegian side and used a magic mirror to destroy people and animals from afar.

Maybe it was from her that Niel had gotten the white powder, which he was so afraid anyone would see. It must be some kind of magic. Would she have slipped and broken her leg at the creek if she had not had the powder in her pocket? No!

*

This autumn Pålsson did not bother with attending the Fatmo-makke church days. He thought that there was no point in wasting time just to be stared at with malicious glares. Of course, he did have a good reason to go talk to the Lapps, but it wasn't too much to ask that one of the mountain people would come down to his homestead and inquire if they had seen Vanni.

The days went by, full of chores. Any day now, the beautiful autumn weather could turn into gray rain. The early snowstorm of last year was still well remembered, and it was important to be prepared for the unexpected.

What could still be used of the hay from the marsh fields was now gathered into small stacks, framed by sturdy fences. It was too far to carry home the hay. When the ground froze and the snow came, you could move more with a hay sled in a single day than you could in a week now. Up on the mountain, the grass was still drying in haystacks. The settler intended to haul that hay down after the first good night's frost.

The potatoes were dug up, but the harvest was no more than half of last year's. To make up for the poor potato harvest, bundles of jierja herb were picked, boiled, and chopped according to the instructions Inga had given last autumn and packed into a large barrel, which Pålsson had made especially for this purpose. And it seemed it would be necessary to eat the preserved sour plants. The berries were small this autumn, and one week Pålsson did not catch a single fish from Lake Marssjön. The settler knew what was wrong. He couldn't get his nets out in deep enough water. It would be necessary to build a boat to use next spring.

149

While going about with these daily chores, everything was not as it should be. Something new had come to Marsliden and one evening Britta said:

– You must consider letting the Lapps know. And when Lars did not answer, she continued: They are worried about the girl, I'm sure.

Pålsson nodded seriously. Yes, it would be good to let them know!

But the days went by without Pålsson making any effort to go up the mountain. It was as if he couldn't bring himself to do it.

Britta noticed better than Lars that something had to be done. Maybe it wasn't such a big deal that the Lapp girl looked up to Pålsson as if he was a superior being. She had expected to be treated badly, and not with kindness. At times this seemed to make her quite giddy. But it was a dangerous adoration, and Britta dreaded the consequences it might bring. She gave Pålsson many inquiring glances, but the man did not seem to be impressed yet by the adoration that Vanni was too innocent to be able to hide. But how long could he resist the gaze of those eyes, which radiated warmth, hotter every day?

Britta brought the matter up again.

– We have to think about letting the Lapps know, she said. They will probably think that she has disappeared.

– It wouldn't be too much trouble for them to come here and ask about her.

– They don't know she's here. And it's not easy to get here either, with that wolf prowling around. Maybe it was him who was out looking yesterday… all that ruckus Sappo was doing after dark.

Pålsson didn't answer, but just sat there pondering about something.

– I'll bring the baby and walk up the mountain myself, if you do not feel like it! said Britta.

Her voice was strained, and Pålsson looked up at her.

– There's no need! he said slowly. I'll go by myself soon.

But that didn't happen either, and one evening Britta decided that the next morning she would take the baby and go up the mountain. It couldn't go on like this.

But the planned hike up the mountain did not happen that morning. Pålsson went out to set a few more fox traps before the ground froze. When he came home shortly after noon, Britta gave him a small bag. She said nothing, but her face was red, and her chest was finding it very difficult to get enough air.

– What is it?

– Look!

Pålsson opened the bag, smelled it, touched a little of the greyish-white powder and looked at it more closely.

– Where did you get this?

– Jonas brought it in as soon as you left.

Britta's voice was barely controlled. It was as if she was hiding a bomb that was about to explode at any moment.

During these seconds, Pålsson's face underwent a terrible transformation. He turned almost ashen, a thick vein protruded on one temple, and his eyebrows drew together.

– Where did the boy find it? he exclaimed hoarsely.

– Vanni's skirt pocket!

Pålsson got up. His ashen face suddenly turned a dark red color. He knew what the powder in the bag was and looked at Britta and saw that she also knew.

– In Vanni's skirt? It can't be!

Those last words came out like the crack of a whip, and Pålsson looked at Britta as if he wanted to force her to take back a lie. But Britta didn't back down.

– Ask the boy – and her! she gasped. I know what she would do with it. Poison me and the children!

– You and the children?

– Then she'd have you ... you, all to herself! Pålsson looked sharply at his wife.

– Me to herself – what do you mean?

– Oh, yes, I've seen what has been going on, and why haven't you gone up to the Lapps and told them she's here?

Pålsson mumbled. He did not know how to answer. Why hadn't he gone up to the Lapps? It was no mystery. It was his turn to have the advantage over them. He didn't notice that Britta was looking more and more upset.

– You wanted her to stay here! she exclaimed hotly, and she was close to crying.

– Stay… yes, but not anymore!

Pålsson said no more but put the poison bag in his pocket and cast a long look at the baby. The other children were outside. He seemed to have regained his composure, and calmly grabbed his hat and headed for the door.

– Where are you going?

– Up the mountain, so I might be a little late getting home.

With long strides Pålsson half ran up the slope between the mountain hills. Out here he didn't need to control himself, and he had to walk fast to shake off all this nastiness. Oh, he really should have gone in and confronted her! But best to just get her to leave. Britta and the children… oh, no, it was about all of them! How could Britta think he would be spared? It was clear that the insidious poison was intended to destroy everyone in Marsliden. The more Pålsson thought about it, the more furious he became. Appearing sweet and innocent but carrying the means to kill nine humans in her skirt! On her way to Marsliden with the stuff, when she broke her leg… would come as a friend… be allowed to stir their stew pot…

It was morning before Pålsson returned from the mountain. The boiling rage had gone away, and there was only a hint of grimness on his face as he opened the heavy door to the front room. He heard sobs from inside, and after a few moments of hesitation, Pålsson stepped into the room.

Vanni was curled up against the headboard, and her cheeks were streaked with tears. When Pålsson entered, she stretched out her arms towards him.

– Lars... oh, Lars! What's the matter? Britta says you've been gone, and Britta looks so strange... and... and...

– Do you want to know what happened? Pålsson's voice cut off the girl's gasps like a knife, and he took a few steps towards the bed. Do you recognize this?

All the color drained from Vanni's cheeks when she saw the small bag in the man's huge hand. Her arms dropped, and she crawled against the wall.

– You were going to finish us off with this!

– No... no!

The words were more terrified sobs than sounds formed with the tongue.

Lars gripped the girl's shoulders tightly, paying no attention to her trembling legs. His face was barely a foot from hers and his eyes blazed.

– Is it true? he gasped. True, that you didn't mean to...

Vanni squirmed under his grip.

– Yes! she groaned! It's true!

Pålsson felt the girl's body go limp between his hands and saw her terrified expression disappear. With a deep groan, he released his grip and gently laid her down. The girl's forehead was damp with sweat, and on her lowered eyelids small, fine veins protruded.

Lars left the unconscious girl and went into the kitchen. Britta was out milking, and with a bowl of water Pålsson went back into the room to try to bring the girl to consciousness. He was far from convinced that she was innocent.

– Well, but what was the bag for? he asked when Vanni was able to answer.

With stammering, disjointed sentences, Vanni told him that she had been on her way to Grytsjö to show Sari the powder and ask if it was dangerous. Olofsson's wife was a close relative of hers and knew a lot of things.

– Did you get the powder on your own, or did someone else give it to you?

Vanni delayed answering but then said in a whisper that she had taken it. Pålsson was told no more. Despite all his stern attempts at persuasion, Vanni stubbornly refused to say who actually owned the bag of poison. Finally, Pålsson left the room with a shrug, deaf to the suppressed sobs that sought to keep him there.

At noon two Lapps came to Marsliden and brought with them four reindeer and sleds. It had been chilly during the night, and now it was snowing.

Few words were spoken, while Vanni was carried out and put in one of the sleds. It was like an armed standoff between the settler and his neighbors in the mountains. Vanni's face was hot with tears, and she looked deeply unhappy, as if she had been held in the cruelest captivity here in Marsliden. To the two mountain men, the matter was quite clear in their minds. Pålsson had his own opinion of the situation as well, as Vanni was tucked into the sled. Not a single person could be trusted up here. There was only falsehood and malice wherever you turned. He nodded curtly as Vanni stretched out her hands in a final pleading gesture, and the next minute the reindeer set off eastwards.

Pålsson was still standing there, watching them in the distance, when he was suddenly startled by what he saw. Up on the heights of Mount Såttan were gray dots. The reindeer were migrating eastwards. Filled with foreboding, Pålsson took his sled and hurried up the mountain. This morning he had not seen a single reindeer east of the pass, and now they had already been driven forward, not allowed to graze as they wished. At least two weeks earlier than last autumn, the reindeer had arrived at the borders of Marsliden.

The settler ran up the long slope and stopped panting, dripping with sweat by the hay meadow in the mountains, when the first dusk of the evening came drifting in. All the hay drying racks had been obliterated. The poles were bare. Some were still in their places, but most were either completely demolished or stood at an angle with one end pointing towards a gray sky. The grass, not already moving eastward in the reindeer's stomachs, had been trampled into a crushed mixture of shredded hay and snow.

CHAPTER EIGHTEEN

It was a few weeks into the New Year, and a violent blizzard swept across the wilderness with furious force. Where the pine forest stood dense, a chorus of broken twigs rattled, mingled with squeaks and howls from the tree limbs rubbing against each other.

It was a little quieter in the birch forest. The storm was just as fierce, but here the sounds were more subdued. Sighing and groaning, the gnarled birch trees stood bent like bows, reaching for each other as if in anguish.

Up on the bare mountain moors, the storm had free rein. It came crashing down in mighty waves, sometimes merging into spinning whirlwinds, where the blowing snow rose like dancing smoke against a sky that no longer seemed to exist.

*

Defying the storm, Jon arrived in Klimpfjäll with his horse and sled on the road from Norway. He had left Kroken early in the morning in the company of Pålsson. Then there had been no sign that the wildest snowstorm of the year would break loose before the evening. He had parted from Pålsson before the first snow flurries had swept in, for the settler had steered his skis up the mountains to take the nearest route home. The two men had not accompanied each other on the journey but had met by chance in Norway.

Without hesitation, Jon forced his way through the storm.

Several times he had taken a good sip from the tin cask he had bought in Norway and felt up to the task, despite the challenges. Warm and tipsy, he tromped forward through the deep snow in a valley west of the Dårronskalet Pass. Here the birch forest stood tall and thick, and the man from Klimpfjäll had not yet fully realized what kind of weather he had encountered.

Jon trusted his horse completely and paid little attention to where he was. The reins were untied, and he walked carelessly a few steps behind the sled. He breathed effortlessly, and the wind gusts could not erase the satisfied expression on his face or disturb him in his thoughts. This thing with Marsliden was working out well. Now the settler over there had only half a year to get his affairs in order, and if he hadn't thought of doing it before, he probably wouldn't now. That fool didn't know that he had settled by Lake Marssjön without legal permission. Abraham – that fool, wasn't willing to work with Jon concerning the claim to the settlement when Jon had last seen him in Åsele, but that didn't matter now. This summer it would be five years since Abraham had had the place inspected, and soon Pålsson would see what happens to folks who let themselves be tricked into buying worthless papers.

He was going uphill, and it became more and more difficult for the horse to move forward, but Jon hardly noticed it. He pondered whether he should move to Marsliden himself or let his eldest son take over the settlement. Maybe this winter things wouldn't be so plentiful over there. Pålsson had only brought two foxes and a half sack of grouse with him to Norway. But maybe he had been down in Åsele. Jon was upset because he had forgotten to ask him but consoled himself that it seemed Pålsson had not talked to the authorities. If he had, he would surely have said something.

Fifteen minutes later, Jon had other things on his mind. Now there was no longer any shelter from the storm, and panting, he struggled behind the sled with his head tilted to protect his face from the worst of the wind gusts. He could only see the horse occasionally. It was almost completely engulfed in a swirling whiteness that threatened to bury everything in its path with a single blast.

Jon now fully realized the gravity of the situation and had sobered up completely. Time and again the horse stopped, and Jon had to grab the reins and the whip to stop it from turning around. Meter after meter, the sled pushed upwards, and the roar from the giant mouth of the Dårronskalet Pass was heard more and more clearly.

Again, the horse stood still, and Jon had to crawl and take shelter behind the sled to avoid being knocked over by the wailing storm. For a moment he thought of turning back, but then fear came over him, the fear that was always lurking as he traveled alone near the desolate mountain pass.

Jon got up and stood swaying in the roar of the storm. Don't turn around… not down there again… Forward, forward! … Away from this horrible place! If he could only get through the Dårronskalet Pass, he would soon be home in Klimpfjäll. He roared and shouted and cracked his whip without seeing if he hit or missed.

Suddenly the horse jerked, and Jon gasped, grabbing the back of the sled to not be left behind. The sled rose up and then became completely covered with snow. Jon hung on through the huge drift, groaning under the pressure of the wind that threatened to squeeze all the air out of him.

The sled stopped again, Jon opened his mouth to yell at the horse, but a storm gust stifled the scream to a wheeze. The man could not see a foot in front of him. He was right in the middle of the howling hell of the Dårronskalet Pass.

Groaning, Jon crawled to the side of the sled. He realized that the horse could not go any further with the sled behind it. He felt around for the drawbar but got all the way to the horse's head before he found anything except snow. The animal stood panting and was almost buried. A few more minutes and neither horse nor sled would be visible.

The animal seemed to understand that it was to be freed from the heavy sled, and stood still, while Jon clumsily unhitched the sled.

As Jon reached for the reins, the horse got up on its hind legs, made a full circle and disappeared into the roaring, whirling whiteness.

Jon had been thrown a few meters to the side by the terrible gust of wind and was gasping for air. He got up, stepped up and down without getting anywhere – sinking, sinking, as the snow packed around him. A moment ago, the snow had reached only to his waist, and now it covered his shoulders. It was only Jon's head that stuck out above the surface of the swirling snow.

With superhuman effort, Jon managed to work his way out of the snow's hard grip, tumbling and rolling to get to the sled and find shelter. Tonight, it was not humanly possible to make it through the Dårronskalet Pass. Where was the horse? Was it pushing its way through enormous drifts or was it buried only a few meters away?

Jon didn't have time to think about the horse. He searched like a possessed man for the sled but could not find it. In a blind daze, Jon raced westward. He had to get to shelter while he had some strength left. With the rest cabin at Tjåkkolafjället Mountain as a vague goal, he wandered down the slopes.

For several hours Jon trudged through the deep snow with the storm sweeping around him. He did not know where he was. His eyes ached in the stinging gray darkness surrounding him. It was only when he bumped into a tree that he could make out anything.

Blinded and lost, Jon suddenly stopped on a small level area. He trembled with fatigue. The treacherous liquor had helped the storm drive the strength out of his powerful body. He cried out a couple of times – wild, hoarse cries, which the storm turned into pitiful little moans, that hardly carried a few meters away. He wanted to run, but his legs refused to carry him, and now he saw – saw clearly the face of a Lapp.

– Mikael! he groaned and sank to his knees.

The answer came in a long, drawn-out howl from a crevice in the mountainside next to him, and as if whipped by evil spirits, Jon got up, only to vanish the next second in the smoke from whipping snow gusts.

*

Britta lay awake, listening to the wailing wind howl down the chimney. Occasionally she got up and put a few sticks of wood on the embers. She felt a little calmer when the fire was alive. Paul didn't sleep either. He lay tossing and turning in the upper bunk, and suddenly he sat up and stared at his mother, who had been standing by the fireplace, wringing her hands together.

– Isn't father back yet?

Britta shook her head, and a concerned look crossed the boy's face.

– Maybe he's still in Norway because of this weather!

– Yes, he's probably still in Norway.

Britta's voice was convincingly firm, but she didn't dare look the boy in the eye, and her hands felt cold and sticky, though she held them in front of the fire.

– Then he won't come home tonight, Paul said, and when he got no answer, he crawled back into bed and lay staring at the ceiling.

Britta sat down by the fireplace. If only she could be sure that Lars had not left Kroken, or that he had arrived at the settlement at Lake Gikasjön, before the raging blizzard broke out. If he was up in the mountain…

Britta trembled. Tonight, no man could cross the mountains, and Lars was no more than a man. She tried to reassure herself that Pålsson had not left Kroken, but this fragile hope was torn apart by the sinking feeling of fear within her. She felt intuitively that her husband was wandering around somewhere in this terrible storm, fighting for his life among the wind gusts and snow drifts.

The longer the night went on, the more anxious Britta became. The storm was still blowing with unabated force. Fierce smoke sometimes blew back down the low chimney, so that the ashes swirled among the embers, and now and then fierce gusts of wind shook the logs of the cabin.

Britta had reason for her worry. If Pålsson succumbed to the blizzard, the entire homestead was doomed to a merciless demise. There was no feed for the cows until spring, and even if Marsliden had been full of haystacks, Britta had no chance of making it in this place, where hostile people combined with harsh nature to create so many difficulties. There was no mercy in the wilderness. Those who couldn't handle it, died.

Britta lay thinking about this and wished they had stayed in Fjäll-boberg. At least they had had someone to turn to there. Their disagreements back there seemed so pitifully small and insignificant to her in comparison with all that was heaped upon them here.

If she lost Lars...

The thought was so horrible that Britta had to bite her lip to keep from screaming out loud. She tried to pray.

– Our Father, who art in heaven...

Her whisper was drowned out by a roar from the chimney, an angry roaring gust of wind that threatened to tear the roof off the cabin, and while the wind gusts continued their howling whirlwind dance, Britta knelt and prayed to Our Lord for mercy.

The storm was still raging when Britta went out to milk the cows. When she opened the front door, a pile of snow fell against her. The snow was packed all the way up to the roof, and if the door had opened outward, they would have had no choice but to climb through the chimney.

The barn had almost disappeared, and it took Britta several hours to dig a hole down to the door and get inside to the cows. Before she had time to finish tending to the animals, the hole was almost filled up again. If she had not had Paul and Aron to help her, she would hardly have been able to get out.

Just before noon it stopped snowing, and an hour later it was completely calm. The clouds dispersed, revealing a few sunbeams in the southern sky before the great ball of light disappeared behind Borgafjällen Mountains.

Paul and Aron worked determinedly to dig down to the windows. When these were free of snow, they began to dig out a wide pit in front of the door, but they didn't get down very far before their arms were not long enough to throw the snow out of the hole, even though they flung the snow until their joints ached.

Aron was actually delighted with the heavy snow and sometimes stole a few minutes to ski down the roof of the cabin. There wasn't even a "bump" if he skied right across the barn. Paul looked disapprovingly at his brother. If their father had been home, Paul would probably have tried the new ski slopes himself, but now there were more serious things to think about.

– We have to shovel this out before Father comes home! he said, and that's all it took for Aron to fall on his head, making the snow swirl around him.

Britta also helped with the snow shoveling, and when darkness came, a trench had been dug to the barn. It was nowhere close to reaching all the way down to the ground, but it was now possible to go through it without sinking up to your waist in the snow.

Britta tried to stay calm while the children were awake, but once they were in bed, she couldn't stay calm any longer. Lars hadn't come … would never come! If he had been sheltering from the storm at Lake Gikasjön, he would have been home by now. She couldn't imagine that he had stayed in Kroken. Lars was always so eager to get home when he was out on a long trip. This time he wouldn't have a heavy pack either. Nothing to trade with because this winter had been cursed. Grouse were hard to find, and two foxes were all his traps had caught.

The hours passed, and Britta got as little sleep as the night before.

She sat at the table, resting her head in her hands. The room was bright, almost like daylight, and among the fur blankets in the lower bed she could clearly make out the baby's cute nose. It seemed to her as if she was in some kind of a dream. Nothing seemed grounded, everything sort of flowed around her. She was becoming convinced; Lars was not coming back.

Britta sat motionless for a long time. It was only her shoulders that trembled from time to time. No proper thoughts were able to make their way through her tormented brain – it was as if she was obliviously drifting away, to a place where all thinking was erased.

Suddenly, she jolted and looked around with wild opened eyes.

Was that a noise? Yes, there it was, something scratching at the door again!

Britta jumped up as if someone had burnt her with a hot iron and looked out the window. Her body trembled, and she took a deep breath. Was it a ghost gliding like a shadow across the sparkling blanket of snow or was she dreaming? Not until the door opened could she fully realize what the shadow was.

– You're here, Lars! she gasped and rushed up to the man as if to convince herself that she was not the victim of deceptive hallucination.

Pålsson nodded. His eyebrows and beard were white with frost, and he looked like he had walked to the end of the world and back again. Sappo, who had joined him on his trip over the mountains, was now stretched out on the floor in front of the fireplace. With half-closed eyes he gazed into the glowing ashes, pushed his nose against his strong front legs and gave off a faint howl. While Pålsson picked chunks of ice from his beard, Britta lit a big fire and put a pot over it. She was half laughing, half crying and hardly knew what to do. She had been so convinced Lars was not coming back that her mind was in a state of confusion. But she gradually calmed down, and when the food was ready to be put on the table, she was at least outwardly calm.

– What a storm we've had!

Yes. Pålsson agreed that it had been quite a storm. He was quiet like he always was when he had been involved in major events that were more or less life-threatening.

– Did you spend the night at the settler's cabin at Lake Gikasjön?

– No.

– Did you stay in Kroken?

– No.

– But surely you weren't out in that terrible blizzard!

Pålsson cast a long look at Sappo, who was eating a bowl of fish.

– We were neither outside nor inside, he said slowly.

– Not outside and not inside?

Britta just stared. Had Lars' mind frozen after all?

Pålsson now told her that he and Sappo had been in the middle of the mountains when the blizzard broke out.

– It was almost impossible to go forward, and I thought it was best to turn back, when Sappo went behind a large rock and began to bury himself in the snow. I called him, but he sat there with his nose above the snow and howled and wouldn't be quiet until I took off my skis and crawled down. Then he dug even deeper, and I dug with him – and then there we were!

– You… you were lying in the snow with the wolf?

– Yes, otherwise I might not be here now. I couldn't walk forward and going back was not easy either since you couldn't even see your hand in front of you.

Britta couldn't believe that Lars had been lying on the mountain in the snow during this terrible storm.

– But weren't you cold?

– No, we were huddled together, and the snow covered us, so I didn't feel the storm at all. I slept on and off. I probably would not have dared to do that, if Sappo had not been lying next to me – he would nudge me in the face with his nose now and then and wouldn't give up until I mumbled something.

Britta continued with her questions, and Pålsson told her that after a few hours Sappo dug himself out of the snow. The storm was over, and they could continue.

– I felt a little stiff but I was completely rested. We came to Lake Gikasjön at dusk, and after I had something warm, I continued, since the weather was nice again.

Sappo had finished his fish and came and nuzzled his nose against Pålsson›s hands. Lars took the big wolf›s head between his big, strong hands and cradled it, while he murmured kind words. Then he went and opened the door, and Sappo slipped out. The tame wolf had still not spent a single night indoors.

CHAPTER NINETEEN

It looked more and more like it would be a terrible winter of famine in Marsliden. No matter how sparingly they had used the hay that had been salvaged from the fields, there was not much hay left by March. The cows got skinny, and their milk dried up, and without milk the jierja became almost inedible. The children's stomachs were upset by the sour herb, when they weren't able to mix it with anything else. Just like their last winter in Fjällboberg, they found themselves having to use too much water. Their stomachs swelled up, so that their arms and legs looked even thinner than they really were. The baby should be walking by now, but her small legs were crooked and soft like cartilage. She couldn't even sit by herself anymore, which she had done for a bit before Christmas. Even Jonas was getting weak, and now he only wanted to stay in bed.

The children were not the only ones to suffer from starvation. Britta moved around like a living skeleton, and Lars had to stop and rest many times when he was out checking on his traps. But he had nothing to bring home. It was as if the foxes had disappeared from Marsliden, and it was rare to see any grouse tracks in the snow. One day he had found tracks of a wolverine but was too exhausted to pursue it. Soon enough it wouldn't matter whether he got any fur or not. In his current condition he would not have been able to reach a trading post.

Sappo fared the best against starvation. He wandered around on long excursions at night and could sometimes be gone for several days. In February he had been gone for over a week, and a deep chest wound might have meant that he had been fighting hard with his wild brothers over some coveted female wolf.

Pålsson was pleased that Sappo knew how to feed himself. An

ordinary dog would have mercilessly succumbed this winter when there wasn't even food for humans.

Something had to be done. Without food, the cows would soon not be able to get up, and if it came to that, there was little hope of saving them.

– I guess there's no other choice but to go over to Saxnäs, Pålsson said one morning.

For the longest time, he had avoided seeking help from his neighbors, but when faced with the threat that his whole family may not pull through, all apprehensions had to be put to the side.

With the sled behind him, Pålsson set off down towards the muorke. He did not have any money to buy hay, but surely they would give him a little feed anyway. He could pay with skins, when he came across something, or leave double the hay in exchange next fall.

Pålsson hadn't been to Saxnäs for long until he realized there was no help to be had here. They laughed at him when he told them that the reindeer had destroyed his haystacks last autumn. Well, that's how it goes! Next time he probably wouldn't come and complain about reindeer being stolen. A little reindeer meat wouldn't be so bad now, would it? It was all right to be a do-gooder when your stomach was full, but let's see what you do when it was growling with hunger.

Pålsson was silent. At that moment he didn't feel up to discussing reindeer thefts, and after a while he left Saxnäs with long, tired steps. Without any hay on his sled.

The next day Pålsson made a desperate attempt to get help over in Grytsjö. Olofsson sat silent and listened to him. He knew full well what it meant for a settler not to have feed for the animals.

– You've already been to Saxnäs, you say. They should have had enough to spare a little, right?

Pålsson shrugged dejectedly. He knew well enough that they did, but they had no willingness to help!

– We didn't get much grass last fall, Olofsson said slowly. The flood destroyed an entire hay meadow.

You could tell he didn't like saying what he had to say.

Pålsson nodded. He had actually gone to Grytsjö without much hope. It was the people here who wanted them to leave Marsliden.

Olofsson's wife told him to come to the table and eat a little. There was nothing special about the food she had to offer. It was salted fish, which had soured in the barrel, some potatoes and a piece of bread.

The potatoes tasted so good to Lars. If he could have, without being rude, he would have stuffed them in his pocket for the children. It was many days since they had eaten the last potato. And the bread! Pålsson's teeth chewed the bark-mixed bread as if it had been manna from heaven.

– You were kind to Vanni! the woman said suddenly.

Ever since Pålsson had stepped through the door, her eyes had been fixed on the tall figure like she was trying to figure something out.

Lars mumbled, not knowing what to say.

– She was here for a few days and told us *everything*! The last word was said with a peculiar emphasis, and she looked intensely at Pålsson.

– Oh, really?

– Vanni cried a lot, the woman continued. She cried because you believed she intended to hurt your family with that powder.

Pålsson darkened. He had thrown the bag of arsenic into a mountain crevice and didn't want to hear any more about it. There was already enough misery to worry about.

– But she wasn't planning to harm you. She had the powder with her because she wanted to keep you safe.

– Keep us safe! muttered Pålsson, and when Sari assured him that the Lapp girl had not come to Marsliden with malicious intentions, he gasped.

That was something incredible – that someone wanted to do something good for them!

Olofsson sat pondering, and suddenly he said:

– We will try to scrape together a little hay for you.

– Because you were kind to Vanni, his wife emphasized.

Pålsson's gratitude knew no bounds, and he was speechless when Olofsson offered to take the horse and bring a load to Marsliden. There was something so unexpected about this friendly gesture. When Pålsson had recovered from the initial surprise, he found it hard to shake off the suspicion that something wasn't quite right. There must be something underneath all this, some insidious danger that he could not see.

Olofsson couldn't spare that much feed, and when the hay load was unloaded in Marsliden, it was still not possible for Pålsson to feel confident that the cows could be kept alive until spring. At least the next few weeks were secured, and the settler warmly thanked his neighbor to the east. In time he would know if the hay had been left with good intentions.

The cows seemed to do just fine with the feed from Grytsjön. One even began to give a little milk, and when Pålsson managed to also shoot a couple of hares, the future once again appeared slightly brighter.

*

In early April, Britta woke up one morning to a terrible bellowing from the barn. She jumped up, and the sight she saw through the window made her scream, which woke both Lars and the children. Pålsson got up abruptly and asked what was wrong, and he immediately put on his pants. For a second, he glanced at the gun on the wall. But the weapon was useless. The last gunpowder had been burned the other night against a stealthy wolverine.

Pålsson snorted in annoyance. Wasn't this just great! No gunpowder, with the biggest predator in the wilderness standing and scratching itself on the corners of the barn! He stood by the window and looked grimly at the furry beast, which was roaming around the barn. Pålsson recognized it. It was the same bloodthirsty carnivore that had bothered their homestead earlier.

There was no real danger from the bear. The cows were not under a spruce tree anymore, but well protected behind sturdy log walls. Pålsson viewed the brute only as prey. There was a lot of meat on that giant beast, and the skin was worth money. But all his thoughts of trying to kill the bear crashed against the impossibility of such an undertaking. An axe wouldn't do much good if the forest giant started swinging its big paws around.

Despite the enormous risk, Pålsson trembled with the desire to rush out with the axe and try to get close to the beast. But Britta clung to him. He couldn't go after the bear with an axe! He must remember not to risk his life when he had the children and her.

Pålsson had no choice but to yield to the circumstances. If he had been perfectly healthy and strong, he would not have hesitated to fight the beast. But now that starvation had almost squeezed all his strength out of him, there would be no point in having a dead bear, if he himself was also lying there torn to pieces beyond recognition.

The huge bear stood scratching and clawing at the manure pile, so that snow and cow dung sprayed up around it. It had been two days since it had broken out of hibernation, and it had not yet come across anything to eat. Gnawing on bitter and woody willow shoots was not appetizing. Furious with hunger, it dug its way through the manure pile, buried its nose in the warm dung, snorted and growled. There was such a wonderful smell of cow that drooling gobs of saliva dripped from its mouth.

Suddenly the bear seemed to realize the futility of clawing at this pile, which smelled good but was impossible to eat. It stood up on its hind legs and put its broad front paws on the eaves. But the cow smell came from below. The bear slid down and put its nose next to the small manure hatch. The bear had been sniffing at it before but had learned that it wasn't worth bothering with these kinds of covered openings. But now it was angry and tore the wooden hatch away with a single swat.

A hot, moist steam flowed out of the hatch. The cows bellowed and pulled at their bindings, but this did not frighten the bear. It stuck its head into the opening and sucked in the appetizing aroma, its eyes gleamed with desire at the three dark lumps that loomed in the half-darkness of the barn. But just looking wasn't enough. The bear pulled out its head and stuck in one of its paws. It groaned longingly. Saliva flowed from its mouth, while its huge paw clawed at the delicious smelling cows. But its spread claws did not make the slightest contact with their warm flesh, and roaring with rage, the forest giant bent its paw as if to tear down the whole barn. The sturdy timber wall held strong, and the bear was panting as it removed its heavy paw.

Now the monster was angrier than ever. The hot air, still pouring out of the opening like white steam, was driving it mad. Its small eyes glittered, and its tongue stuck out like a bloody rag between its frothy teeth. It tossed its head here and there and began to trudge around the barn searching for a suitable point of attack.

After circling the barn a couple of times, it stopped, roaring at the door and whacked it with one paw, so that pieces of wood flew. But the door held firm. It was as strong as the cabin's front door and would withstand many blows. The furry beast gave up trying to break the door down and angrily glared up at the roof, stomped up and down and suddenly made a jump. The eaves creaked from the tremendous weight. The bear's hind feet scratched and scraped against the wall, and after a few seconds the bear tumbled down.

The failed attempt to get on the roof did not calm the agitated giant. It ran back a few steps to get a better perspective, darted away to one corner of the barn, and a few seconds later stood roaring on the roof.

So far Pålsson had stayed quite calm, since it was unmistakably clear that he had no possibility of taking the bear down. The beast would surely get tired of running round the barn, and the settler hesitated to try to frighten it away. It was as if he had been waiting for a miracle to happen – that the bear would get caught in something and become an easy prey or would submissively lie down and give up its breath in the middle of the yard.

But now things had changed. The second after the bear had climbed up on the roof, Pålsson rushed out with the axe, followed by Britta, who flailed her arms and shouted, drowning out all the noise from the barn.

The bear cast a furious look down but seemed to have a remarkable sense of what was dangerous and what was not. Scratching and clawing, it stayed on the roof. The snow was swept away. The torn bark crackled, and a pole snapped like a pistol shot. It would not take many seconds for the beast to break through the outer roof, and then it would not be long before it would fall through – down to the cows.

Suddenly the bear gave a terrible howl, hit in the middle of the nose by a piece of wood, which Pålsson had flung with all the force he could muster in his excitement. Then another hit -right above the eyes. Log after log hailed around the bear's head, and suddenly it came tumbling down from the roof. Raised on its hind legs, it charged the bold folks, who had dared to disturb it.

Panting with excitement, Pålsson retreated towards the cabin with a gnarled log in each hand. He glanced quickly for the axe, but it lay out of reach by the log pile. A chorus of screams rose from the cabin, where Britta and the children were beside themselves with fear.

The bear replied with a wild roar, which echoed mightily from the stone walls of the mountain. Its eyes glowed like fire, and the huge body lurched forward, attempting to get a hold of Pålsson in a crushing embrace.

The settler kept his distance, and suddenly a violent throw shot out from his right hand. The hard birch log struck the bear square in the mouth, and howling with pain, it came down to all fours the moment the next log struck it across its ear. That was at least one hit too many. The beast turned and lumbered away towards Ropenbäcken Creek, followed by Pålsson's wild threats.

After the bear had disappeared, Lars and Britta went to the barn. The animals, which had exerted all their strength to stay on their feet in the face of the impending danger, lay there collapsed with sweat covering their backs. They couldn't get up when Britta brought them the scanty hay left over from the load from Grytsjö. Pålsson tried to get the cow up, which was milking a little, but did not succeed. They would have to wait with the milking until the animal had regained its strength.

Pålsson grimly looked at the scratches on the floor from the bear's claws, went to the manure pile which was now strewn about and picked up the hatch and covered the opening with it temporarily. The pieces of leather which had been used as hinges, were torn apart and could hardly be used any more.

The roof had to be repaired, but the settler went inside first to eat his meager breakfast. The children were still so frightened that it was difficult for them to dare to sit down at the table, and Britta's cheeks were blazing red.

– This is when Sappo should have been home! she said suddenly.

Pålsson grunted. He was actually grateful that Sappo was out roaming around. If he had been home, he would now be just a bloody spot on the ground. A single blow from the bear's paw would have squeezed the life out of the wolf.

– He may not come back again.

– Who?

– Sappo.

Pålsson nodded. Yes, that could be. Sappo hadn't showed up very often at the homestead since the famine had begun to show its ugly face. He had to get food the best way he could and seemed to be getting more and more of a taste for the free life in the wilderness. He would probably soon be completely wild. Pålsson thought of this with regret. If only they could give him a meal sometimes, he would stay close to home more. Now there was a risk that one of the neighbors would think he was a threat and shoot him.

Aron had been outside and now came running inside, yelling:

– He's coming!

– There's no reason to shout like that! snapped Britta. Open the door, so he can come inside!

– It's the… the bear! gasped the boy.

It really was the bear. It came striding with long steps from the birch grove by the lake and headed straight for the homestead. Its angry eyes were peering out from its face, and its whole body showed resentment from having been driven away by some harmless firewood. Or was it the glorious scent from the cows still tickling its nostrils? Whatever it was, here it came striding towards the barn like an unstoppable disaster, while the news of its arrival struck the cabin like a bomb.

Pålsson tried to get up from the table but sank back down. His teeth chattered against each other, and cold sweat broke out on his forehead. A wave of dizziness danced through his brain. It was the bear fever that came over him, the worst terror that could befall a wilderness man. And the fever found an easy victim. The famine, the hardships, the recent battle all combined to create chaos within him that drove all the strength from his limbs.

It wasn't just Lars who was horrified. The children were almost paralyzed, and Britta groaned and collapsed by the fireplace. Her shoulders were shaking, and she was nearly out of her wits. Marsliden's settlement had never been so defenseless before.

After a couple of minutes, Pålsson felt the paralysis subside enough to be able to move towards the door. But he did not feel able to fight the monster. The wood logs would not hit it if he tried to throw them. His arms seemed as heavy as lead.

The bear was now only a few paces from the barn and stepped purposefully towards the corner where it had previously jumped up on the roof. Pålsson cried out. It was a hoarse, sickly cry, and for a moment the beast turned its head, snarled, and showed its teeth. It had no intention of being frightened by empty threats.

It was clear to the settler that if the bear got up on the roof again, there would be no cows left in Marsliden. He shouted again, but the bear would not be swayed. It backed up to get a running start and shook its head, making big blobs of drool fly all around.

Suddenly a piercing howl came from below the birch grove. It was

Sappo, who came bounding with furious speed in the bear's tracks, and for a few seconds the whole settlement held its breath.

Sappo looked fierce when he came running into the yard. His bristles stood straight up, and his upturned lips revealed two rows of shimmering wolf teeth. Without hesitation, he charged at the furry mountain of flesh.

Standing on its hind legs, the bear stood ready to make short work of the insolent wolf, and, roaring, flung out one of its paws. The mighty blow, which could have swept an ox to the ground, came a few inches from Sappo's head, and the next moment the bear and wolf were dancing about in a whirling circle. Sappo ran around his opponent with such speed that the bear was forced to get down on all fours to be able to protect his back. Roaring with fury, he charged and swung, but Sappo was constantly out of reach of the whipping paws. Jumping and bouncing like a ball. Lunging at lightning-fast speed, he suddenly managed to rip open a large gash in one of the bear's hind legs.

A white cloud of steam hung over the combatants. Sappo's attacks began to slow, and suddenly he ran a dozen steps back and threw himself down and laid panting on the snow. The bear rushed forward to destroy its enemy. Sappo flung himself out of the way at the last moment, as he passed behind the bear, he took the opportunity to strike its hind leg and then took up a new place to rest some twenty meters away. The bear followed. The maneuver was repeated, and after a few minutes the uneven battle had moved at least fifty meters away from the barn.

Pålsson had stood mesmerized for the first few minutes of the battle, every second waiting for Sappo to be crushed between the bear's paws. Only when the wolf showed signs of fatigue did his mind start working again. He shouted something into the cabin, a few words that no one could quite make out, ran down to one end of the barn where some poles stood up, drew his knife, and hurriedly began to sharpen the sturdiest of the poles. All concerns were swept away. A man, weakened by months of starvation, could safely attack an irritated bear. The beast had to be stabbed, impaled – everything else was irrelevant.

Without heeding Britta's cry, Pålsson rushed to the battlefield with the pole drawn like a lance. But before the newcomer got there, the bear had had enough. One eye hung in shreds, and roaring with pain, the beast took off, running wildly towards the valley between the mountain hills.

Sappo lay panting on the snow. Perhaps he was content to have driven away the intruder, or perhaps he felt that a bear was not a sensible risk for a lone wolf to take on.

But the matter was more serious than that. When Pålsson got to the wolf, he saw that Sappo was lying on packed-down snow in a pool of blood. A huge gash had been torn in his chest, and it looked as if the brave pet wolf did not have many minutes left to live. He howled faintly as Pålsson gently lifted him up.

– Is he done for? Britta gasped when Lars came inside carrying the bloodied wolf.

– Not yet! Pålsson answered grimly and told her to make a bed in the room and light a fire.

Pålsson almost forgot to fix the roof of the barn that day. After he had bandaged the wolf to the best of his ability, it was almost impossible for him to leave the room. It was as if he was waiting for Sappo to open his mysterious wild eyes and make one last request before he closed them forever.

There was a strange mood in the cabin that day. Britta whispered when she spoke to the children, and they were so quiet that they barely dared to breathe. It wouldn't have been quieter if a person lay dying there.

As so many times before, Britta found it difficult falling asleep when night came. She was overwhelmed with too much worry. What if Sappo hadn't come to the rescue! She shivered at the thought. The cows would now be dead – and maybe even Lars! She clenched her hands, and wetness shone in her brown eyes.

That blessed wolf!

CHAPTER TWENTY

Sappo recovered unexpectedly quickly after the adventure with the bear. It was worse for the humans. The famine, which had been overshadowed for a day by the attack on the barn, became increasingly difficult. Only a few poor remnants of the hay from Grytsjö remained. It could not be significantly stretched by the occasional bundle of reindeer lichen that the settler scraped out from under the snow up on the mountain. None of the cows milked. They lay dormant – living skeletons, which for some strange reason could continue to breathe. Their shiny eyes grew dimmer every day, and their tails lay motionless in the manure gutter.

Even worse was watching the children. It seemed like none of them would make it until spring came bringing open water. The baby's breath fluttered like a dying flame, and it was miraculous that she hadn't already fallen into a slumber that knew no awakening. The strength of the other children was almost as exhausted. It was only Paul who, with difficulty, could get across the floor without falling. But he didn't leave the bed for long.

In reality, the hardest part was over – the terrible days and nights when Britta had been close to losing her mind from all the crying and whining for food. The children were no longer hungry. They fell asleep and woke up, whether it was day or night, had a sip of water or chewed on their fur blankets, until they were sucked back into a merciful slumber.

Britta was in bed for most of the day too, dragged herself up now and then, but just couldn't do much of anything. Her eyes shone unnaturally large in her sunken face, almost terrifying with a strange glow. Her dark hair had grown gray in these weeks, making her cheeks look even more wrinkled and old.

Many times, Britta had been pulled into the room as if by a hypnotic power and had stood for long moments looking at the potatoes that lay covered in a corner. But they must not be touched. What would they plant if this corner was empty?

Today Britta stood in the room again, staring at the oblong root vegetables. She wondered if it was noticeable that she had taken a few of them and cooked them up without Lars knowing. She had done that a week ago when the children had been crying the worst.

The settler's wife bent down almost unconsciously and took a potato in her trembling hands. Small sprouts had begun to grow on it, greenish-white little tops, which when put into the ground would almost immediately sprout up into leafy greens.

But Britta wasn't thinking about potatoes growing. Saliva flowed from the corner of her mouth, and without her knowing how it had happened, she suddenly stood there, chewing. Her greedy teeth bit and chomped on the raw potato. Her saliva stood like foam, while a merciless hunger flared in her eyes.

Half the potato was eaten when Britta's jaws stopped chewing. Her eyes reflected a growing anxiety, and she dropped the half-eaten potato as if it had been a glowing piece of metal. Groaning, she covered up the forbidden fruit and for a moment nearly collapsed from the shame and embarrassment. She staggered towards the door, leaned against the wall for a few seconds and ran her hand over her forehead. Then she closed the door tightly behind her, shrinking back as if it had been the gateway to some evil for which there was no forgiveness. Shaking with sobs, she stepped out onto the stoop. The barn seemed to be surrounded by a sea of bright sunbeams, that cut through the daze which stung in her tear-filled eyes.

Lars and Britta had never considered slaughtering any of the animals. Killing the cows was just as unthinkable to them as it would be to sacrifice some of their children so that the others might live. They had both been brought up in settler homes down by Lake Malgomaj and followed strict principles. If things went badly here in Marsliden, it wouldn't be the first time a settler family starved to death along with their cattle. They simply could not be slaughtered in the spring. It would defy all reason and come back to punish them a thousand times over. In the autumn, when the animals were fat – was the time to slaughter, if you had any to spare. In the spring – no! The animals were lean, and the meat was tough and dry at that time. It would be like blasphemy against Our Lord to slaughter animals when the grass was beginning to sprout or would soon do so.

Even if Lars and Britta hadn't had these principles to follow, slaughtering animals was such a grave matter that it stood like a wall against all temptations to do so.

Only if they were certain that it was absolutely impossible to avoid starvation in any other way. But what if Pålsson came home the next day with game from the forest! Then there you'd be with a dead cow and still have hard times ahead.

*

That same day while Britta felt guilty about eating the raw potato, Pålsson stumbled around in the birch forest. He was more of a skeleton than a human and breathed heavily, even though he moved extremely slowly. In one hand he held a pole, which he had sharpened a couple of weeks ago. He carried it with him at all times, both to have something to lean on and to not be completely unarmed in case the bear should show up. The settler still had the wild dream to be able to kill the bear. He talked about it in his sleep sometimes and smacked his lips. It was as if a different animal wouldn't be big enough to make a proper meal.

Pålsson sat down. Facing south, the sun had burned holes in the snow here and there, so that the ground was bare in patches. No grass was to be seen, but there were swelling buds on the willow branches, and crowberry shrubs and purple mountain heather were waking from their winter sleep.

Lars sat in the midst of the burning sunshine, chin resting on one hand. That day he could not come home without something to eat.

If this continued another couple of days, he would have to break up the boat he had built during late winter and make coffins out of the wood. The children couldn't last much longer – and what about Britta? She didn't say anything, but he could see she was having trouble staying on her feet. And such a strange look she had every time he came home empty-handed! Maybe she didn't think he was doing all that he could. She maybe thought he should go to one of the neighbors and ask for help. Tomorrow he would… tomorrow. If he couldn't find anything to eat today, he would drag himself off to Grytsjö. Though there might not be any help. Everyone had their own concerns to think about, and he had been to Grytsjö once before – could he keep coming as a beggar time and time again without embarrassing himself?

Suddenly there was a rustle at the settler's feet. A little lemming, short and fat, ran carefully to a heather tuft and began to gnaw on it.

Pålsson stared at the animal and suddenly had an idea. He lifted the pole, and a second later the lemming was killed. The settler gave out a little grunt and picked up the catch. It wasn't exactly a small mountain rat he had intended to bring down with the sharpened pole.

A couple of minutes later, Pålsson had another lemming in his grasp, and now he was trembling with eagerness. He crouched and watched, and as soon as another small rodent appeared, he brought down his pole.

There seemed to be plenty of lemmings this year, or else this was a particularly lucky occurence. One rodent after another came peeking out, and after a while Pålsson had eight lemmings in a pile. But now he had to stop. His heart was pounding so violently that he could hardly breathe, and his knees trembled. He put down the pole, sat down on the ground and began to skin his catch.

When all the lemmings were skinned and gutted, the settler tied them together in a bundle. He left the skins behind. They were certainly beautifully colored in black, yellow, and white but without any value.

Pålsson was almost grateful that Britta was in bed when he came home with his catch. She was sleeping, and no sound was heard from her, while Lars built a fire and put a pot over it. Everyone else in the cabin seemed as if they were dead. There were only a few wheezes, which betrayed that there was anyone alive in the room.

The silence frightened Pålsson. Was it already too late? He tried to distinguish the different breaths but could not make out whether there were three or four sets of lungs breathing. He did not dare to go over to the bed to see how things were. Instead, he fed the fire under the pot as if it was necessary to cook the meat in the shortest possible time.

They had salt. That item had not been in great demand this winter. Pålsson put in a couple of pinches and then stood hesitantly with his fingers in the salt jar. He didn't really know how much salt was needed for this kind of meat – probably another pinch!

The fire burned briskly, and now a juicy smell from the meat began to rise up to the ceiling. Pålsson stirred the pot – because who knows, this meat might burn if it was cooked like regular meat. He smelled it. Something was missing, yes, pepper! Pepper wasn't really an everyday spice, but he had gotten a paper cone at Kroken, and it ought to be here somewhere. He found the paper cone on the shelf above the door. Lars put a couple of dozen of the black-brown peppercorns into the pot and continued to stir, slowly and laboriously as if it was a witch's brew, while his gaze lingered on the floating peppercorns. Maybe they could mask the taste of the meat, if the meat didn't taste like they were used to.

It boiled and simmered in the pot, and for a moment it was as if the strong smell had awakened the sleeping people. Britta sat up in bed, staring at the man and the pot, her nostrils flared as she smelled the air.

– Did you catch anything? she gasped faintly.

Pålsson nodded. Yes, he had caught something!

– What did you put in that smells like this?

– Pepper!

Pålsson didn't say anything else. He couldn't stand there and tell them that he had lemmings in the pot!

Even the children, except Jonas and the baby, had sat up. Pale and hollow, they stared at their father and the boiling pot. Not a sound came from them, only dull, sighing breaths. But their jaws were moving – their skinny cheeks twitched spastically – and from Aron's mouth a few drops of spit fell onto his thin arm.

For Pålsson, the children's awakening was even more terrible than the complete silence a while ago. Here they sat like gaping baby birds waiting for food – and what did he have to give them? He positioned himself in front of the pot to prevent the demanding eyes of the children from seeing what was over the fire.

He took a ladle and skimmed the pot. Strange – just like froth? But when he had gotten rid of the foam, the fat covered the broth with a smooth, shiny film – a shimmering, yellow layer, making his mouth water.

By now the meat ought to be ready. Pålsson picked up a piece of meat with his knife. A small cloud of steam came from it, and the settler blew on it. But it was still too hot to bite into, and Pålsson laid the meat on a wooden board and began to cut it into fine strips. But what a strange color it was! Not red like meat from four-legged animals, nor white like bird breasts were. Wasn't it almost a little bluish? Pålsson stared. There were moments when he thought the meat was not blue either, but yellow.

Piece by piece, Pålsson took them out and cut them up, because he felt that the children could eat the meat better if it was finely chopped and mixed with the broth. They wouldn't have to chew it and notice a strange taste but could just swallow the mixture like soup.

Britta had dragged herself out of bed and wanted to take charge of the cooking, but Lars grimly pushed her away. This was not food to be cooked by womenfolk! Instead, he told her to set the table with the children's bowls. The food was almost ready.

It was dead quiet in the room, while Pålsson filled the bowls with the greasy yellow soup, and when Lars returned to the fireplace with the pot, he was no longer followed by the eyes of the children. Their eyes were glued to the table, where eight bowls stood in two rows, emitting steam, rising to the ceiling like the smoke of sacrificial bowls.

One minute later, Pålsson was lifting the children from the upper berth. They hung like rags in his arms, and they could barely sit upright at the table.

Sipping and slurping, the children devoured the soup, and after Britta helped Jonas and revived the baby with a couple of spoonfuls, she also began to eat the filling broth with its swirling pieces of meat.

– Aren't you going to eat, Lars?

Pålsson jerked as if he had been slapped, but then hesitantly grabbed the spoon. Well, could he eat it?

The children had already finished their bowls and were licking their spoons. Their cheeks had a little bit of color now, and their eyes had lost some of their ravenous expression.

– But why don't you eat while your soup is hot, Lars?

A drop of sweat appeared on Pålsson›s forehead. Should he tell the truth and say that he couldn't bring himself to eat this soup… that it was made from… No, he shouldn't tell them. Then the children might throw it up.

The first spoonful made Pålsson›s stomach turn. Such food wasn't fit for humans. But before he knew it, another spoonful was in his mouth, and suddenly he sat licking his lips with an empty bowl and went back to the pot to see if there was more left.

After a while, the children began to complain of stomach aches, and Pålsson worried that he had given them food that would make them succumb to tetanus. But Britta knew better. There was no danger to their lives. It was just that the meat soup had been too rich for their hungry stomachs. Eventually the pain subsided, and when Pålsson went to bed that night, he could fall asleep safe in the knowledge that the children wouldn't starve to death at this time either.

*

181

For the next three days the people of Marsliden lived almost exclusively on the lemmings gathered on the slopes of the mountains. Britta didn't gag or throw up when she found out what kind of meat it was; it wasn't very pleasant to think about, but it was edible, and Britta knew of more ways to prepare the meat. There was a little bit left of the sour grass. It wasn't usable on by itself but mixed with meat and broth it made a dish, which the children greedily devoured. They were hungry all the time again, since their desire to live had been re-awakened by that first steaming bowl of soup. Even Lars ate the dish with a voracious appetite and would probably have continued to go out and catch lemmings, had he not made a pleasant discovery.

Strengthened by the hearty food, Pålsson was now able to walk further and came to a spot, which was brown and black from trampled bird droppings. The settler knew at once what he was seeing. It was a large wood grouse courting ground, a place where the huge forest birds gathered this time a year for their spring mating.

Pålsson drew his knife and began to cut branches from a number of young spruce trees. He stuck the branches in the snowy ground, so that they made fences in the snow in the open area. These paths led to bushes, where Pålsson set up snares everywhere. The work took several hours, but the settler was so eager that he hardly noticed that it was late evening.

Early the next morning he went to the grouse courting area, and for the first time in a very long time a slow smile spread across his face. Almost all the snares contained dead grouse. Some had their feathers almost completely pulled out, for there had been a tremendous fight here a few hours ago. The roosters that had gotten caught in the snares had become an easy target for the other ones competing fiercely for the hens' favor. Pålsson gathered them into a bundle, which he could barely drag home, and from now on the lemmings were left alone.

The days passed. Pålsson had another couple of good catches at the courting area. He would've been able to look ahead to a brighter future again if the cows weren't doing so poorly. These days Pålsson would have undoubtedly exchanged meat for hay – pound for pound. If they lost the cows, their own recovery was not worth much.

The weather turned rainy. It was stormy and windy, and Lake Marssjön broke free from its heavy ice shackles. An occasional water bird began to settle in the open bays, and before they knew it, all of Lake Marssjön was clear of ice and slush.

Every morning Pålsson stared at the ground. Wouldn't it ever turn green this year? He felt the dirt, sort of begged the seeds to hurry up and sprout and didn't get around to putting the boat in the lake.

But at last, the solemn moment came, when the barn door was thrown wide open. All the children, even the youngest one, were outside to see the cows being let out to pasture. But no cows came tumbling through the doorway, and Stina, sitting on the steps with her little sister on her lap, picked up the baby and walked with her down to the barn to see what this meant.

Lars and Britta tried in vain to get the cows to stand up. There was nothing else they could do but to drag them out. The boys helped, and now the first cow was pulled over the threshold and dragged a short distance up onto the grass.

After a while the bull and the second cow were also dragged out of the barn, and Pålsson looked at their miserable bony bodies. They would probably never be decent animals again. They were too far gone. The last cow they had dragged out lay gasping for air like a fish thrown up on land. Its eyes were covered by a dark film, and it lay with its head on the ground, unable to raise it. But suddenly it was as if the sun's rays brought it to life. Groaning, it lifted its head and began to nibble on the fresh spring grass.

CHAPTER TWENTY-ONE

This spring it seemed as if the Lapps did not dare to approach Marsliden. The reindeer were carefully guarded and driven up along Mount Såttan without a single animal coming south of Ropenbäcken Creek. It didn't help that Vanni swore that the settler meant them no harm. What did she know about it anyway? It could be that the tall man at Lake Marssjön had meant no harm in the beginning, but now it was probably different. The Lapps certainly knew what damage the reindeer had caused last autumn and knew settlers too well to believe that such a thing would remain unavenged. Now they had to make sure to drive the reindeer cows out of the way and get themselves to relative safety on the other side of the pass.

The Lapps' fear of a terrible revenge was understandable from several points of view. There was some mysterious about the settlers of Marsliden. After the disaster with the hay, the mountain people had expected to be summoned to court and ordered to pay a hefty amount in compensation, for in such disputes it was always the settler who had the law on his side. But the winter had passed, and they hadn't heard anything. The reindeer people became more and more convinced that the settler considered receiving compensation to be too lenient of a punishment, and that he himself intended to exact some kind of bloody revenge. And did he have only the hay to avenge? No! They all knew about the forest fire, but there was even more that had happened, which they considered with trepidation.

These events had not come to their attention until this winter. Niel had taken to drinking more liquor than was good for him and had lived like a wild man in a drunken stupor, and then collapsed like a ragdoll, wailing, tearing his hair, and swearing that he was haunted

by evil spirits. That's when they had learned about the "magic balls"
he had put out, the attempted arson and the astonishing spear throwing incident down on the muorke. The last one they had almost refused to believe. Catch the spear midair and then return it – no!

During the migration to the mountains, all this was discussed
around smoky fires. The settler had much to avenge but had so far
done nothing – only pretended that nothing had happened. That he
had brought Vanni back to their home last autumn and taken care of
her was incomprehensible. Perhaps it was not enough of a revenge
for the grim man of Lake Marssjön to leave a Lapp girl to perish in
the wilderness. Perhaps he was gathering all these evil deeds into
a big pile, so that when the time was right, it would make a bigger
impact. Otherwise, he would have let the wolf loose on Vanni, when
he found the powder in her pocket! The Lapps shuddered when they
thought about the powder. Niel had told them about this too and
complained about it being lost so that he had not been able to put
an end to them over there. Only when the reindeer had started to
move west had Vanni told them that she had brought the powder
with her to the settler's cabin.

Vengeance would come. Vanni was not as sure anymore of Pålsson's goodwill as she had been when she was in their home at Marsliden. Since then, two terrible things had happened – the discovery
of the poison bag and the destruction of the haystacks. Sometimes
it was as if she was more afraid than the others. So good in friend-
ship – how terrible would he not be in his anger!

Vengeance would come – but how? Each of them had their own
suspicions, but for the most part they were united in the opinion
that this summer the reindeer would not be left in peace for one
single day. He would come, that mighty man, and bring the wolf
with him – for a wolf is what it was! Perhaps he had acquired several wolves this winter – large, gray wild beasts that did not fear
humans, and which were perhaps as unaffected by steel as their
master. Everyone had heard Niel say that the settler was protected
from fire and steel.

But would destroying their reindeer be enough for him? Maybe he would come to the goahtis and sit down, unsettling them with his presence? Look at Vanni!

She had been acting strange all winter, sighing, crying sometimes and had a look in her eyes that did not look human.

*

During the Midsummer weekend there were two funerals in Fatmomakke. A small child from the settlement at Lake Gikasjön and Jon from Klimpfjället Mountain.

Jon was found at the end of April, lying as if in prayer beside the path between Dårronskalet Pass and Tjåkkola Mountain. At first some suspicions were directed at Pålsson, for in Norway it was said that the two men had accompanied each other to Kroken. But no signs of violence could be found, and when the horse and sled were found between the threatening stone walls of Dårronskalet Pass, the matter began to be seen in its proper context – although some wondered why such an experienced man as Jon had sought to cross the Dårronskalet Pass in one of the worst snowstorms in living memory.

Perhaps the Lapps drew some conclusions, for they looked at each other and nodded gravely. Wasn't it right there at Fjällfjällen Mountain that Mikael had disappeared a few years ago? And the dead, who hadn't been buried in consecrated ground, had certain powers. They could attract and destroy; they had the ability to dole out punishments themselves.

But no one was thinking about punishment when the pastor lowered the three shovels of dirt to Jon's simple wooden coffin, and it was from the Lapps that the most desperate weeping and wailing came. Perhaps it was not grief in the true sense of the word. It was not the dead but Death that caused the Lapland people to bend down to the ground. For them, Death was a being that must be appeased by wailing and crying wherever it appeared.

The gathering this spring weekend did not have the right feel about it. It was hard to get a laugh down among the goahtis, and eyes were occasionally drawn out to the bay to see if the settler from Marsliden was coming. But Pålsson was nowhere to be seen, and with every hour there was more and more unrest in the Lapp camp. When they sat in the chapel and listened to the pastor preaching, they did not listen the way they usually did. They couldn't really focus on the sermon. They sometimes looked at the windows and turned around in their benches at the slightest creak from the door. Sweating and panting, they tumbled out of the chapel when the service was over, and their faces looked almost confused when they saw that their goahtis were still standing, that the bay lay gleaming in the sunshine and that Marsfjället Mountain had not been wiped off the face of the earth.

There were not many people in the goahtis this weekend. Some of the men had stayed on the mountain, because this year they dared not entrust the reindeer herds to just the boys.

Vanni's father was not down here, nor was Niel and several others.

Niel was not on Marsfjället Mountain either. At the big market in Lycksele he had joined up with a different Lapp family, and when the time came to migrate, he had already married one of their daughters and was now watching reindeer up among the snowy peaks of Mount Tärnafjäll, determined not to approach Lake Marssjön until he was completely certain he would be able to achieve something.

More often and eagerly than anyone else, Vanni looked to the east. But it was not an avenger she expected. Her cheeks were deeply colored, and her eyes shone with a strange radiance. Just to see him! Now and again, there was a flicker of anxiety that came over her soft face. Was he as stern as when she had left Marsliden last autumn? Would he look at her with those cold, sharp eyes that could freeze blood to ice?

Pålsson did not come, and in her despair Vanni sought out Sari and brought her down to the beach, so that they might be left alone.

Olofsson's wife looked at her niece with a sharp eye when they were alone. She guessed what the girl wanted to talk to her about.

Vanni didn't look at her. She sat with her hands on her knees and looked up at Marsfjället Mountain, where the snow still glistened on the highest peaks. Suddenly she said:

– Did you see the Marsliden people last winter?

Sari's thin lips twisted into a grimace. She knew that when Vanni said "people", she meant "him".

– Yes, he visited early this spring and got a little hay. I thanked him for being kind to you.

Vanni's face blushed brightly.

– What did he say?

Her voice was so low that Sari could hardly hear it.

– Say …? Not much. He was skinny and starving, it seemed strange that he could stay up on his feet.

Vanni gasped. Skinny and starving – how merciless he would be to those who had destroyed his hay!

– Did he say anything about … about us? Was he angry? Olofsson's wife shook her head. No, he hadn't said anything about being angry!

Had he not felt strong enough to, maybe?

Vanni's face expressed all her fears and feelings, while her questions sought helplessly to find their way to some clarity. Sari looked at her more and more sharply and suddenly said:

– You shouldn't care about him like that!

– Care… care about?

– He can't marry you.

Vanni stared, and her bosom rose in deep gasps.

– Ma … marry!

She didn't understand anything.

– Well, isn't that what you had in mind?

– In mind… me?

Vanni had confusion written all over her face, but suddenly she understood what they were talking about.

– How can you think, that … that…

– One has eyes to see with! said the older woman sharply.

To Sari's surprise, the Lapp girl insisted that she hadn't meant anything of the sort. He is already married! She tried to explain how she viewed the settler at Lake Marssjön but was not quite successful. Her opinion of him was that he was beyond ordinary.

Sari frowned. Beyond ordinary! She knew all about that – that's what everyone was saying! But when she looked at Vanni, she was still half convinced that her niece did not think of Pålsson as an ordinary person. In her eyes he was a saint — not a man to whom a woman showed her adoration in the usual way. Sari suspected that the "saint" would soon show his true colors. After all, the settler at Lake Marssjön was no more than human, and after last winter…

When the two women stood up, Vanni seemed to agree with her, and if Pålsson had rowed into the bay just then, she might have run away to hide.

Inga from Klimpfjäll would have handled seeing him better. She, too, had been eagerly looking for the man from Marsliden. There was so much to discuss with him. Had Hans been up there at all, or was he planning to? And would anyone else be able to settle in Marsliden?

Since Jon had met his demise in the howling blizzard, it had become clear to Inga that she must now find a way to move away from home. Her eldest brother had taken over the farm and was getting married today. A funeral and a wedding on the same day in the same family was not an unusual event in Fatmomakke. A new woman had been in Klimpfjäll for several months, and that was more than Inga could stand. Neither she nor her mother would have a say over the house and the barn. This was normal her mother, now that she was a widow, but Inga's hot temper was revolting against it. She was entitled to two cows; she could take them with her any time she wanted and find a different place.

Inga had hoped that she would meet Pålsson and perhaps Hans in Fatmomakke. If there was no room for another family in Marsliden, she was not afraid to go further up the Ransarån River or look for another place in the wilderness where a new settlement could be built. If she was left with no other choice she might take her cows, shovel, and axe and go into the wilderness alone. If there was a woman in the entire Lapland countryside who would be up to this task, it was Inga from Klimpfjäll.

But leaving by herself was a last resort, and Inga was not seriously considering it yet. When it was apparent that Pålsson was not coming to Fatmomakke this weekend, she asked Olofsson if he had seen Hans walk past Grytsjö.

– Hans? Who is he?

– The man who helped Pålsson build his cabin during their first summer.

Olofsson didn't think that there was a visitor in Marsliden currently, and Inga decided to go down to Malgovik to see Hans. There was a family here from Bångnäs, and if she could accompany them, it would not be more than fifty to sixty kilometers to travel alone. After Inga had decided this, there was not much that could sway her, and when evening came, she was in a boat heading for the mouth of the Ångermanälven river.

The fact that no one from Marsliden had come to Fatmomakke was also noticed by the farmers and settlers. Not last fall – and not now! What kind of heathens were they? Once the liquor had gotten their minds going and loosened up their tongues, they were better able to put words to their thoughts. After all, maybe there was something suspicious about Jon's death. The Saxnäs farmers had some interesting things to tell. Jon had intended to move to Marsliden. He had clearly said that to them once when he had been a little tipsy. There was something wrong with the deed for Marsliden. Jon had made it sound like the settler had moved there without legal right. Who knew if he had even bought any papers from Abraham, who had been a farmhand in Klimpfjäll? Stolen them maybe... or ... They nodded grimly, and one of the men gestured with his finger across his throat. Had anyone seen Abraham at any market in Åsele in recent years?

But several of them had seen the former Klimpfjäll farmhand in Åsele as recently as last winter, so that question was resolved. But this thing with Jon still demanded an explanation … because the question was if he wasn't the reason Pålsson hadn't come here. It wasn't so easy to appear unmoved at a funeral, which you yourself had caused – best to stay at home!

They became more and more convinced of their opinion that something had happened up in the mountains. The matter seemed very clear. Jon and Pålsson had left Kroken together – there were witnesses to that! – and so the settler had realized that his papers were worthless, and that Jon could drive him away from Lake Marssjön. Someone should give the police chief a tip about this. It was not wise to have such a person in the area. You yourself might not be safe, when it came right down to it.

The settlers and farmers left Fatmomakke with that mindset, but there were some who, on sober reflection, felt that it was all nonsense. It was hard to say what the situation was with the papers, but Jon was not the first to have perished in a snowstorm. Furthermore, how could you explain that the horse had been unhitched from the sled up there in the Dårronskalet pass?

Long before the settlers were ready to go home, the Lapps had left Fatmomakke and hurried up to their reindeer herds, occasionally jumping at a sound as if expecting a sudden attack.

*

It was close to midnight but still bright like daytime, when Olofsson and his wife rowed their boat across Lake Marssjön. Sari sat staring toward the settlement, which seemed dead and abandoned.
– What do you think happened?
– What?
– Could Pålsson have…
– Nonsense!
– But some people don't think it's nonsense!
– Maybe not.
– Do you think the police chief will come?

191

Olofsson rested on his oars for a second and swept his eyes over the shiny surface of the lake, where the mountains were darkly reflected.

– Yes, I'm sure the police chief will come! he snapped and rowed, making the water splash around them.

CHAPTER TWENTY-TWO

It was not until a couple of weeks after midsummer that Pålsson learned that Jon had perished in the terrible storm that had almost done him in too. It was Olofsson, who had rowed over to Marsliden to warn the settler.

– There are those who believe that there was foul play involved, he said.

– Oh, really?

– They say that you and Jon left Kroken together.

– Sure, we traveled together for a while, and if we had known that the weather would get that bad, we probably wouldn't have gone up the mountain. If I hadn't had Sappo with me, I don't know what would have happened. Sappo and I spent almost a day in a hole in the snow on the mountain. The weather was terrible, and I don't know what Jon was thinking, trying to get through Dårronskalet Pass – he could have used the cabin at Tjåkkolafjället Mountain.

Olofsson was tormented. The fact that Pålsson had been holed up with a wolf on the mountain was a piece of information that sent shivers up his spine, but it was not this that worried him the most. He did not believe that Pålsson had anything to do with the incident on the far side of the Dårronskalet Pass, but he should probably warn the settler so that he would know what to expect.

– You'd better be prepared for the police chief to come here! he muttered.

– Police chief? Why would he be coming?

Olofsson explained what had been discussed at Fatmomakke, and a grim look came over Pålsson›s face.

– And it also sounded as if your papers for the deed aren't in order.

– Not in order – how so?

– Well, that you have no legal right to live here.

– Who told you that?

Pålsson's voice was sharp, and a vein began to slowly swell at one of his temples.

– The Saxnäs farmers made it sound like Jon had said something about it. It sounded as if he was trying to arrange things, so that this place would eventually become his.

Pålsson's face had become even gloomier. So, that was why Jon had been so elated after reading his papers … left Inga to stay behind and him trying to cozy up to Pålsson! And always so curious and asking how things were in Marsliden.

– In a few days it will have been five years since this place was inspected, Olofsson continued. In my inspection papers it stated that if I had not been a resident of my settlement, when five years have passed since the inspection, I would no longer have had the right to settle here. I would think it says the same thing in the papers you have, and since you bought them from Abraham, it's probably his name that is in the papers. You had best go down to the police chief and sort this out before it's too late.

Pålsson muttered something, but said neither yes nor no, and when Olofsson left Marsliden, his face showed more worry than when he arrived. Did the settler not understand the issue with his papers, or was it that he didn't dare go see the police chief?

The rest of the day, Pålsson was brooding about the papers for the deed. They couldn't come and make them leave Marsliden just like that, could they? Maybe there was some paper that was missing after all… something that had his name written on it. It must still be in that book that they were writing in at the courthouse in Åsele. They had asked what his name was and where he was from. And if the paper was still there, there was no point in going to the police chief in Vilhelmina. It was one hundred seventeen kilometers to Åsele, and he didn't have time to walk that far now. It was probably not in Åsele either, when he thought about it, because papers like that were usually issued by the county governor in Umeå, which was seven hundred kilometers there and back. Long trips like that had to wait until winter.

Pålsson was not worried about the police chief coming to Marsliden due to Jon's death. He knew he had done nothing wrong and didn't think there would be any reason for suspicion.

*

This summer the people of Marsliden worked as if they had been whipped by invisible demons, and when fall arrived, so much hay had been harvested that there should be enough winter feed for twice as many animals as there were in Marsliden. Lars and Britta were driven by the fear of starvation. They couldn't bring in enough. Thanks to the boat, it was possible to put out their nets in more productive places, and lots of fish were dried or salted. For several days in a row, Britta and the children were out in the marshes picking cloudberries, and although the potatoes this year seemed to be plentiful, they brought home whole loads of mountain grass for preserving. When the first snow came, there may not have been a family west of Vilhelmina as well equipped against famine as the settlers at Lake Marssjön. After the summer's grazing, the cows were shiny and fat, and Pålsson looked longingly at the bull he had gotten in the trade in Klimpfjäll and wondered if he should slaughter it – they couldn't have too much food!

Feeling the pressure to have enough food, which almost increased the more their supplies grew, Pålsson began to see to his traps out in the fields. Now it was primarily fur animals he wanted to trap, for he would not rest until he had traded and brought home a few sacks of flour. This year he could expect to catch more with the fox traps. There had been a great number of lemmings in the fall – almost to the point of it being impossible to reach some areas because of them, and that meant that there would be plenty of game. During lemming years, the foxes gave birth to more cubs than usual, and not only foxes – all kinds of predators, both birds and four legged animals became more numerous. When the lemmings multiplied so much that they were forced to migrate they became like a constant smorgasbord for all the carnivores of the wilderness.

The reindeer stayed up in the mountains for a long time that autumn, and Pålsson bitterly realized that he could have brought all the hay home during the winter and avoided the difficult toil of carrying all of it home before the ground froze. And it wasn't just him – Britta and the boys had had to work hard these past months too! Carrying home huge loads of hay across the wet marshlands.

As the days went by, the settler began to wonder what mischief the Lapps would come up with this year. That they would leave the homestead alone was more than they could expect after all that had happened in past falls – and anything could happen on a dark night. A piece of meat could be thrown to Sappo, covered with white powder, and then … There were nights when Pålsson rose trembling from his bed to see if the storeroom remained on its posts or if the barn door was open and the cows had been killed. The more the settler thought of the Lapps, the clearer it became to him that he had to get tough with them. He couldn't just turn a blind eye to it any longer. You had to fight evil with evil – then it came down to who was the strongest or could come up with the most cunning attack! Without Pålsson really realizing it, it was the hunger of last winter that still gnawed within him. His body was healed, but there was something still broken in his soul. Sometimes ghostly images flashed across his eyes – the half-dead children, Britta's gaunt, tear-covered face, the cows, the lemming meat… never again!

One morning Pålsson walked towards the birch forest. There was only a thin layer of snow on the ground, and it was still easy to get around. In several places he saw the tracks of both fox and wolverine, but the tracks were of no importance. He had no rifle to shoot with, even if he would happen to catch a glimpse of an animal. Although he had borrowed some gunpowder from Olofsson, both rifles hung at home in the cabin, loaded with bullets, intended for the big furry one, if it came wandering by. However, he was not completely unarmed. He had carved a stake into a smooth spear, put a sharp spike on it, and he always had it within reach when he went out. On a day like this, he didn't let it out of his hand.

Pålsson had gone farther and farther up into the birch forest when he stopped suddenly. Not fifteen paces from him stood a snorting reindeer. Heat rose in the settler's face, and his hand gripped the spear tighter. He took a few steps without the reindeer moving.

For a few oppressive, unbearable seconds, Pålsson stood motionless as if carved in stone, while the hunger of winter pressed on him with a strength that was almost paralyzing. It was only right that he took this reindeer. He should have some compensation for the destroyed hay. Right and wrong were stirred together in his brain into a seething mass. Go hungry – never!

Pålsson raised his arm – a single whistling throw, and the reindeer would fall to the ground with the spear in its chest.

At that fateful moment, a tremor ran through the mighty figure of the settler. He lowered the spear with a groan, waved his arms and scared away the reindeer. A few drops of sweat appeared on his forehead. Was this the way that revenge would be laid to rest? No! One evil deed would only bring on more evil deeds.

Pålsson continued upwards. He was both pleased and not pleased that he had let the reindeer go. His old hunger wrestled with an even older feeling, which didn't want to have anything to do with violence.

When the settler was a few hundred meters above the big rapids in Ropenbäcken Creek, he suddenly saw a couple of Lapps disappearing into a hollow in the ground. He steered his steps grimly in that direction but did not get far before a figure appeared on the edge of the hollow and came skiing down towards him. Pålsson's chest constricted as he saw who it was.

Red-faced and panting, Vanni braked with her skis while her eyes revealed both fear and joy.

– Lars? she gasped.

– Yes.

Pålsson's voice was cold and harsh, and his gaze involuntarily turned to the girl's coat pocket. Sari had said that Vanni meant them no harm – but was that to be trusted?

– I... I was just coming down to see you! said Vanni, giving the settler a confused look.

– I see. And who is with you?

Vanni blushed and stared trembling at the ground.

– It's... it's just Turi! she whispered softly. He needed to come with me, because they didn't dare to let me go alone.

– Well... what is it about then?

– I was just going to ask, if you want some reindeer because... because...

– A reindeer! Pålsson growled.

He had been so close to taking a reindeer a few minutes ago!

Vanni whimpered! Her fear had been building up for many days and now it came pouring out.

– Five reindeer! she exclaimed desperately. Because... because they destroyed the hay for you last fall!

Pålsson grunted. Five reindeer! He didn't mind having his supplies increased. Suddenly he remembered something.

That Turi... is he the same person who was with you that night, when our place nearly burnt down?

– No, no, Vanni gasped breathlessly. Turi... he... he means no harm!

Pålsson was still just as grim.

– Call him over here! he said darkly.

Already twenty meters away, the young Lapp took off his hat, and you could see that he was performing one of the bravest acts of his life, far more nerve-wracking than attacking a pack of hungry wolves. Pålsson could not recall having seen Turi before, but the young man seemed decidedly more sympathetic than the boy who had thrown his spear at him down on the muorke.

After Turi stammered and confirmed that they were indeed going down to the settlement to offer them some reindeer, Pålsson went with them up the mountain. He was not fully convinced of the good will of the Lapps. This could be a trap! He kept Turi and Vanni in front of him as they skied along. He felt it was necessary to not have his back turned to them.

The reindeer were just above the tree line, almost at the same spot where the haystacks had stood last year. Some of the drying rack poles accusingly remained there, because last summer there had been such an abundance of feed in the hay meadows near the settlement, that it had not been necessary to go to the mountains.

Now some older Lapps arrived, just as humble, and the settler again received confirmation that they intended to give him some reindeer. At this moment it would have been possible for Pålsson to get – not just five but maybe a hundred reindeer. The settler didn't know what trepidation the Lapps had been in all summer, a dread which, when nothing had happened, turned into a spellbinding belief that a terrible catastrophe would befall them when the reindeer passed by Lake Marssjön. In their darkest moments the settler was no longer a human being in their eyes, but some kind of deity who patiently bided his time, just as Our Lord saves the burning sulfur lakes until the day of judgment.

Not many words were spoken between the Lapps and the settler. The Lapps seemed to want the matter settled as quickly as possible, and Pålsson was not in the mood for an exchange of opinions either. He knew full well that this was not going to reconcile them to each other.

No matter how grim Pålsson felt, he could not help admiring the flawless agility Turi displayed when Vanni pointed, and he caught the reindeer with his rope. All five were large, magnificent animals. The settler had to admit that he would not have been able to select them as well in the moving, gray herd, where it was almost impossible to keep your eyes focused on any particular animal.

Vanni, her father and Turi followed Pålsson down to the settlement with the reindeer. Sappo came rushing and might have scared the living daylights out of both Lapps and reindeer, if Pålsson had not anticipated his charge and reduced it to a passive growl.

An hour later the reindeer were slaughtered, and Britta stood nearly overwhelmed in front of the fireplace with blood and entrails in buckets and bowls. The largest pot stood simmering over the fire, spreading a fragrance around it that made the children's nostrils flare.

None of the Lapps came inside the cabin. Only Vanni had gone in to talk to the children while the men slaughtered the animals, and her visit had been closely monitored by Britta. The settler's wife had never for a second taken her eyes off Vanni's hands. She remembered last autumn's bag of poison far too well.

Pålsson grunted contentedly, after he had hung up the five reindeer carcasses in the storehouse. Out there, the meat would freeze and stay fresh and nice until spring.

– How come the Lapps gave us so many reindeer? Britta asked later.

– Can't really say. They said it was because of the hay, but this must be the first time they've ever voluntarily given any compensation for that kind of a thing, so I don't really know what to think of it.

– Vanni was not herself, I thought.

– Not herself?

Pålsson looked curious at Britta.

– She looked so worried somehow.

– Oh really? Yes, I suppose, Lars said thoughtfully.

He remembered that Turi had looked at Vanni with strange shining eyes. Maybe that meant something.

After Pålsson had walked out to the store house again and in the frosty moonlight seen that he really did have five reindeer hanging there, he was ready to go to sleep. The next morning, he had to get up early, because now he had to trap enough furs, so that he could go down to Åsele and find out about his deed. He did not dare to think what the situation might be. This thing with the reindeer was not really a good sign, because after lucky days there was often something bad lurking.

CHAPTER TWENTY-THREE

Pålsson and Olofsson were going through the desolate mountain area near Mount Stalon on their way to the market in Åsele. The weather was neither bad nor good. It was overcast, and a foot of fresh snow made it hard to see the front of Olofsson's sled. The horse had snowshoes on its feet and sweat steamed off it on the steep uphill slopes. But it was calm, and towards evening large holes began to form in the cloud cover.

Pålsson was skiing behind the sled and had warned Britta that it might take several weeks before he returned home. Paul and Aron were now big enough that they could easily go together to Grytsjö and pick up some things, which he intended to ask his neighbor to bring back with him, if he himself had to continue to Umeå.

If the settler hadn't been so worried about his papers, he could have been quite content. He had two wolverine skins, a marten and eight foxes bundled on Olofsson's sled, and on his back hung a bundle of white ermine skins that alone were worth a pretty penny. But they needed money. There were so many necessities that were needed at the homestead. The most urgent need was clothes, and if Britta did not get some wadmal wool fabric, the children would not be able to go outside all winter. She hardly had a scrap of cloth to put on the younger ones.

Slowly the men went east, and Olofsson was deep in thought. The fact that he had received double the hay in return for what he had given Pålsson last spring was not really that strange. It was much more remarkable that the Lapps had given up five reindeer to the settler. Although it was now several months since Vanni had told Sari about the incident, the man from Grytsjö had not stopped pondering over it. Such an event was so extraordinary that it seemed like something wasn't right about it, and there were times when Olofsson seriously suspected that the settler had used secret powers. It was obvious to him that the Lapps had been frightened, and yet they had insisted that the settler had not raised a hand against either them or the reindeer – hadn't even set his wolf loose on them! Even if Olofsson had had all the facts laid out in front of him, he still wouldn't have understood it. Compensation for the hay – then you had to go to court first, no matter how much you were related to them! And it was about feed that had grown up on the mountain, where the settler had no rights to it at all. No court would have ordered the Lapps to pay compensation for those haystacks – and so they had voluntarily handed over five reindeer – no!

Equally remarkable was the story of Jon. The police chief had not been up to Marsliden, and Olofsson knew why. No one had dared to tell him! But now it would depend on whether someone drank a little too much at the market in Åsele and began to rant to anyone who would listen – if someone started to share their thoughts, it was hard to guess what would happen. During the market, the police chief had sharp ears. Olofsson did not usually drink much alcohol, and now he had promised himself that not a drop would pass his lips during these days in Åsele, for at this market it was important to be in control of your tongue.

On the second night the two travelers stayed overnight in Malgovik, and the next morning they were joined by farmers from the village who were transporting goods to the market. Pålsson stayed with his relatives, and there was a lot to catch up on because he had not been to Malgovik since their first summer in Marsliden. There had been both deaths and births in the village during that time, and after Pålsson had heard about these events, people began to wonder how they were doing up there.

Pålsson answered in short sentences. Yes, they were doing fine! He didn't mention a word about the fact that they had been close to starving to death last spring. It was none of their business.

Later that evening Hans came home. He was still unmarried and hadn't had time to get a place of his own. Like before, he wandered around the villages. Helped build a cabin here, a barn there and got "thank you!" but no more for his trouble. Every year it became more and more clear that he wouldn't amount to anything, at least that was his parents' firm opinion.

After Hans had eaten, he took Pålsson outside. There was something he wanted to talk to him about. They went over to the stable, and now Pålsson heard that Inga from Klimpfjäll had been there.

– What did she want?

– Well, she thought I should come to you and ask if we could build near you.

Pålsson drew in his breath a little uneasily. He well remembered what Jon had been thinking about in regard to Marsliden. Perhaps Inga was no stranger to the subject, either.

– I said I didn't want to, Hans continued, but she wouldn't give in until I told her… well, that I intend to marry Greta, when it's a good time.

– Maybe it's about time! muttered Pålsson with his uncle's sharp remarks fresh in his mind. You're wearing yourself out working for others instead of getting your own place.

It was the first time Hans did not laugh at such a warning.

– Yes, that's exactly what I want to discuss with you, he said seriously. Greta thinks it's about time now, and I've been meaning to go and see you and Britta to hear what you think. Greta has a heifer and three goats, and a few people owe me money, so we're not entirely without means to begin with.

– Hear what we think…? said Pålsson slowly.

He was not quite clear what this meant.

– Yes, if there could be room for Greta and me to settle and build up there with you.

Pålsson was in a tough spot. Hans was probably the last person he would refuse to settle in Marsliden, but it was no good to promise anything, when he didn't even know whether they themselves would be able to stay. And in the midst of all this, the fear of hunger still haunted him. If one family had been starving – how would two fare?

– We haven't come up with anything else, Hans said. We don't want to leave and be completely isolated in some place we don't really want to live, and in these parts, there are no fields available.

This last part was something Pålsson was well aware of. It was almost fifteen years ago since he himself had been wandering around these parts in search of land to claim with fields and fishing waters.

– Yes, there is certainly room for you, he said hesitantly, but we don't know how things stand right now. The deed we have may not be correct.

Pålsson explained the situation in more detail, and Hans asked if he had the papers with him. Pålsson nodded. Of course, he had the papers!

– Let's go in and have a look!

– Do you understand such things?

– Oh, yes!

They went inside. Pålsson took out his papers, and Hans began to study them eagerly. Last summer he had helped the police chief in Vilhelmina with some construction work. He had a grown daughter, and she, like nearly every other girl around, was eager to teach Hans something. Despite her teaching him to read, it took Hans a couple of hours to spell his way through the sixteen pages of writing, and when he finished, he was sweatier than after a hard day of haying. However, it was clear to him that something was missing from the papers, and now all that remained was to hear what they would tell them at the courthouse in Åsele.

Hans accompanied them to Åsele the next morning. He had some fur to sell too, but might have sent them with somebody else, if it hadn't seemed so necessary for him to be present and see how things would work out with Marsliden.

They arrived in Åsele at dusk the next day. It was the evening before the actual market, but the fur traders were already busy, and Pålsson was so worried about his papers that he immediately sold his furs. There was plenty of furs this year, the skin buyers claimed, and the price was a bit on the low side. Pålsson didn't think about whether he was being cheated or not. His eyes went up to the courthouse, which stood there dark and threatening. There it would be decided whether he had the rightful claim to Marsliden.

Lots of settlers and farmers from the mountains crowded into booths and stalls, and the smell of furs and people combined into a foul stench that made people's stomachs turn over for the first few seconds. The liveliest place was the inn. Beer mugs and glasses of liquor were filled and emptied, and one frost-covered face after another was thawed into a reddish glow. People drank with a clear conscience. They sat for months at a time on their lonely farms and settlements – sometimes they had to relax and feel like a regular person.

Pålsson was not at peace indoors. There was hardly any question of sleeping tonight. A small miserable room with a dozen men left little space for rest, nor did anyone consider sleeping sitting up. One left, another came, and there was an incredible number of stories to tell.

Pålsson was standing down by the stables, when a hand was suddenly placed on his shoulder, and the next second he was looking into a gaunt, dull face which he hardly recognized.

– Oh, it's you! he said softly, his ears feeling hot.

The other person breathed heavily. At first Pålsson thought he was drunk, but he did not smell a drop of alcohol.

– How are things in Marsliden?

He sounded ill and was almost groaning when he spoke.

– Well enough! replied Pålsson

– Have... haven't the Lapps done anything?

– Why do you ask? wondered the settler.

The other hesitated and began digging in his pockets. He pulled out a pouch and handed it to Pålsson.

– Here's the money back! It wasn't right of me to sell that place.

Something red and black flashed before Pålsson's eyes. What was the meaning of this? The money back – return the claim … no!

– I knew that it was not possible for anyone to live there, Abraham continued, and the papers didn't cost me more than one and a half riksdaler coins.

Pålsson refused to take the money. He didn't know that Abraham had looked for him at the market every year, didn't know that his involvement in Mikael's disappearance and selling the claim to land where no one could actually survive, had in the long run become too much to bear for the boy from Hälsingland. Abraham had heard that Pålsson had moved up there with six small children, and it was hard to know if it was Mikael or those children that most haunted and bothered Abraham's conscience. Maybe it was the children, for he was now married himself and had little ones. He pleaded with Pålsson to take the money.

– Are the papers not valid, then?

– Yes, they are valid!

Abraham sounded fully convinced of this, and Pålsson nodded grimly. He had no intention of handing over any papers. And he said so.

Abraham replied that he did not want the deed back, and Pålsson looked at him murderously. Was this too good to be true? Was it some kind of trap, perhaps – or was this man out of his mind? He had a peculiar look on his face.

When Abraham asked the settler to come with him closer to the river, Pålsson followed with some hesitation. But it was necessary to move if they wanted to talk more, because here they were not left alone for a minute. If not to look after the horses, there were plenty of other things to do at the stables.

No danger seemed to threaten Pålsson at the sharp river bend. However, his face turned more and more grim. Abraham had not previously uttered a word to any man about the event on the other side of Dårronskalet Pass, but a couple of hours ago he had learned that Jon was dead, and now he no longer needed to keep any promises. Slowly and sickly he now told what had happened in the mountain areas before Pålsson came up there – the bloody incident – the transfer of the deed it had brought with it – his own failed attempt to settle in Marsliden – all the fear and curses that lay hidden in the shadow of Marsfjället Mountain. Every word from Abraham's lips seemed to be the result of his conscience bothering him, and Pålsson began to understand why he wanted to return the money. But instead of accepting the money, he said:

– Did you know that there was something wrong with the deed? The question surprised Abraham.

– Something wrong with the deed… no!

And that was true. Just like Pålsson, Abraham hadn't realized that the inspection papers had been issued in a specific name and actually couldn't be sold. He still didn't understand that now, and Pålsson wasn't able to explain how things were either.

– But then you can take the money, exclaimed Abraham.

Pålsson did not take it. He thought it would be harder to settle the matter at the courthouse unless he could say that he had paid for the claim with honest money, and he did not intend to make things worse for Britta and the children in order to ease someone's heavy conscience.

– We'll see how it goes tomorrow, he said, no longer listening to what Abraham had to say.

The next morning Pålsson and Hans went to the courthouse, gloomy and serious as if they had been on their way to a place of execution. The settler showed his papers, which were quickly leafed through.

– Well, what about this?

– There's apparently something missing in the papers, Pålsson answered heavily, and the head clerk looked more closely at the notes.

– No, Jacobsson, this looks correct. Pålsson gasped, and it was with difficulty he told them that his name was Lars Pålsson and he had previously lived in Fjällboberg.

– Then of course this is wrong if you're the one who lives in Marsliden. Where did you get these papers from?

Pålsson told them about the purchase and said that he had been at this courthouse and had the papers read to him and that someone had asked questions, written them down in a book and said that everything was in order.

The assistant clerk started to leaf through large books, becoming more impatient by the minute. Suddenly he said:

– Who wrote it?

– It was a short, fat man with a black beard. The head clerk nodded, as if confirming his suspicion, but he perhaps thought there was no reason to tell the settler that this man hadn't kept good records and had long ago since been relieved of his duties. He leafed through the books a little more, but it was mostly for show.

– There seems to be no record of that transfer. You'll have to bring Jacobsson here or get a letter from him, and maybe this can be fixed.

Pålsson got his papers back, and Hans and he hurried out to find Abraham. After they had searched in vain for a couple of hours, they were informed by a settler that the Hälsingland man had left Åsele early in the morning. Pålsson and Hans stared at each other – now all hope was gone!

They walked slowly back to the courthouse, and on the way there Pålsson suddenly let out a groan. He felt around in his pockets for a wad of chewing tobacco, which he had bought the night before, and instead found the pouch Abraham had tried to force on him. The fact that Abraham had managed to slip the pouch into his pocket later that evening was not so remarkable, but Pålsson took it very seriously. With this money in his hand, he had no right to Marsliden. Pålsson also began to understand why Abraham had disappeared – he had of course feared that something would be revealed to the police chief about Mikael.

On the courthouse steps, they met Hellgren, the police chief in Vilhelmina, and Hans asked him if he would be so kind as to look at some papers.

The police chief followed them in, and Pålsson again explained his situation, while Hellgren from time to time looked at the notes from the inspection he himself had carried out six years ago.

– We just went looking for Abraham, but he left.

– Abraham has nothing to do with this! said the police chief very grimly. His right to the deed expired last year.

Pålsson groaned. It became more and more complicated. Now it didn't even help to find Abraham.

– How… how do we take care of this then? he stammered.

– Well, there's nothing to do about it but for Pålsson to apply for a new inspection.

– Is that possible?

Pålsson looked at him questioningly.

– Of course! You'd better submit the application as soon as possible.

After Pålsson had regained his strength for a few seconds, he asked if Hans and he could have the place inspected together. There was no objection, and the police chief helped the two men to draw up an application to establish and jointly farm a homestead at Lake Marssjön. When this was ready, the police chief wanted to speak privately with Pålsson.

What Olofsson feared had happened. Someone had made insinuations, which had reached the police chief, and he had already earlier that day questioned a couple of people about Jon. They had said that it was just rumors. Jon had been frozen to death and nothing else, for they had not seen any external injuries when they found him in the snow. Hellgren was, however, interested in hearing what the settler had to say about the matter.

Pålsson told him about his journey from Kroken, and the police chief seemed to lose interest in everything else, when the settler talked about his journey on the storm-whipped mountain.

– Were you really holed up with a wolf up in the mountains for a whole day and night?

– Yes, I had no other choice!

The police chief nodded. Well, maybe not! But the impact was still visible on his face when the settler's broad back disappeared through the doorway. He sat muttering for several minutes, and when a farmer an hour later made a polite remark about the beautiful weather, he replied that men like that are what is needed up there.

CHAPTER TWENTY-FOUR

Pålsson came walking back from the wood grouse courting area he had found last spring. This year, the place was again a haven for cocks fanning their tail feathers, and gracefully crouching grouse hens, and the settler carried a large load of snared forest birds on his back. But now he was not in a weakened state as he had been during the last mating time, and there was a look of satisfaction on his weather-beaten face. The last remnant of his fear of hunger may have been melting away.

All winter long, Pålsson had suffered from this terrible feeling… a creeping, icy fear of running out of food. It was only in the springtime that he had begun to feel calmer. Only a couple of weeks ago he had woken up from a horrible dream and could only drive his anxiety away by getting up and shining his lantern on the children.

Slowly and burdened down the settler approached home. He was still lost in thought, when he suddenly was startled by a scream. Aron came running, hatless and with his arms swinging wildly. He was close to falling on his face in front of his father's feet.

– Pa… ul has shot… shot, he gasped.

– Shot …?

– Up there!

Aron pointed eagerly at the valley, which crept up between the hills, and got out a couple of choppy sentences, which made Pålsson half-run towards the cabin. The huge bundle of grouse flapped around on his back, leaving behind the occasional feather.

In the cabin there was great excitement. Britta's face alternated between pale white and red hot, and she ran back and forth as if she were dizzy. The children were hollering about "Paul" and "shot",

crowded in front of the window and could barely contain themselves. But two of the children were not inside – Paul and Jonas.

Pålsson didn't stay inside for many seconds. He ran to the wall
of the barn to get the hay sled, and pulling it after him, he hurried towards the forest with Aron running a few steps ahead like a
panting hunting dog.

Half a kilometer from the settlement, Pålsson received confirmation that Paul had "shot" something. In a small clearing lay a large,
black-brown lump, guarded by Sappo and the two boys.

Pålsson looked serious when he arrived and saw that it was Marsliden's old troublemaker, the bear, who had been shot between its
eyes. It was unbelievable that the boy had shot this one!

– How did it happen?

– I shot it!

Paul looked much more confident now than the time he had shot
the wolverine in Stalon's mountain pass. Now he was not ten but
thirteen and had permission to use a gun.

Pålsson was not satisfied with the answer, and Paul told him that
it was Jonas who had first seen the furry beast.

– And so, I ran in to get the rifle and called Sappo.

– Wasn't mother inside?

– No, she was in the barn. Sappo got wind of the bear at once and
was jumping around it when I fired.

Pålsson grunted, still looking very stern, as he rolled the huge beast
onto the sled with the boy's help. This spot was not far from the place
where he had to be contented with hunting lemmings last year.

*

The settler spent the next few days in deep thought. He gave the
boys – even Jonas – long, serious looks. Pålsson was convinced that
the boys had not viewed the bear as a dangerous animal, but only
viewed it as a source of meat. But if the boys saw all the animals in
the area as mere pieces of meat to be hung in the pole shed, then

bad things might happen here when the reindeer came roaming. He had to have a serious talk with Paul about this.

Pålsson found an opportune time, when a few days after the bear was shot, Paul and he went out to bring home all the snares, before the reindeer arrived.

– But what if we run out of food?

– Still no, Pålsson said sharply. It's stealing to shoot reindeer.

– The reindeer destroy the hay! muttered the boy.

The father tried to explain to him that this was not a good enough reason either.

Paul did not answer. His gray eyes stared into the distance, and his lips were drawn together, edged with grim lines, that made him look many years older. And in that moment, the settler realized that the famine had scarred his oldest boy so badly that he would never again allow himself to go hungry for weeks on end. The mere threat of a winter of starvation would cause him to sneak out on his own with a rifle to get some meat. There was only one way to keep Paul from becoming a filthy reindeer killer. Pålsson himself had to get enough food so that the boy realized that he didn't need to steal other people's property.

– We probably will never have such a difficult winter again, he said slowly. Now Hans is coming here too, and two are always better than one.

Paul nodded, but he looked far from convinced. His father was right. The famine had scarred him too deeply.

Britta might have noticed that Lars was worried if she hadn't been so filled with anticipation that Hans and Greta were coming. Ever since she had learned that the two young people were to share the settlement with them, her spirits had been lifted. She could stand for long moments looking at the great pile of logs that lay rolled up a short distance from the cabin. That pile was proof that they were coming. A couple of times during the winter, Hans had been up here with a borrowed horse and sled and on one occasion stayed more than two weeks hauling timber from the forest.

Every day Britta looked more and more eagerly to the east. She could hardly concentrate on her chores, even though she had more to do than ever. Mostly she thought of Greta. Just to see and talk to another woman seemed like heaven to her. Oh, how she had longed during these years in Marsliden for a woman to talk to and confide in!

The thaw was over, and Pålsson began to expand the clearing. This spring, more potatoes had to be planted, and he would try to grow a small field of barley. The boys helped as best they could, but Britta couldn't manage to roll away even one stone. She looked more brooding with each passing day. It was now June, and Hans and Greta had not come.

– Perhaps they've changed their minds, she said one evening, when all hope seemed to be lost.

– Well, I don't think so, Pålsson answered slowly. They will come.

Pålsson was not as sure as he sounded. A lot could have happened since Hans was last here. Someone might have warned them and said that it was not possible to live at Marsliden. They didn't know a lot about what to expect here, and it maybe wouldn't take much to make them change their minds.

– You'd better go down and see what is going on. We can't keep waiting like this.

Pålsson nodded. He understood that Britta would take it hard if the young people changed their minds. And what would happen with the new papers, if Hans didn't move here? They had applied to have the settlement together.

Before the children woke up the next morning, Pålsson headed east. Britta admonished him repeatedly not to give in. They must come here! Lars muttered. It wasn't easy to say that they must come, if there were some serious obstacles in the way. But he would do what he could, and with that resolve he hurried through the pathless wilderness.

CHAPTER TWENTY-FIVE

Pålsson found Hans and Greta at Mount Stalon. They had been delayed by strong spring flooding, and one of the cows had calved just as they were about to leave.

The young people were grateful that Lars had come to meet them. Although Hans had previously been up in Marsliden with supplies, they still had heavy packs to haul, and the animals were difficult to lead at this time of year. After Pålsson had strapped Greta's pack on his broad back and taken charge of one of the cows, the journey went twice as fast through the rugged mountains.

*

A week or so after Hans and Greta had arrived in Marsliden, Pålsson and his wife went to Fatmomakke to have their youngest one baptized. The newlyweds couldn't spare the time to join them, and since there were adults staying at home, Paul got to accompany his parents to the church site for the first time. Pålsson had expected the boy to be beside himself with delight, but there was only the hint of a twinkle in Paul's gray eyes, and that twinkle vanished instantly when his father said that this time it wasn't necessary to bring his rifle.

Pålsson didn't have much to say during the journey to Fatmomakke. He walked heavily and steadily behind the quiet Paul, wondering if they would face the same hostility now as two years ago. Maybe it was foolish to let the boy go with them. If he got the impression that everyone looked at them with spiteful eyes, it would be one more injury he would need to recover from.

When the people from Marsliden arrived at the bay, they didn't even have to shout for a boat to come over from the other side. It was Olofsson who came to meet his neighbors. He was sweaty and excited, and it was the first time Pålsson saw a smile on his face.

– Are you here already?

– Yes, we came here yesterday, when Vanni and Turi got married. Britta glanced at Lars, but not a look on his face indicated that this affected him in any particular way.

– Oh, they got married? she exclaimed.

Olofsson grimaced.

– Yes, and if I may say so, I have seen happier brides than Vanni.

– How so?

– Sari says, it's mostly due to you folks from Marsliden. The poor girl still believes you think she brought that bag to make trouble. But you mustn't think that about her!

– And we don't.

Olofsson was fully satisfied when Britta said that she would talk to Vanni if she found the opportunity.

– You should, he said. She asked for you both yesterday and today, and she's the one who spotted you first.

Pålsson's arrival at Fatmomakke caused as much attention as the times before, but at least the demeanor of the Lapps was different, although the joy of the wedding celebration became somewhat subdued. It was as if strangers had arrived, and it was now important to behave as respectfully as possible.

Vanni and Turi had met them at the beach, and it wasn't long before Lars and Britta sat with lots of food in front of them. Britta warmed up to the others immediately, and that gave the Lapp women the courage to show an astonishing interest in the youngest resident of Marsliden. Everyone must see what color her eyes were and feel how heavy she was. Never before had a settler child been passed around so much among the Lapp women, and Britta finally began to worry that she would never get her little one back.

Lars didn't display the same joy as his wife. He was slower to warm up and still held on to some of his mistrust, but slowly his stern look began to disappear from his face. He sat and talked to

Vanni's father and a couple of the older Lapps. There were no sensitive subjects discussed, mostly the weather and market prices.

Paul refused to loosen up. He steadily ate his fill. All attempts at conversation were shut down by his one-syllable answers and the stern look on his face. But he attracted more attention than his parents. Olofsson had talked about the bear Paul shot, and the older boys in the Lapp camp formed a reverent circle around him.

The farmers and settlers stayed in the background and talked to each other and wondered what all this might mean. That the people from Marsliden would receive such a reception from the Lapps was the last thing they had expected. There were several of them who agreed with Olofsson – that the settler possessed some secret power that could crush all resistance. Some felt uneasy since they had participated last autumn in speculating about Jon's death and wished they could somehow cover it up. They would have felt more at ease if the settler had walked up to them and shaken his heavy fists threateningly at them. Then at least they would have known that he was just an ordinary man. This church weekend, there was not really a single visitor who didn't wish to get on the good side of the secretive man by Lake Marssjön. Pålsson discovered this when he took a walk around the chapel before the service. Every one of the groups eating at the tables wanted him to join them at theirs. Lars stopped to visit with them but did not accept any food from anyone.

Paul was also walking around after his hearty meal with the Lapps. People didn't ask him to stop at their table, but just stared at him as if he was a wonder child.

It was thanks to the bear that Paul received this flattering attention. Many of these men had cursed angrily when the furry beast killed their animals, but now a half-grown man had walked a few steps away from his cabin and shot it. No one believed that he had used ordinary gunpowder and ordinary bullets.

Sitting at the top of the hill were the Saxnäs farmers and a few others, and when they saw Paul come up, one of them wondered if they should offer the boy a couple of drinks.

– Don't you dare! said Ericsson sharply.

– Oh, it might be fun to see how he would act.

– It may not be so funny afterwards.

– Pålsson will come and see it, you mean?

– Well, I wasn't thinking of him. I certainly don't want to be the first who offers that boy alcohol.

– Why?

– You'll find out in a couple of years, because it won't take long before everyone will have to be careful before taking on that bear killer. They say he's thirteen, but have you ever seen a thirteen-year-old like that before?

Paul was still standing in the same spot, and another one of the farmers asked if anyone really knew why Hans Persson had moved to Marsliden.

– Pålsson and Hans are said to have applied to farm the settlement together, Ericsson replied.

– That's strange – to have such a good place and to share it with someone else without a second thought. He must not be in his right mind!

– I'm beginning to think that he is smarter than we are. Here we have walked around thinking that he is simple-minded, but he seems to have good reasons for what he does. No Lapps have ever come to us with five reindeer! I don't know what kind of tricks he used to make that happen. Maybe it's something that not just anyone can learn.

– He hasn't done anything, from what I've heard!

Ericsson glanced up at Marsfjället Mountain with a thoughtful look, and then said that perhaps his approach was to handle matters gently, although it was hard to see how one could do that.

– Now we know how Pålsson handles things, and we know Hans a little from before, but again, best not to have any bad blood with them when they're riled up. They won't hold any punches; I can tell you that. Paul is coming here now, and I warn you not to offer him any liquor!

Paul came slowly walking towards the five men and was about to pass them by, when Ericsson stopped him.

– So, you're here too!

Paul nodded in the same serious manner that his father usually did. Yes, he was here!

– Sit down and tell us about when you shot the bear.

Paul sat down reluctantly. His nostrils flared, and his gaze was hard and fixed.

– Weren't you scared when you saw it in front of you?

– I shot it!

That was all Paul had to say about the matter, and then he looked calmly and steadily at the men from Saxnäs.

– Did you have enough hay last winter? he asked.

– Hay… what… do you mean?

Ericsson's voice was thick, and he gave his neighbors a strange look.

– Well, because then you could have come to our place and gotten some, so you wouldn't have had to eat lemmings.

– Lemmings! What are you talking about?

Paul did not answer but got up slowly and walked steadily down to the chapel, where a service was about to begin.

The chapel was filling up quickly, and Paul elbowed his way over to his parents. His breathing was a little heavier than usual, but perhaps that was because of the crowds, and when the pastor began his sermon, he sat there tensely and listened.

Perhaps the pastor sensed a different mood in the church this time, or maybe he had chosen his sermon text after deep introspection. Today he spoke not so much of punishment and hell, but more of reconciliation. All people were brothers, and happiness on earth and in heaven could not be gained in any other way except through reconciliation and brotherhood. It was not sufficient just to believe that there was one God and one heaven. Salvation was not won simply because Jesus Christ had died on the cross. You had to work towards goodness yourself, and the foundation for that was called brotherhood. If mankind did not act like brothers, ready to help one other, then all the supplication and prayer would be in vain. It was by doing good deeds that the blessings would come in abundance even here on earth. The more men and women came together in reconciliation, the sooner the kingdom of heaven would come.

Pålsson did not take his eyes off the pastor's face; at that moment he thought he had been vindicated for all the evil that had befallen him. He could sit and listen to sermons like this for any amount of time.

After the service and after the little one was baptized, the Pålsson's got ready to go home, but Vanni asked them to stay a little longer, and the young Lapp woman looked so radiantly happy that they couldn't refuse. There was more food, and this time the pastor's words seemed to have reached further than the church door. While Britta was almost dizzy from the women's goodwill, Lars held conciliatory talks with the men. A couple of hours passed quickly, and when Pålsson finally started to get ready to leave, Paul was gone.

Pålsson went around asking, but the boy was neither among the goahtis nor with any the groups of people on the hillside, and there was almost a small commotion. At last, someone remembered that he had seen Paul and a Lapp boy walking down by the bay a little while ago.

Paul was found down by the shore, sitting on a rock with Vanni's fifteen-year-old brother by his side. It was hard to know what the two boys had been talking about, but they looked solemnly serious, and Paul had a large Lapp knife hanging at his side.

– Did he give you that?

Paul looked calmly up at his father's face. Yes, he did!

The people from Marsliden walked home quickly. Both Lars and Britta felt that a new day was dawning. At home, Hans and Greta were hard at work. It was true that there would still be many hard times ahead, when trouble would come calling, but now they were two families, and working together would make it easier to keep the ghost of starvation at bay. Pålsson had thought about it before but hadn't seen it in the same clear light as he did now, after the church visit to Fatmomakke.

Brotherhood! A more beautiful word could not be imagined by the settler at Lake Marssjön. He walked and thought about it all the way home. If people could come together as brothers, everything else would work out in the end.

Appendix

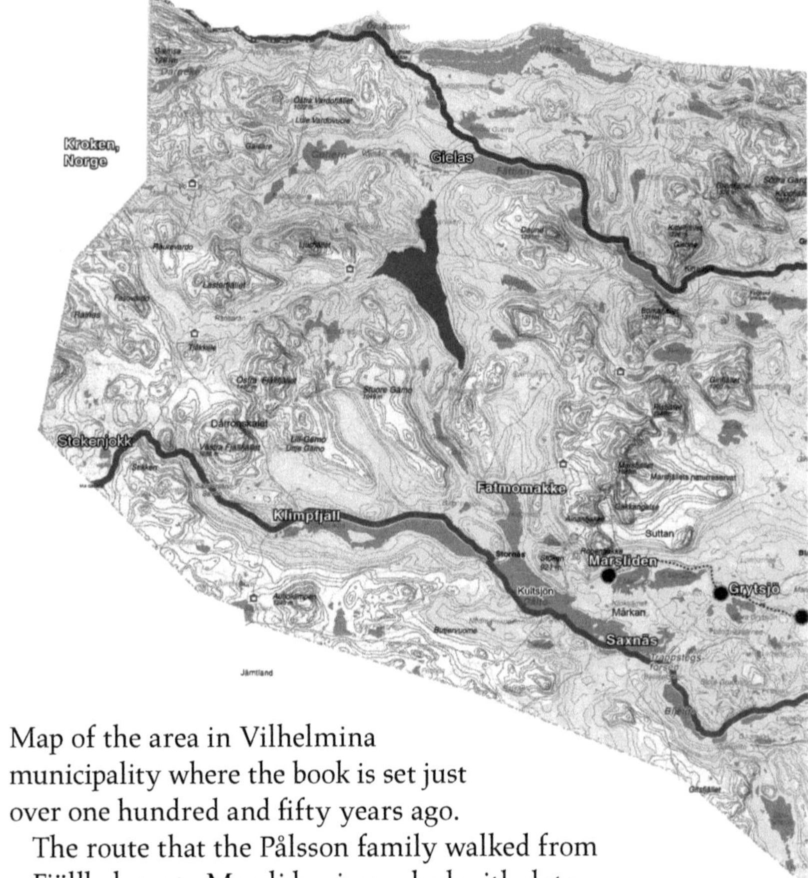

Map of the area in Vilhelmina
municipality where the book is set just
over one hundred and fifty years ago.

The route that the Pålsson family walked from
Fjällboberg to Marsliden is marked with dots.

At that time there were no roads, only footpaths and some trans-
portation paths. Marsliden was not accessible by road until 1954.

Now the area is accessed by these roads: *Vildmarksvägen*; Vilhelmina – Strömsund via Stekenjokk, *Sagavägen*; Örnsköldsvik –
Brönnöysund via Vilhelmina and Dikanäs and *E45*; Sicilien – Kare-
suando (and Nordkap) via Vilhelmina.

The map is taken from the Bernhard Nordh Society's brochure:
"A literary journey in the shadow of Marsfjället".

Grönfjäll
Dikanäs
Bergland
Västansjö
Dalkarlvik
Blaikliden
Erikberg
Grytsjö
Dorris
Fjällboberg
Kroksjö
Heligfjäll
Västansjö
N Tresund
S Tresund
Lappudden
Strömnäs
Gränsnäs
Näslandsjö
Ormsjö
Malgomaj
Malgomajsjön
Mark
Skog
Naturreservat
Malgoviken
Malgomäsel
Malgovik
Laxbacken
Vilhelmina
Lövliden
Forsnäs
Blaikfjället
Djupdal

Seeking to escape starvation and unfriendly neighbors, the Pålsson family journeys through the Lappland wilderness for five days to the foot of Marsfjället Mountain to create a better future for themselves as settlers.

Bernhard Nordh had this book's incredible stories told to him by, among others, Jonas Larsson in Marsliden, who himself took part in the journey as a three-year-old in the spring of 1856.

All people and places in the book are referred to by their real names. The book was Bernhard Nordh's big breakthrough as a folk writer; it was translated into five languages and has so far sold nearly 300,000 copies in Swedish.

In 2014, Professor Annelie Bränström Öhman wrote about the book: "…it's not wilderness romance, it's for real. Bernhard Nordh's stories have that quality – and it still stands today; you can taste, smell, and feel the emotions.